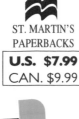

ST. MARTIN'S
PAPERBACKS

U.S. **$7.99**
CAN. $9.99

P9-DCJ-309

Look for these other novels in the
Black London series from
CAITLIN KITTREDGE

Soul Trade
Devil's Business
Bone Gods
Demon Bound
Street Magic

...and don't miss Kittredge's
Nocturne City series

Daemon's Mark
Witch Craft
Second Skin
Pure Blood
Night Life

Available from
St. Martin's Paperbacks

ISBN 978-0-312-38826-3
50799

EAN

"KITTREDGE IS A WINNER!" —Jim Butcher

DARK
DAYS

A BLACK LONDON NOVEL

CAITLIN KITTREDGE

Bestselling author of *Soul Trade*

characters, and a lead character you can actually care about—Kittredge is a winner."   —Jim Butcher

"I loved the mystery and the smart, gutsy heroine."
     —Karen Chance, *New York Times* bestselling
     author of *Claimed by Shadow*

"A nonstop thriller laced with a ferociously deadly menace. Count on Kittredge's heroine to never say die!"   —*RT Book Reviews*

"Kittredge takes readers on a dark adventure complete with thrills, chills, and a touch of romance. Well written . . . and impossible to set down."   —*Darque Reviews*

"Fast-paced, sexy, and witty with many more interesting characters than I have time to mention. I'm looking forward to reading more stories in the exciting Nocturne City series."   —*Fresh Fiction*

"Wow, I am still thinking about this book. The last time I reacted to a book this way, it was the first Mercy Thompson book by Patricia Briggs. If you are looking for a book that seamlessly blends a police procedural with a paranormal, go out and get this book."
     —*Night Owl Romance*

"A tense, gritty urban fantasy that grips the audience from the onset."   —*Mystery Gazette*

"Caitlin Kittredge just keeps honing her craft with each new book. *Second Skin* has some pretty creepy elements and page-turning action. Readers who enjoy good solid urban fantasy will enjoy this installment."

—*A Romance Review*

"*Night Life* dived right into the action, and carried me along for the ride . . . If the following books are written with the same care and interest as *Night Life*, they will be a welcome addition to this fantasy genre."

—*Armchair Interviews*

"Kittredge's amazing writing ability shines through in this wonderful tale of murder, magic, and mayhem . . . The intriguing plot grips you from the very first page and takes you on a roller-coaster thrill ride with an ending that will leave you gasping for more."

—*Romance Junkies*

"If you're looking for a good paranormal mystery and enjoy reading about shapeshifters, give Caitlin Kittredge's work a try!" —*Bitten by Books*

"Hot, hip, and fast-paced, I couldn't put [*Night Life*] down. Don't go to bed with this book—it will keep you up all night. It's that good." —Lilith Saintcrow, national bestselling author of *Working for the Devil*

"Luna is tough, smart, and fierce, hiding a conflicted and insecure nature behind her drive for justice and independence, without falling into cliché . . . a lot of fun to read." —Kat Richardson, national bestselling author of *Poltergeist*

Also by
CAITLIN KITTREDGE

BLACK LONDON SERIES

Street Magic

Demon Bound

Bone Gods

Devil's Business

Soul Trade

NOCTURNE CITY SERIES

Night Life

Pure Blood

Second Skin

Witch Craft

Daemon's Mark

DARK DAYS

CAITLIN KITTREDGE

St. Martin's Paperbacks

This is a work of fiction. All of the characters, organizations, and events portrayed in this novel are either products of the author's imagination or are used fictitiously.

DARK DAYS

Copyright © 2013 by Caitlin Kittredge.

For information address St. Martin's Press, 175 Fifth Avenue, New York, NY 10010.

ISBN: 978-0-312-38826-3

Printed in the United States of America

St. Martin's Paperbacks edition / May 2013

St. Martin's Paperbacks are published by St. Martin's Press, 175 Fifth Avenue, New York, NY 10010.

10 9 8 7 6 5 4 3 2 1

CHAPTER 1

Everything tastes like ashes. The air above London is black no matter the time of day, smoke billowing from the burning districts south of the Thames. Sirens scream, echoing from building to building. People scream as hungry things chase them through the street, now the graveyard of cars long abandoned.

Not all people are victims. Some roam the darker, narrower parts of the city in packs, falling on man and creature alike.

Jack Winter watches the fires as they flourish and die. He watches the wraiths flit out over the water. He watches the zombies and the gangs alike feast on the flesh of men.

He tastes the ashes, the only thing that remains of a world that was once daylight and free of the knowledge that things like this existed, nearly close enough to touch.

But that wall fell, like all walls do, victims of time or pressure or circumstance. Now there is no division, no dark and daylight. There is just this world, burning and broken, and in it Jack Winter is alone.

Jack hated waking up. At times, he would keep his eyes pressed shut and imagine that when he opened them he'd see the ceiling of his old flat, stained and blank. That instead of a car fire or raw sewage, he'd smell coffee and a fry up. That instead of the constant sirens and blared announcements from the Territorial Army tanks roaming the streets, he'd hear his daughter and his wife laughing.

He opened his eyes. He could see straight through to the sky. It was as black as the rest of the place, and he sat up and looked around at the hundreds of other bodies scattered across the floor of King's Cross. Some slept, some smoked or ate tinned food with furtive expressions.

A few aid workers walked among them, and one started toward him with a vile meal-replacement bar that was quickly becoming the only thing you could reliably find to eat in London, if you weren't into roasting stray cats or cannibalism.

Jack waved her off. The other poor bastards in this place needed food a lot more than he did. King's Cross was one of the last safe zones in London, surrounded by holdouts from the army who hadn't cut and run when they started getting ripped apart by lycanthropes and zombies.

He hated the safe zones. Nothing but sad civilians, dirty and battered, always with fear in their eyes as they scoured each individual face for signs that it did, in fact, belong to a human.

The psychic frequencies in King's Cross were calm, though, and it was the only place he could get any sleep. Whitechapel used to blank out his second sight with the sheer volume of static from the many bad deeds wrought on its earth, but now it was alive with ghosts, poltergeists, and wraiths—guaranteed high-octane nightmare fuel for someone like Jack.

Besides, he didn't want to go back there. Lily and Pete had been there. And now . . .

"Are you sure you're not hungry?" The nurse held out the wrapped bar to him. Jack caught a whiff and wrinkled his nose.

"Food's not really a priority these days, luv."

She shoved the bar against his chest, until he was forced to take it or let it drop and shatter. He had to hand it to the civilians—they'd figured it out pretty quickly. Chop the head off a zombie, ward your safe spaces against the dead, and don't make skin-to-skin contact with anyone. Magic, especially black magic, used touch as a contact point, and everyone in the city had taken to swaddling up.

"Try to keep your strength up," the nurse said, and moved on.

They all believed in it so quickly, Jack thought, watching a little girl sitting next to her sleeping parents, reading a coverless book with burnt edges. *In magic, in the people who used it, in the creatures it spawned.*

Sure, it had caused a mass panic and destroyed London as they knew it, but they all believed.

He could never have imagined such a thing when he was the girl's age, still realizing that seeing and speaking to the dead wasn't something every snot-nosed brat could do.

She caught his eye. She and her parents were Indian, but he could see Lily in her face.

Who am I kidding, Jack thought. He saw Lily in *every* little girl's face.

"Here." He gave her the protein bar. She frowned at him.

"Don't you need this?"

Jack stood up and shouldered his kit, the stuff he'd managed to grab from his flat before they had to run. Before . . .

"No, darling," he told the girl. "Not where I'm going."

CHAPTER 2

The safe zone extended from King's Cross to the Ice Wharf on the canal, and down to Clerkenwell Road. A tiny slice of what had once been the most alive city in all the world, at least as far as Jack was concerned. London had so many layers of magic and death and blood and sex all piled on top of one another, you could never plumb the depths. That city, the one kept safely out of civilian gaze, and the daylight London, made it a place he'd never wanted to leave.

Now he *couldn't* leave, because from all reports the rest of England was just as fucked.

Just shy of the barrier, Jack slipped through the wire and down the boarded-up steps to the Angel tube station. He could take the tunnels to Blackfriars and from there one of the ferry gangs would take him across the Thames.

He thought about the last meeting he'd had with Ian Mosswood, a Fae creature who was one of the few not to abandon London for their own realm, the Courts. Mosswood, usually a chap who could pose for billboards, looked ragged, wrapped in a black coat, his salt-and-pepper hair mostly white. Fae didn't last long in the Black or the daylight world unless they were ancient and strong, which Moss-wood was.

When they'd met, Jack had had the unpleasant realization that the world was a lot more buggered than he'd let himself believe.

"You know you can't possibly succeed, right?" Mosswood had asked, keeping a close eye out for both the scavenger gangs and the menagerie of flesh-ripping creatures that roamed outside the safe zones.

"Cheers, Ian," Jack said. "Always like to hear that I'm doomed from the start."

Mosswood handed him a scrap of vellum on which was both a liberal spatter of blood and an address.

"I'm dying," Mosswood said. "Do you realize how absurd that is? I am eternal and yet I am dying."

Jack glanced at the paper now, then shoved it back in his pocket. The address was south of the river, deep in Elemental territory, and he remembered the sinking sensation in his gut that he'd been careful not to let Mosswood see.

"We all have to go sometime, mate," he'd told Mosswood.

"You'd do well to remember that," the Green Man replied. "I won't see you again, Jack. This world has only a little time before there's nothing left but the ashes and the demons."

"And the cockroaches," Jack had said, with a lev-ity he didn't feel. His sense of humor had abandoned him on the day he'd left Whitechapel.

"Like I said," Mosswood muttered, and then turned and limped away.

Jack shook off his memories and forced himself

to focus. The tunnels to the river were populated with nasty monsters, of course. Jack had a light, his hexing abilities, and a liberal spray of iron-and-salt packed shotgun rounds for anything that made it past the first line. Pete had had her old service weapon, which he was glad of when things went pear shaped, but the shotgun was better if you weren't a former crack-shot police inspector like his wife. Point and shoot, no skill required.

The things north of the river were mostly scavengers, wraiths and the like that would rather feed on the dead than the living. Then there were the mole people, as Pete had called them, the humans who'd taken to the underground when it all kicked off.

And the ghosts. Thick, packed, like commuters waiting for a train. Many of them had been, when they'd died, and most were so new they didn't even realize they were dead.

Jack sighed, doing his best to avoid brushing against the silent, staring spirits that packed the tunnel. His head throbbed.

He had to get to the south side of the river before dark. He'd been chasing his daughter for months, ever since *he* had ripped Lily out of Pete's arms.

Some of those months, the ones after Pete, had been wasted crawling inside any bottle he could find. He would have gone back to being a dirty smack addict if anyone in the greater London area had any drugs left.

Then he'd picked himself up, and set about getting Lily back. Jack had spent his life on the shadow side, so he learned how to sneak in and out of the safe zones, learned who dealt information and who just played at it, learned the names of all the big hard men who controlled South London now, and he decided that he'd either get Lily back or he'd be dead soon enough.

These days, either option was acceptable.

Of course Jack knew *he* was only keeping Lily alive to torment him. That Jack was being batted around like a cat toy. Jack had decided it didn't matter. All of this had happened. He'd started life in shit; he'd clawed his way into a filthy, miserable existence as a psychic too strong to shut off his own visions, and when he'd finally found a bit of happiness, that was when it really hit the fan.

Jack was acutely aware as he climbed the broken escalator at Blackfriars that if he'd just stayed in his tip and continued shooting up, none of this would ever have happened.

That was the sting of hindsight. Jack couldn't imagine being happy, and then he was. He couldn't imagine his happiness being ripped away from him, and it was, every last bit. And looking back, it was so fucking obvious that it hurt just as much as a boot to the gut. He wasn't supposed to be happy and live his life and kick off as an old man with a bunch of grandkids. Jack had only ever existed to burn the world, whether he wanted to or not.

The demons and the old gods and everyone with sense who'd ever met him saw it. He was the only one who had thought things might turn out differently.

Breaking glass, screams, and bootfalls reached his ears as he exited the station, and Jack sighed again.

Riots were practically an hourly occurance now, but he didn't have time to waste on avoiding this one. The sun—what little could be seen through the constant haze of soot and smoke—was already perilously low.

A broken brick whizzed past his ear, and he saw a human gang—the Front Street Boys out of Twickenham, judging by their colors—converging and beating on a zombie. The thing already had one leg off and its face stove in, thrashing as it struggled to scream through its mouth sewn up with red thread.

The Stygian Brothers were turning out zombies with the regularity of a biscuit factory, some half-arsed gibberish about giving the dead of London a second chance. All they gave the rest of the city was a great big fucking pest problem, by Jack's reckoning, but that was a Stygian for you. Corpse-botherers with no damn sense at all.

Jack avoided the festivities as best he could, heading for the docks where you could find a ferry south, if you were either not human or suicidal.

Before he'd gone far, though, he heard screaming of a different kind—human and panicked. Not that human screams were rare outside the safe zones, but this was bookended by the kind of cackling that Jack attributed to men who enjoyed inflicting pain on smaller, weaker things.

He rounded the corner into an alley that dead-ended at the water. Once, the area had been posh, like most of the wharfs. When he'd first landed in London, the Docklands had been a rotting mass of wharves and junkies and tips falling into the river.

Over the years, the tips had been knocked down and the junkies shuffled off to places like Peckham, and the wharves supported posh shops, restaurants where the prices were longer than the menus, and gleaming towers of flats that Jack always figured cost a quid to even look at.

Now it was all burned or overrun with the gangs and the zombies. He could smell the river from here. It was like London had reverted to its dirty, blood-soaked roots. A river full of sewage, a sky full of smoke, and streets full of people so desperate they were worse than animals.

There were four of them surrounding the source of the screaming, a woman with a backpack which one of the hooligans was busy ripping into.

They didn't sport colors, except for the rusty streaks across their bare torsos. Jack dropped his head to his chest. Fucking cannibals. What was it about people that made them decide the quickest way to deal with the end of the world as they knew it was to turn each other into entrées?

He should just walk away. There were four of them, and often enough cannibalism led directly to necromancers, all too happy to have a band of homicidal nutters who'd work for long pig. Bad enough the cannibals ran about feasting on human flesh; being juiced up on black magic was just unfair.

Still, Jack picked up a length of pipe lying in the street and marched forward. He hit the one rummaging through the pack first, laying him out on his face, and then banged the pipe off an overturned metal rubbish bin. "Oi!"

The cannibals turned as one. Their eyes were as empty as the next addict's, and Jack sighed. They were definitely running on sorcery.

Jack set himself, gripping the pipe so he felt the threads bite into his palm. "Come on, then," he said. "Let's get this over with."

The leader was a skinny bloke with short hair, pasty and small. He might have been one of the posh twats occupying this stretch of the wharves before it all kicked off. Jack threw a leg-locker hex on him and watched him go down, one of his friends falling with him. Jack took the brunt of the third's charge on his shoulder, the cannibal glancing off and going past. He responded with a hit to the kidneys with the pipe, and another to the back of the cannibal's skull when he went down.

And another, just for good measure.

The woman screamed something, and Jack turned to see the leader up and bearing down on him. He wondered, as the man closed his teeth on the sleeve of Jack's leather, why she hadn't done a rabbit as soon as he'd shown up. Might explain why she'd gotten caught by cannibals in the first place—she was too fucking stupid to live.

Jack let himself fall. The bloke wasn't big enough to pin him, and Jack rolled them and pressed the pipe across the bloke's throat. He kept pressing until the bastard twitched and went still.

He realized he'd forgotten about the leader's friend when he felt a waft of air across the back of his neck as the cannibal wrapped his hands around it.

Then there was a report, a sting in his ears as the

shot echoed back and forth from the narrow alley walls, and the woman straightened up from her pack holding a handgun, an old-fashioned revolver that gits in movies called a .38 Special.

The cannibal dropped, the exit wound in his chest the size of Jack's balled fist.

"Fuck," he said, sitting down hard. The woman picked up a piece of gauze from her pack and approached him, wiping what turned out to be cannibal blood off his face.

"You know," she said. "You have a shotgun strapped to your back. Why go to all this trouble?"

Jack blinked at the nurse from King's Cross. Her face was scratched and dirty, and the collar of her scrubs hung in rags, but she looked a lot more together than he felt. "What the fuck are you doing out here?" she asked, tossing the gauze away, sticking the gun in her waist, and gathering up the wreckage of her pack.

"I could ask you the very same question," he said.

"Not everyone who needs help made it to the safety line," she said. "And now the army won't let them in if they make it, so I'm out here."

She hauled Jack to his feet with surprising ease for a woman who'd almost been turned into carpaccio. He let her. He wasn't young any longer, and a dust-up like that belonged to the Jack Winter who strode through the streets in steel toes and black leather, daring someone to give him an excuse to shed blood. His own or the other bloke's, it hadn't mattered.

"How about you?" she said. "You one of those

mages? The ones who claim they aren't doing sorcery even though everyone knows they fucking are?"

Jack shook his head. If she'd seen the leg-locker hex, he'd deny it. People in the safe zones hated mages. They hated magic, period. Believed in it, saw it with their own eyes, and hated it. That bit hadn't changed—give the human race something it didn't understand and it got right down to the business of burning it out of existence.

"Just heading across," he said.

The nurse's light brows drew together. "That's demon territory."

Jack nodded. "I know," he said. "And to answer your other question, luv, I didn't ventilate those cannibals because I didn't want to also ventilate you."

She snorted. "Glad you're concerned with my safety, because you sure as hell don't care about your own, going over there." She pointed at the columns of smoke rising from across the Thames. "You go over there, you're dead."

Jack sighed. "Look, what's your name?" He didn't want some gun-toting Florence Nightingale to stop him from crossing in the mistaken belief that his life was worth saving. He had to shift her before she decided they were friends, or worse, that she needed to help him.

That was how people ended up getting hurt. There'd already been enough of that.

"Ida," she said. "Ida Higgins."

"Christ, what did you ever do to your parents?" Jack said.

Ida Higgins shrugged. "My grandmother's name. What's yours?"

"Jack," he said. "Jack Caldecott." Ida hated mages, and he was one of the big names on the list. He figured if Pete were here, she wouldn't mind him using her maiden name to save his arse.

"You want to tell me why you're bent on feeding yourself inch by inch to demons, Jack?" Ida said.

While he'd been wasting time saving Ida, the horizon had started to bleed red. The smoky sunset was already in full, apocalyptic swing. It would be almost night by the time he made it across.

Fuck it, Jack decided. It wasn't like he was planning to come back anyway. "Because my daughter is over there," he said. "If I go after her, I may die. If I don't, she will for sure."

CHAPTER 3

"Take the baby." Pete shoved Lily into Jack's arms while she screamed and thrashed, her face several shades darker than the pink onesie he'd dressed her in that morning.

Jack tried to breathe, but there was nothing, no air, and his vision began to spin. Pete snatched Lily back. "Jesus, Jack! If you don't want to quiet her, then go pick Margaret up from school. Either way, get off your arse and be a bit useful."

He blinked at Pete. His eyes were dry, gritty. *As if he were still standing in the smoke.*

"Was I asleep?" he asked.

Pete rolled her eyes. "How should I know? I've been dealing with our darling daughter's fit for the past half hour."

"Yeah, sorry," Jack said, taking Lily back and bouncing her until her screams became merely complaints.

He wanted it to be a dream, and for now, it would be. He'd had dreams before that were totally real in the moment.

"Thank you," Pete said. Her hair dusted her eyes, the new pixie cut she'd adopted standing on end, and her face was flushed. "Sorry," she said. "I'm just in a rotten mood, I guess."

Jack shifted Lily to one arm and used the other to pull Pete close. She smelled like baby powder and shampoo. When he kissed her, she smiled against his mouth. "So I take it all is forgiven?"

"I'll keep the baby occupied," he said. "Go get Margaret."

He waited until Pete flew out the door of their flat, keys jangling, before he collapsed into a chair with Lily on his chest.

Dreams about being dead were nothing new. He'd been having those since he was barely past puberty. Dreams about Pete being dead and Lily gone . . . those were new.

If it was a dream at all, and you know it wasn't, something treacherous whispered inside him.

Visions and prophecy were a load of shit, as far as Jack was concerned, but he couldn't change the fact that what just happened had been real, a direct line from his second sight into some sort of apocalyptic ripple reaching out from the Black and disturbing things so much that the whole thing had rung his skull like a bell.

Or, he convinced himself more and more as Lily settled down to sleep on his chest and he managed to pour a glass of whiskey one-handed, it really *was* just a dream. A horrible, vivid, shit-your-pants dream, but just the same, nothing but his own frayed neurons firing out of sequence.

He'd almost managed to talk himself into believing the whole nightmare had been just that when a bird crashed into the glass of the flat, sending spider cracks across the heavy pane. Half of the wavy panes had survived the Blitz and everything since, and Jack felt his hand spasm as the whiskey glass shattered in it. "Fuck!" he hissed.

Lily woke up and began to wail as the crow fluttered on the windowsill outside, helpless with a damaged wing. Jack started to get up and help the silly thing, cursing up a blue streak as he put Lily in her bounce chair and took off his shirt to wrap around his hand, sliced to shit and dribbling blood all over the floor.

He stopped when he saw the rest of the crows. Not just crows—ravens, sparrows, all the other birds in London, too. They alighted on rooftops, on wires, on the awnings of the money-changers and the mobile phone kiosk below his window. People on the street stopped and pointed, and even the cars on Mile End Road slowed as their passengers stared.

Birds, as far as the eye could see, just sitting and staring toward his flat. The crow righted itself and tapped its beak against the glass over and over, as more and more cracks appeared in the pane.

"Fuck off!" Jack shouted, and thumped on the glass with his good hand. He felt the constricting panic of a bad attack of sight coming on, the throbbing in his skull that he'd do anything to quiet, the tides of magic all around him converging into a drowning wave.

As one, the birds took flight, and Jack felt the wave of magic choke him and take him under. Blackness took him before he hit the floor.

CHAPTER 4

"Jack?"

Water hit him in the face and burned when it went up his nose. Jack choked and bolted up. Margaret Smythe, the teenage girl he and Pete had saved from an apolcalyptic cult, crouched next to him, her school water bottle upended over his head.

"Sorry," Margaret said. Beyond her, Jack saw Pete standing with her mobile, talking to the 999 service.

"No problem, luv," he said. He started to swipe the water off his face, but Margaret shook her head. "Don't. You'll get blood everywhere."

Jack saw the red puddled on the floor next to him, then took in the broken glass and a window ledge newly covered with bird shit. "Is Lily all right?" he asked.

Margaret went and got a dish towel, which she wrapped around his hand. "Fine," she said. "What happened?"

Jack wasn't sure himself, and he definitely wasn't going to get Margaret all worked up over nothing. She was only thirteen, and she had endured one set of crap parents already.

"You're good at that first aid thing," he said instead.

Margaret shrugged. "My mum used to crack her head on stuff all the time when she passed out. At least you're just clumsy."

"Might need some work on the bedside manner, though," Jack said.

Pete hung up and came in. "I'm just going to skip asking what happened," she said. "There was a pile-up on the M25, so it'll be faster to just drive to the A&E. Think you can manage it?"

Jack nodded. He'd welcome anything that involved a lot of normal people and lights and noise, even though he usually hated hospitals.

"Stay with Lily," Pete told Margaret. "I'll call you as soon as I know anything."

The A&E was packed and busy, but between Jack's steadily dripping dish towel and Pete's insistence, they were put in a curtained cubicle almost immediately.

When the nurse pulled the screen, Pete slumped in the plastic chair opposite him. "You want to tell me what happened now?"

Jack shrugged, even though his cut throbbed with every motion. "Window broke, I cut my hand, it was worse than I thought and I fainted." He leaned back and shut his eyes. "Humiliating, yes. Cause for alarm, no."

"You should know by now you can't lie to me." Pete's weight shifted the mattress next to his. "You've been pale as a sheet ever since we came in."

"Blood loss?" Jack offered lamely.

"Bullshit," Pete said. Jack sighed. He was going to have to tell her. Maybe saying it out loud would make the whole thing seem like something kicked up by the intersection of his talent and a hiccup in the flow of power winding under this world, full of its hospitals and traffic wrecks and everything mundane. Something weird, but not worthy of worry.

"I had a dream," he said. "It was . . . it was the future. Things had gone wrong. And you and Lily . . . you were dead."

He thought Pete might be about to smack him, or that she'd walk out, until he felt her head cradle against his chest, her small frame sharing the skinny hospital bed. "And how did that lead to you making the flat look like a crime scene?"

"I hate birds," Jack grumbled. He didn't want to think about what the birds meant. He knew. It wasn't exactly a subtle hint.

The Morrigan, the bride of war and death, was sending him yet another love note. She'd never been so direct, so out in the open, but her tricks were all designed to make him piss himself and fall in line.

It hadn't worked before, and it wasn't going to now.

"It was just a dream," Pete said. "At the risk of sounding soppy, dreams can't do anything to you, Jack, unless you think about them afterward."

"You were dead," he said again, not liking how small his voice got.

"But I'm not," Pete said. "And I'm not going to be. You've known me a long time, Jack." She sat up and pressed her lips against his skin. "You know I'm far too mean to die."

The curtain whipped back, and Pete moved back to her chair at the knowing smile from the nurse.

"Right," she said, pushing her cart ahead of her. "Let's get that hand fixed up, Mr. Winter."

"It's Jack," he said. The nurse took away the towel and examined his cut, clucking.

"I'm Ida," she said. "This is a nasty scratch, but it's not deep. I'll stitch you up and a doctor can make sure you didn't damage your nerves, but we'll fix you up with some pills and you can go on home."

"No pills," Pete said. "He used to be addicted to opiates."

Normally, Jack would have given her a dirty look at that—just because he used to shoot smack didn't mean he was going to start popping handfuls of housewife's helpers.

He didn't, though, because he'd gotten a good look at the nurse's face, and her name tag: Ida Higgins.

It was her. Same face, minus dirt and tear streaks. Same tall lanky frame, only clad in pink and yellow scrubs rather than dirty, torn green ones.

Ida returned his stare with an expression that told Jack she was wondering if she should remove herself from biting distance. "Are you on any narcotics right now, Jack?"

"I . . . ," he tried, but there was a rock in his throat, a scream building behind it as the sounds and smells of his dream came rushing back over the beeping and clanking and shouting of the A&E.

Because it hadn't been a dream. What he'd seen had been real, and somehow the Ida Higgins he'd met months or years in the future had converged with Jack now, before whatever led to their encounter on the docks had happened.

His dream was a vision. It was his talent, his inexorable connection to the cataclysms of death that surged through both the Black and the daylight.

The Morrigan had finally gotten his attention.

Jack looked down at the tattoos that covered his skin down to his knuckles, one of them sliced through by the glass. She'd marked him, the ancient thing that fed his talent, and he'd been an idiot to think he could pretend she wasn't going to collect on her mark.

"Jack?" Ida held his palm gently, antiseptic soaked gauze poised over his cut. Nothing sparked when they touched. She was normal, human.

He had to get away from her.

"Jack!"

This time Pete screamed, but he was running, his talent bubbling up through his mind, dropping the veil of sight over his eyes. The A&E was choked with spirits, some fresh and wavering, cast in black and silver, and some were so old they were just voids of black smoke in the background magic of the place.

He burst onto the street, the traffic barely registering, and saw more spirits, from every age of London. Prostitutes; men in top hats, wigs before that; soldiers from the Great War wrapped in bandages and missing limbs; dirty, skinny children who'd died on the steps of a hospital they couldn't pay to enter. Roman dead before that, when the entire East End of London had been a burning ground for Britain's conquerors.

They didn't move or flicker in and out as the dead should.

They all looked in one direction, at him, and then

turned their heads as one, south, toward the Thames, and watched the black clouds laced with lightning roll across the face of London, every church bell in the path of the screaming wind tolling the end of the daylight world.

Jack ran. He dodged the cabs and buses, crossed the street, and kept running until his lungs felt like twin sawblades planted in his chest.

By the time he looked up, he was on Old Street, miles from the hospital. Jack stumbled to the nearest wall and leaned against it, glad that passersby gave him a wide berth.

His shirt stuck to him, and his hands shook. His head felt as if it were full of pistons, thrumming away in time with his jackhammering heart.

At least his hand had stopped bleeding. Small comfort, considering that Pete probably thought he'd finally gone around the bend. He'd always known there was an expiration date on the trust she put in him. She'd helped him find ways to stave off his sight that didn't involve smack, stuck by him when he'd made bad choice after bad choice with demons and the Morrigan and everything in between, but Pete wasn't stupid. Sooner or later, she was going to hit her threshold.

Jack had just always thought that when she left him, only his world would collapse. Now, it looked like everyone in London was pretty well fucked.

He sank down to the pavement, cold now that he'd stopped moving, and wrapped his arms around his knees.

He'd *remembered* so much during the vision. Why things were the way they were, how to get around the city, but not how everything had started. It was as if he'd woken up in the middle of a program he'd never seen, and picked up the threads but not the bigger picture.

Glad he hadn't managed to eat anything, as his shoes would be wearing it now, Jack considered that this was pretty much where everything had started. On a sidewalk, sick and out of prospects, when a man named Seth McBride had plucked him up and told him that he wasn't mad or bad or dangerous to know. He was talented, meant for something bigger.

Something bigger turned out to be the Morrigan, and what Jack was meant for was to usher in her rule. After that, Seth and his ilk hadn't been so enthusiastic, and Jack was on his own again. Besides Pete, nobody before or since had the nerve to get close enough to him to be hurt.

"That's not entirely true."

Jack looked down at the snakeskin shoe that reflected his own face back dozens of times in the shiny hide. He looked up at the pale black-nailed finger proffering a cigarette.

"Stop reading my thoughts," he told Belial. "It's tacky."

"And not very illuminating," the demon agreed, sticking the fag between his own lips and lighting it.

"We're done," Jack said. "Remember? Square accounts and all."

"I did tell you that there's something brewing in

Hell." Belial exhaled. "And that I'm asking—nicely, even—for your help."

Jack narrowed his eyes as the demon leaned against the wall next to him. "You're a Prince of Hell, mate. Why the fuck do you need my help?"

The demon smiled. Jack hated it when demons tried to mimic emotion. The only thing that could put a genuine smile on Belial's face was the pain and suffering of others. Jack's had filled that slot more than once.

"You know that expression, 'only human'?" he said. "Well, I'm not that, but apparently I'm not perfect either, Jack. Because when I floated my opinion to the other Princes that things have gone off the rails, I was unceremoniously told to fuck off. As if I were a junior partner."

It was Jack's turn to laugh. He didn't like Belial—hated him, even, but he liked seeing the obsequious bastard squirm. "I take it ruling the roost isn't as easy as you thought."

"I'm *right*." Belial glared at Jack. "There's a bloke come up through the ranks, got everyone all stirred up, and he's created a right bit of chaos in the Pit that could have been avoided if we'd just liquidated the little shitbird when I suggested it."

"And pardon me, but why should I care?" Jack said. "I hate you, Belial, did you forget that?"

"Your hate is not nearly equal to the contempt I hold for you, be sure," the demon said. He scratched out his cigarette against the brick wall. "This world of yours is shit," he said. "But for as long as anyone can recall, it's all been spinning around as it is. Hell, the Black, this, the Land of the Dead, all stitched together by the in-between places, and aside from the occasional primordial demon jailbreak, quite nice, really."

Jack felt unease squirm in his chest. Belial was chatty, but he usually only talked about either himself, or how thoroughly he was going to fuck over the victim of his attentions. Having a conversation like they were equals was much, much worse than feeling like Belial was about to drop his boot on Jack's head. It was unnatural. Demons were predators, and mages were conditioned to avoid them at all costs.

"Get to the point," Jack said. "I have to walk all the way back to Tower Hamlets before my wife has a fit and bans me not only from sex, our bed, and anything enjoyable for the next six months, but the flat as well."

"I said it to dear Petunia," Belial said, "and I'll say it to you. Nice as this little juggling act is, we've too many balls in the air. Everything that's happened since I met you lo these many years ago, Jackie . . . it's all been leading to this." Belial stood up and faced Jack. His smile was oddly small and calm, no hint of superiority. "It's the beginning of the end, and if something isn't done, then when the end has come and the end has passed us by, we're not going to be on top. This other tosser is."

Jack started to tell him to fuck off, but Belial held up his hand. "You are the only one who knows firsthand what it would mean if this balance of Hell and magic and the mundane fell out of balance, Jack. You've seen the precursors, and you saw what almost happened when those moronic cultists who had little Maggie Smythe tried to slice into Purgatory."

Jack wished fiercely that he'd taken the cigarette when the demon had offered. "Fine, the end is nigh. What am I supposed to do, march about with a sign hanging off me neck?"

"Help me stop it, of course," Belial said. "Because old-fashioned as it might be, I like things the way they are. I don't relish the apocalypse. I'm a contented creature, Jack, and this bastard has threatened to upset all that. So I'm asking. Not cutting a deal. Asking you. Help me put the brakes on this long skid we're on into armageddon. If you do . . ." Belial's smile was bitter this time. "I owe you a favor."

That made Jack pause. Vision or not, Belial was talking about the end, the big show, the falling of all the walls that kept the Black apart from the daylight, and the dead from walking the earth as the living did. Like most things Belial said, it was a load of crap, but a favor from a demon?

Jack had a feeling, if something big enough to send this vision to him was coming, that might come in handy.

And because Jack didn't believe in ignoring the obvious, he thought Belial's shit-stirrer would probably have some part in kicking things off.

Jack shivered at the thought of a world without the Black and the daylight—just one world, rampant with all of the darkness and evil that sprang from magic, and the human suffering and wickedness on the other. No buffers, no barriers, nothing to keep the world sane.

"Fine," he said to Belial. "But that favor? It's going to be the biggest you ever do."

CHAPTER 5

The army evacuated Whitechapel at dawn, convoys of trucks miles long rolling down Whitechapel Road, spreading through Tower Hamlets ahead of the fires and the looters.

The corpses weren't all human, or even mostly. Scavengers from across the river had made it to the Docklands in the night, and Jack had been listening to the screams of people too stupid or unlucky to make it inside before the legions of Hell fell upon them.

They were mostly scavengers, carrion feeders or elementals that crawled inside human hosts and left the street littered with corpses.

The trucks didn't care. They crunched over flesh and skulls, the long dead and the ones that were still warm.

By the time Jack held the door open for Pete and Lily and Margaret, it was chaos all around. Trucks were on fire, the army had taken cover anywhere they could, and the streets were filled with mobs of panicked civilians and looters all struggling to run from the demons.

Pete tried to turn with the baby and go back inside, but a flaming bottle shattered against the building, and flames sprouted so close Jack could feel the heat singe his eyebrows.

Magaret screamed, and he grabbed her hand while Pete shielded Lily, and they ran down the alley where they'd kept Pete's Mini Cooper. The car had been looted weeks ago, was just a spray-painted corpse now, no glass, no tires, and no engine.

Gunfire chattered from the road. The army hadn't figured out yet that bullets didn't do much good against things that weren't human. Jack hoped, at least, that they'd put a dent in the looters.

"Where are we going to go?" Pete panted. "If we can't evacuate, we're fucked."

"If we go back that way, we're fucked," Jack said. Margaret's grip on his hand was so tight that he could feel his fingers going numb. "Maybe we can try to get to a tube station. At least we'll be off the streets."

"They shut down the stations weeks ago," Pete said. She looked up at him, pulling Lily tight against her. "Jack, what are we going to do?"

Jack didn't get to tell her he had no fucking idea. A cluster of looters appeared at the far end of the alley, and the leader let out a sharp whistle, pointing at Jack and Pete.

"Oh, shit," he muttered. He could see it now— they'd be beaten, anything useful would be taken, and then if they were lucky it would end there. If they weren't, they'd be taken or killed, or left alive but too weak to fight off the demons that hid in every dark spot in the city.

It was Pete who acted while Jack was still frozen.

She shoved Lily into Margaret's arms. "Run," she told Margaret. "Get to a truck, and go with the evacuation. We'll find you."

"But Pete . . ." Margaret's eyes filled up with panicked tears.

"Don't argue!" Pete snapped. "We *will* find you, but you need to take Lily and you need to run."

Margaret turned and fled, Lily wailing. Jack looked at Pete, panic forming a bubble in his chest and making his heart thrum. "We should have stayed together," he said.

Pete turned back toward the looters, who were taking their time. They knew Jack and Pete had nowhere to go. It was either the gang, or the demons out on the main road. Magaret could find her way to the army, as long as they bought her some time.

"I'm sorry," Pete said.

Jack felt the panic burst abruptly, replaced with something that felt like a blade to the gut. "We're not going to meet them, are we?"

"Maybe," Pete said. "But the important thing is we give them time to get away."

She didn't look upset or afraid, but then, Pete never did. She was strong. If it weren't for him, Jack thought, she probably would have survived even this without a scratch.

He threw a leg-locker hex on the first looter, but there were more and more of them, and he and Pete got pushed, slowly, back toward the body of the Mini. Jack was about to say fuck it and hex up a fire that would incinerate every last looter when one sprang forward and grabbed Pete, pulling her forward into the forest of grasping hands and cold, frenzied faces.

Pete screamed and kicked at the looter, but before Jack could do anything, a shot rang out, snapping off the walls of the narrow alley. The first was followed by another volley as three soldiers with machine guns advanced, mowing down the looters until none of them moved.

Jack caught Pete as she swayed, and he didn't understand for a moment why she was falling. The looters hadn't had blades, just tire irons and cricket bats, things left over from when they'd been rational people, before the advent of the demons and the dead had driven them over the edge.

Then he saw the two blossoms of red on her shirt, and he started screaming. Pete fell, and she didn't move, didn't breathe, didn't do anything. Her eyes stayed open, but she didn't look at him, and there wasn't enough breath left in her lungs to say anything.

He'd never imagined this. That it would be quick, unexpected, that one moment Pete would be in his arms and the next she'd be gone, just another body out of the hundreds he'd seen in the preceding weeks. He'd never imagined that Pete would die before him.

Jack wanted to stay with her, right there on the bloody pavement, but the soldiers grabbed him and forced him onto a truck. He fought them. They'd killed her, and now he was alone. Finally, one of them hit Jack on the skull with the butt of a rifle, and he tumbled into the merciful void of nothing.

CHAPTER 6

Belial was watching him when his eyes flickered open. "It's a little weird when you go out like that, just so you know," he said. "People are staring."

Jack sat up and immediately wished he hadn't. "You might want to move unless you want me redecorating that ugly suit of yours," he told Belial.

The demon pulled Jack to his feet and hailed a cab. Once they were inside, he looked Jack up and down.

"You going to tell me what you saw?"

Jack pressed his forehead against the glass. "No." The gunshot still echoed in his ears, and he could still see Pete lying at his feet, silent and bloody.

Belial shrugged. "Suit yourself. But it might interest you to know that what you're seeing isn't certain."

" 'Always in motion is the future?' " Jack grumbled.

"More like, you're going to come down to the Pit with me and we're going to convince the Princes that they can't bargain their way out of this," Belial said.

That made Jack sit up. His head was still thick and muzzy, but a day trip to Hell was the one thing worse than the visions that had started knocking him on his arse. "I don't fucking think so," he said. "The last time I was there, if you'll remember, the Princes didn't exactly take to me."

"I'm one, and I certainly don't," Belial said. "But you're tied up in this now, whether you like it or not."

Jack wanted to argue that this was a demon's mess, and that Belial could piss off, but much as he hated to admit it, Belial was right. He was tied up in it. The things he was seeing couldn't be written off. If there was even a chance that what he'd seen could happen, he couldn't do anything but try to help Belial stop it.

Pete and Lily weren't going to end up in the place he'd seen. *He* wasn't going to be that man, drifting through the end of the world with nothing to anchor him except the fact that his heart was still beating.

The cab stopped at the entrance to Regent's Park, and Belial stepped out. Jack followed him, and Belial held out his hand. "Let me do the talking," he said. "Things with the Princes haven't exactly been smooth since all this kicked off."

"You mean you found someone besides me who thinks you're an insufferable twat?" Jack said. "Imagine that."

Belial heaved a deep sigh. "The day the first human crawled out of the mud was the day the rest of the universe went to shit," he muttered. "Just stick with me, and try not to get both of us turned into furniture, all right?"

"Sure," Jack said to himself. "Sweet-talk the Princes of Hell. What could be easier?"

CHAPTER 7

Jack hated the way the air smelled in Hell. The City belched smoke from its furnaces and factories, and the heavy, hot winds borne out of the surrounding white bone deserts invaded his nostrils with the worst elements of both a garbage tip on a hot day and a vigorously burning tire fire.

He hated the sounds, too. The clanging of the heavy iron trains that ran on tracks fifty stories above the cesspits at street level. The snarling and hissing of the elemental demons that prowled every alley and dark byway like packs of especially hungry dogs. And the screaming. It was like flies buzzing, after a time—the screams of tormented souls floating from every corner of Hell.

Belial's new quarters, as a Prince, were two thirds up the tallest spire in the City, the triple-towered fortress that, to Jack's eyes, had always resembled a pitchfork. Jack wondered if that was on purpose. Demons weren't known for their sense of humor.

"Nice place," he said, looking around the flat. Twenty-foot ceilings and black glass floors aside, the space wasn't what Jack had imagined for a ruler of Hell. Everything was black or white, and aside from a rug made from the hide of some furry white creature

that had three curling horns sprouting from its life-
less head, everything was made of stone or glass.

"It'll do," Belial said. Jack examined himself in
a mirror framed in interlocked skeletal hands. He
didn't bothering asking if the bones were real.

"Bit severe, isn't it?" he said. "Sort of reminds me
of a monastery by way of a gay nightclub."

"You implying something?" Belial asked, standing next to Jack so their reflections overlapped.

Jack turned his head. He didn't like the demon
that close. "You working up the courage to tell me
something?"

Belial flashed him that grin and slapped him on
the shoulder. "Get it all out of your system now. The
Princes aren't nearly as tolerant of that sewage pit
you call a mouth."

"You know," Jack said, brushing Belial's grip off
him, "you're one of them now. Still getting used to
that heavy crown?"

"I include myself in that statement," Belial said.
"Now shut up and stay close."

The first and only time Jack had stood before the
Triumvirate, he'd seen them in a dull sort of corpo-
rate office, which fit his imagining of the Princes as
a stodgy bunch of bureaucrats obsessed with bargains and rules and divvying up Hell so they all got
an equal slice of the pie.

This time, Belial led him through smooth black
hallways, arched at the top, which looked as if they'd
been carved by the passage of some great serpent
rather than any tool.

The room he opened the black double doors to

was smaller than Jack had expected—too small for comfort. The remaining duo of Princes sat on either side of a long table inlaid with the bones of a winged creature, floating in clear resin like a fossil chipped out of the ground. The walls held a selection of paintings depicting medieval tortures, in graphic and colorful detail.

Jack sucked in a breath to dispel the tightness in his chest. They needed him, for whatever reason, he told himself. And he needed them, for the time being, if they were going to call a halt to the event sending him nervous breakdowns through the frequencies of the Black.

"I'll never understand your proclivity for running to the humans whenever something goes wrong, Belial," said the Prince on the right. Baal, Jack remembered, a bloke who did an even more piss-poor job with his human form than Belial. Baal had snake's eyes and sallow skin spotted with sores. His tongue was twice as long and thin as a man's, which gave his voice a curious sibilance. Bald, he resembled something that lived in the dark and popped out at night to eat unwitting household pets.

"You don't understand a lot of things." Belial took his seat at the head of the table. "You still think this can all be smoothed over."

"He's just an elemental, for fuck's sake," said the other Prince, Beelzebub. Where Baal couldn't be bothered to look human, Beelzebub looked almost *too* human, slick and blond as a film star, and about as plastic. Belial at least looked like he had blood pumping through his veins. Beelzebub resembled one of those dolls that came to life and tried to carve up your family with a chainsaw.

"Wait, wait," Jack said. Belial slitted his eyes, and Jack ignored the demon's poisonous look. Belial may have managed to oust Azrael, the oldest of the three Princes, but he was still the same tosser who'd made Jack's life a pain in the arse for over a decade. "This problem of yours is an elemental demon? Not even one of you Named fuckwits?"

"He is one of the legion, yes," Baal hissed. "Is there a problem, skin sack?"

"No," Jack said, spreading his hands. "No problem. Impressed, actually, that one of your office drones managed to get you three in such a tizzy."

"Do yourself a favor, Mr. Winter, and stop talking before I turn your tongue into an appetizer," said Beelzebub. "For fuck's sake, Belial, do you think it's funny to torture us with breathers?"

Jack kept his mouth shut. Baal was creepy and Belial was irritating, but he'd always had the sense that Beelzebub might actually be unbalanced. For a demon, that was saying something.

"You two knobs know full well how far his influence has spread into the Black and the daylight," Belial said. "Face it—we're demons. We need a man on the ground if we're going to nip this in the bud."

"Maybe we should give him something," Beelzebub said. "A token concession so he'll stop all this nonsense in Hell. Maybe something like . . . Europe."

Belial's fist hit the table, and the resin cracked. "We are not," the demon snarled, "giving one fucking inch to something that crawled out of the ashes and the mud and challenged the rule of the Named. He's spitting in your eye, Beelzebub. If your head wasn't so far up your own colon perhaps you'd have noticed."

"Listen, you upstart prick . . ." Beelzebub began, but Baal opened his mouth and let out a long hiss that landed in Jack's ears like scalding water.

"Enough." Baal's tongue flicked in and out, tasting the air. "This matter will not conclude if we are eating one another's entrails like the carrion birds above this city. It will only turn out in our favor if we can all agree."

"Excuse me." Jack held up a finger, and thought by the intensity of the glares turned on him that it might not have been his brightest idea ever. Still, he had their attention now, so there was nothing to do but press on. "This is all fantastic," he said. "Believe me, I love watching you two gentlemen rake Belial's pale hide over the coals, but I'm not in your little loop. You maybe want to bring me up to speed, since you're asking for my help?"

"Are you going to shut him up or am I?" Beelzebub snarled at Belial. "You know, you may have gotten Azrael in the back when he was weak, but I know what you are, Belial. You're as much of a bottom-feeder as our little problem is."

Belial pushed his chair back, the screech making Jack flinch, and came around the table to grab him by the arm. "Couldn't just keep your gob stopped, could you?" he snarled.

Jack didn't argue as Belial dragged him out of the

room. "Tough crowd, those two," he said. "You'd almost think they were plotting your death behind your back or summat."

"Of course they are," Belial said. "And if I get the chance, I'll throw both of them off the top of this building and take the whole pie for myself. That's how it works down here, Jack. And now you made me look weak in there."

Jack wrestled himself from the demon's grip. "I didn't do shite to you, Belial. You wanted me to dance, but you didn't tell me the steps. So either you fill me in on *all* the lines, not just the alarmist crap about the end of days, or I'm going home."

He held his breath, feeling his blood throbbing against his neck and his temples. Bluffing with a demon was something he never would have concieved of a few years ago. Back then, Belial owned his soul and scared Jack shitless. Now, though, he'd seen that there was so much worse out there than demons, even one with as much power behind him as Belial.

Belial sighed. "Come with me," he said, leading them back through the smooth halls, past occasional white-uniformed servants who pressed their bodies against the wall when Belial passed. They were all sorts of common demons—berserkers, scavengers, others that Jack had never clapped eyes on—but they all shrank back from Belial like he was contagious.

Jack could see how someone as power hungry as Belial could get used to this, and how any threat would be like a gun held to his head. He was also starting to wonder if their problems were even connected, or if Belial had manipulated him again into doing the demon's scut work like he had with Abbadon.

Then again, Abbadon *had* almost ended the world as Jack knew it, so he followed Belial up and up, through lifts and steps until they finally came out to the top of the spire, the noxious wind stealing Jack's breath and hearing.

Belial pointed down toward the City spread out before Jack like a dissected corpse. "Look!" he shouted above the wailing wind.

Jack had been to the City before, and while it had been full of smoke and chaos and suffering then, now it looked as if it were actually burning, the figures on the elevated streets and tracks and into the open sewers below churning in a panicked mass.

It was a lot like his vision, Jack realized. People—or demons—with their lives reduced to destruction and misery struggling to survive just long enough to get away.

Gazing down at the broad avenue leading up to the spire, hundreds of feet below, Jack saw a mass of demons, elementals, and even the damned frothing outside the gates of the palace. Vehicles and shops were burning, and even from here he could hear the crunch of bone and the screams of pain as the crowd tore into both one another and the black-suited thugs arrayed in a line before the gates. The guards were Baal's troops, the Fenris, bone-breakers who were probably having the time of their lives.

Belial took Jack's arm again and guided him

inside, down the lifts, and back to Belial's flat. The demon stalked across the empty space and poured out two glasses of ruby-red liquid from a black decanter. "Drink?"

Jack eyed the liquid. It moved in a suspicious, oily manner remniscent of spoiled salad dressing. "You think I'm stupid?"

Belial lifted one dark eyebrow. "You really want me to answer that?"

Jack waved the glass off. Belial shrugged and sipped from it. "Your loss."

"I know you're never going to give me a straight answer without that babbling brook of bullshit you relish so dearly," Jack said. "So I'm just going to guess this bloke who has your knickers in a twist started that riot down there?"

He watched Belial, but the demon had a good poker face even for a resident of the Pit. He just drank his drink, staring unblinkingly back at Jack. Jack sighed. "I'm further going to guess he's someone who didn't take kindly to you plopping yourself down in the vacant seat on the Triumvirate." The ruling body of Hell had been unchanged for millennia, until Belial had stuck his upwardly mobile nose into it. The demon who'd once been a bottom-feeding soul-scrounger was now one of the most powerful beings in the universe. Jack had to admit that he was impressed with Belial's acumen. Say what you wanted about the bastard, but he knew how to step on you to get up the ladder.

Belial sucked his teeth, his ruby tongue flicking over his pale lips. "Maybe."

"You take out the oldest Prince, and his loyalists bash your windows in?" Jack said. "I don't mean to be rude, but what'd you expect? A gift basket?"

Belial gave a smile that wasn't directed at Jack, but at the chaos below. "Those aren't Azrael's boys."

Jack shrugged. "No offense, but it's hard to tell you bastards apart."

"Some are, of course," Belial said. "He commanded more legions than anyone. But there are the Egregors—that's Dagon—and every other kind of fuckwit follower you could name." He turned that smile on Jack now, and Jack felt the chill in his gut that would never go away, as his warm, beating human heart let him know that no matter how slick and mannered Belial's demeanor, he was a predator and Jack was a meat sack.

"This isn't a little upset that can be solved with a few thousand bodies and somebody's head served up at the dinner table," Belial said. "This is just a slice. It's everywhere in Hell, Jack. Do you think anything that's happened in the last year would have been allowed if everything was fine and dandy?"

Jack shrugged. "Considering the way you lot blather on about the end times, I figured you weren't too worried."

That was a lie. Things upstairs had been fucked for a long time. Old gods wandered with impunity; the original demon, Abbadon, escaped his prison to try to kickstart the apocalypse; slices of Purgatory, the one spot uncontrollable by demon, man, or force of nature, seeped into the daylight world and nearly sucked all of England into a plane filled with wild magic and ancient entities starving for human flesh.

"Hell used to rule all," Belial said. He didn't sound angry, or even boastful. "The Princes and the Named would never allow anything—in the Black, the daylight world, or anywhere else—to happen without weighing the impact. And if it didn't serve our interests, it wasn't allowed. That's gone now. And it's not just outside the Pit, it's at our doorstep." He pointed at the crowd. "Half of Baal's Fenris have gone rogue. The damned everywhere have started turning on the Named who rule them. And the Named . . . they're all too busy figuring out how they're going to axe me from my seat to pay the slightest fucking bit of attention. Not to mention that those two soft-headed shite-for-brains I sit on the Triumvirate with think the way to make all this unseemly upset go away is to cut this fucker a deal." He knocked back the drink and handed it to a stooped, bat-winged creature who appeared with a tray.

"Still not getting how your problem controlling your people translates to the end of my world," Jack said. "And frankly, if this is a demon-on-demon problem, I couldn't care less. You lot have always been squabblers."

Belial braced himself on the railing. "We can't rule from the shadows any longer, it's true," he said. "And the world is going to end, sooner rather than later. But if Hell falls, Jack . . . it will be so much worse than even I can imagine. Hell is the one constant of existence, from as far back as anything has a memory. If the realm collapses, then everything will. Every plane will blend into one, and then *everything* will go dark."

"Waiting to hear what you think I can do to stop this," Jack said. He knew Belial was right, of course—if too much magic was allowed to bleed into the daylight world from the Black, or too much of the Land of the Dead was allowed to bleed into the living, and you got things like . . . well, exactly like what had been going on for the last year. If Hell ceased to be Hell, that didn't even bear thinking about.

"Everything you see before you is the result of soft-headed fanaticism," Belial said. "The result of one demon—not even a Named, mind you—who has somehow convinced an astounding swath of idiots that he will be the *one* ruler of the Pit. That the Triumvirate was never meant to rule, and that the Princes, me especially, need to be skinned alive."

"Welcome to my world," Jack said. "Every one has its share of zealots."

"I don't know how he's turning these people to his side," Belial said. "Named, legions, everyone. But I'm going to find out, with your help. And then I'm going to make a tartare out of his balls in the public square, and all of this is going to stop."

"Again," Jack said, "this bloke sounds rather more muscular than what somebody walking around in a human body, with bones and internal organs and whatnot, would be smart to tangle with."

"That's the trick," Belial said. "He's hiding out on Earth, and sometime in the near future, something he does while hiding there sets off those nasty little clips that have been playing in your head. But I don't know what, and in order to find out I need someone he won't see coming. It can't be a demon, and for a human, you're pretty useful."

He grabbed Jack and dug his nails into Jack's palm, drawing a little blood. Jack started to protest, but his mind filled with images, like photographs falling down into a chaotic pile, and his tongue tasted of burning penny. He felt vomit boil up into his throat and tried to scream, but the onslaught stopped as quickly as it had begun.

Belial wiped his fingers on the lapel of his suit. "Like that? I can transfer memories via blood now. Perks of being a Prince."

"Fuck you," Jack groaned, clutching his forehead.

"Lucky you have that second sight," Belial said. "Only works on psychics. Normal blokes would have beans on toast for brain if I did that."

"I feel so special," Jack grumbled.

"Everything my spies have been able to gather about where he's hiding is there," Belial said. "I need you to find him, and I need you to use your particular talent for being a sneaky cunt to help me smack this bastard back to the Middle Ages before whatever he's got planned goes down, and he flips the switch on the end of everything."

"If he figures out that I'm spying on him and turns me into a leather jacket?" Jack said. "I have a wife and kid, you know."

Belial shrugged. "I suggest you don't let him figure it out," he said. "Because I don't think I need to spell out what'll happen to your lovely wife and darling daughter if this fuckwit manages to bring down Hell."

He didn't. Odd as it was to know his survival depended on a race of creatures as despicable as demons, in a place as dark and dingy as Hell, Jack didn't argue that Belial had a point.

But that didn't mean he was going to his mission with a smile on his face.

"If you want me to tangle with the demonic version of Jerry Falwell, I'll need something to defend myself with besides my good looks and charm," he said.

Belial inclined his head. "Of course. This way to the armory."

Jack cast one more look out over the city before they went inside. Thunderheads had built up over the desert, and they rushed in on the screaming winds, bathing the street below in rain, sending rioters scurrying for cover and washing the black blood into the gutters.

CHAPTER 8

Belial led him deeper into the palace than Jack had
ever wanted to go. The whole place was like slices
of different centuries stacked as high as the low black
and red clouds that constantly roiled above the City.
One floor was as opulent as an art deco hotel, one
floor was the dirty lino and buzzing light tubes of a
dole office, one floor was the sterile white of a labo-
ratory. Belial brought him to one of the white floors,
through a door that recoiled soundlessly into the floor.

Inside a narrow room, Jack saw a variety of ob-
jects on glass pedestals. Weapons, chunks of stone
carved in demonic languages, books, an eyeball that
blinked at him from its nest of flesh and severed
optic nerve.

Belial stopped next to one of the cases and
pressed his thumb against the pad. Within lay a flat
black disc that looked like lava rock, with a hole in
the center for a strap or chain.

"You're one of the only living men ever to see this
place," Belial said. "The Princes' vaults are secret,
even from the Named."

Jack shivered. He could feel the black energy
creeping off most of the things under those glass
domes, and he didn't want to get any closer than he

had to. "The armory is only a small part of the vaults," Belial said. "But this is all you'll need."

He handed Jack the disc. It was oddly light and sat flat in his palm, not giving off any particular sting of magic, demon-spawned or otherwise.

"This is cute and all," Jack said, "but are you sure I couldn't have a knife or a gun or something? Even that eyeball would be better for shock value."

"If you touched the Allfather's Eye, your tiny little dish sponge of a brain would come straight out your nose," Belial said. "That's not for you, boyo. This will ensure that once you've found our little self-proclaimed Messiah, you can bring him straight home for a spanking."

Belial folded Jack's fingers around the disc, and Jack fought not to pull away. Belial's skin was cold and dry like a snake's, none of the warmth Jack associated with a living thing. "The first demons carved the gates of Hell from living rock," Belial said. "And they bound the rock with spells to make it indestructible. Any man who possesses a piece of those gates may pass in and out of Hell freely."

The demon let go of him, and Jack sucked in a deep breath, ordering himself not to throw up on the spotless white floor. Belial swiped his thumb over the dome again and gave Jack one of those grins that would have made the shark from *Jaws* weep. "You've got the keys to the kingdom now, Jackie. Don't make me regret giving them to you."

CHAPTER 9

The first thing Jack did when he returned to London was find a pay phone and call Pete. "I'm sorry," he said. "I know that I worried you, and I'm all right." He paused, flinching a little. "You going to scream at me?"

"Just get home," Pete sighed after a moment. "I can't even begin to express how sick I was when you went running out of there, but I hope you feel bad."

"You have no idea," Jack said. The memory Belial had given him rested in his mind like a splinter in his foot, aching and sharp and causing his vision to blur. "I'll be home soon," he said, and hung up.

When he was still shooting up, Jack had frequented the south side of the river, crappy little shooting galleries from Southwark to Peckham. He didn't need smack, but he needed privacy, a place where he could behave like a freak without anyone caring.

The last time he'd let his sight have free rein, he was much younger, living in Dublin, and the things he'd seen had driven him to try for suicide rather than keep seeing the parade of dead that were drawn by his talent.

This has to be different, Jack thought as he walked from the Queen's Road station to Rye Lane. Peckham had been a tip for as long as he'd been in London, but this was a city where you could never really fight the creeping disease of gentrification. Where there'd once been fly-tips and vacant lots there were now wine bars and shops selling precious little trinkets for you, your flat, or your pet. The street-level folk were recent immigrants or working-class, and the gangs and yobs had been pushed back onto the borders of the council estates that rose like drab monuments to a bygone London, though one less than the ancient London of the Tower or Newgate Prison.

Jack left the shopping high street and moved toward those estates, the ones that had once made North Peckham the British equivalent of Watts or Cabrini-Green. Posh folks—the ones who weren't quite posh enough to afford flats in that thin belt of yuppie paradise north of the Thames but south of the sooty gray expanse of North London—hadn't ventured here yet, and broken-out windows and bums stared at Jack as he walked.

He cut down a narrow walkway between two townhouse flats, both just brick husks but gamely plastered with estate agent's listing signs. *Two bedrooms, an en suite, and three junkies living in your kitchen,* Jack thought. Just the sort of "colorful" venue some twat from the City would snap up in another six months or so.

Now, though, it served his purpose. He kicked in the back door, which was rotten, the latch hanging by a few splinters, and stepped inside. One thin body wrapped in an overcoat slumbered in the back hall, and Jack surprised a prostitute and a blobby, sweaty john in the front room.

"Never mind," he said, seeing the look of outrage on the man's face. "Just looking for the loo."

He climbed the creaking steps as far as he could go and found the skeleton of an armchair in an upstairs bedroom that looked toward the river and the council estate towers to the north.

More than anything, Jack wanted to grab Belial by the neck and shake him until there was no life left. The demon must have known what he was doing, making Jack use his talent to find the demon that had Belial's knickers in such a twist. Belial probably thought it would be funny.

Jack shut his eyes. He had been fighting against his talent for so long that there was a moment, just a heartbeat or two, when there was nothing. Quiet reigned inside his head, and all he could hear was the tick and click of the wobbly house settling and the soft sounds of the girl and her client through the floor.

Then, like plunging into freezing water, the sight washed over him. It felt like biting a live wire, and Jack's eyes flew open. The room was the same trashy wreck, washed now with the shimmering silver of the world that lived beyond physical sight, open only to the dead and those who could touch them.

A small boy, not more than ten, sat on the floor pushing a toy car back and forth. The marks on his neck were in the shape of fingers, and the veins in his eyes had burst, making them appear black in Jack's washed-out vision. "I was good," the ghost announced. "I didn't tell. Why did he hurt me if I didn't tell?"

"I don't know, mate," Jack said. "And I'm sorry. Nobody should get a shite deal like that."

"I was good," the ghost repeated in a singsong as he pushed his car across the ruined carpet. "I was good, I was good."

Jack tried to blink the sad little spirit away. At least he wasn't a hungry ghost, or a poltergeist, those dead who hadn't taken the news of their demise well. An angry spirit could shred you like a turbine, and Jack had more than enough of those encounters under his belt. Now, he was after the memory Belial had planted in his subconscious.

He looked at the room again, seeing slices of what the place had been like decades before, hearing the wail of air raid sirens from the Blitz, the clatter of carriages on the street below, the tinkle of a piano from a long-ago party.

Psychic echoes existed in dozens, if not hundreds of layers in any place with more than a few years' history, but now they kept Jack from what he was really after—the itch that the demon had planted in his brain.

Using his talent was like feeling along a wall in the dark, fingers rubbing over the echoes of the building. He felt the static of the spirits floating in his orbit, and something else, something shimmering among the many layers of psychic residue.

Jack pushed his talent toward the shimmering ob-

ject that hung before his vision, grazing it like you'd
test a hot pan before you picked it up.

Contact was all it took, though, and the demon's
memory unfurled like a poisonous flower. The room
fell away, and Jack tried to ignore the pain in his skull
and the heartbeat threatening to crack his breastbone.
His talent was far too much for a human body to contain, and he'd always known it could simply clock him
out with a heart attack or an aneurysm if he pushed
too hard.

The visions of the future would end him sooner
than that, though, so he bit down on the inside of his
cheek until he tasted blood and kept his eyes open.

He no longer saw the tip, but a street deep in the
City in Hell. A long black car, belching smoke from
its exhaust pipes and sporting a goat-skull hood or-
nament, idled outside the sort of storefront church
that Jack had seen by the dozens on his last trip to
America. The blue neon hanging from the window
was some sort of demonic sigil rather than a cross,
but otherwise the feel was the same.

Outside, a variety of lesser demons crouched.
Some were missing eyes or limbs; others held themselves and rocked back and forth while they cried
softly.

They weren't human, but Jack had seen plenty
exactly like them on the streets of London. Desperate, broken, looking for solace in a made-up story
gussied up with faith. When you had no hope left,
faith was a strong drug. Jack felt sorry for the poor
bastards, whatever this place was.

Belial stepped from the car wearing his usual black suit and white shirt, his ruby tie pin glowing in the blue light from the storefront. The demon didn't go inside, just stood in the street and waited.

The sad bastards populating the pavement shrank back from him, and a few hopped or limped back into the shadows.

"I know you're in there." Belial's voice could have cut glass. Jack didn't think he'd ever seen the demon in such a full rage, and he was indescribably grateful it wasn't directed at him. Whoever was in that church, Jack figured they'd have a puddle to clean up when this was all over.

"Do you?" A voice floated out from the church. "What else do you know, Belial?"

Belial's jaw clenched, and Jack saw the muscles in his face jump. "That you don't want me coming in after you," the demon said.

The figure that emerged from the church looked entirely human. Jack didn't know what he'd expected, exactly, but not that. The demons of the legions weren't generally very pretty, ranging from the enormous Fenris to tiny imps that were little more than soot-smears. The two-legged, ten-fingered act, though . . . that was reserved for the Named.

"I suppose I don't," the new face said. "You aren't famous for minimizing collateral damage, Belial. I'd hate for my flock to be injured."

"Cut the shit," Belial said. "You think it's funny, stirring up the Fenris and getting them to betray Baal? You think convincing the Named that I'm behind it is some kind of bloody joke?"

There it was, then. The demon had gotten under Belial's skin, and the Prince was looking for a little payback. Jack didn't know why he was surprised. He thought Belial's head might actually explode if the demon tried to tell the whole truth about anything.

"No," said the other demon. "I don't think anything about this is funny, Belial. And what Baal chooses to believe is his own business. Now the question you really should be asking is, why are you being distracted by a puny little rebellion in Hell?"

Snarling came from all around them, and in the shadows, Jack saw Fenris move. Nasty creatures, at least half a head taller than a man, they had long snouts and jaws, wolf's teeth, and clawed hands made for ripping and tearing.

Belial's eyes narrowed until all Jack saw was black, and his own lips peeled back from his shark's teeth. "Is this your idea of an ambush, boy? It's adorable."

"You're so preoccupied with holding on to that Triumvirate seat tooth and claw that you don't see I've already won," the demon said. His delivery was soft and hypnotic, and Jack recognized the particular cadence of an effective cult leader. "I've won the human world, Belial, and you're too stupid to realize it."

The Fenris approached, their heavy feet cracking the worn pavement, until they surrounded Belial and his car.

"And how exactly did you manage that?" Belial asked. Jack was sure, as he watched the memory, that he was the only one who saw a single transparent bead of sweat work its way down the demon's temple.

The demon took something out of the pocket of his baggy trousers and held it up. It was a flat piece of metal, the size of a ruler, with a broken end. It looked like any old scrap you could pick up off the ground, and the only way Jack knew things had gone sideways was that Belial's body got wire-tight.

"Where did you get that?"

"From the vaults, of course," said the demon. "They're really not all that impregnable, Belial. All it takes is enough of the rank and file who believe that something like this belongs in the right hands, and doors have a way of opening themselves."

Belial took a breath in and out, smoothing a hand over his tie. Jack waited, watching the whole tension-strung scene play out, and thought, *It figures.* Jack had something from the vaults, but Belial had only told him half the story. He'd sent Jack flying in blind, and for once, Jack didn't know why. Belial clearly knew this was serious. What possible motive could he have to not tell Jack his rogue demon possessed an artifact that had a Prince of Hell piss-scared?

"You don't know how to use that," he said. "None of us do. And if you try, you're going to end things."

"That's what you'd like to tell yourself," said the demon. "But I know how to use this, Belial. I, a rank-and-file member, have bested you. I've gone to the human world. I've set things in motion. I've destroyed your credibility, because you're the only Prince who could possibly have the stones to stop me. And now . . ."

Belial started to laugh. "And now you kill me? You have any idea how many times I've heard that line from pissants like you?"

The demon shook his head. The Fenris snarled, their breath misting in the cool air.

"Now I leave you here," the demon said. "To see what focusing only on your pride has wrought. Enjoy ruling what's left of Hell, Belial. It won't be around much longer."

The demon withdrew into the church, and the Fenris followed, forming a protective barrier that even Belial would have to be a nutter to try to penetrate.

Silence reigned again, except for Belial's own hard, rasping breaths as the street went still, bathed in blue.

CHAPTER 10

Jack came out of his psychic wormhole with a start, finding himself on the floor, grit and glass shards clinging to the side of his face.

He choked and spat out a little bile, and he felt a wet dribble work its way from his nose over his upper lip.

"Fuck you, Belial," he muttered. His body felt like he'd tangled with a lycanthrope and lost badly, but he forced himself up. His skull was throbbing so hard that bright light collected at the corners of his vision.

Jack couldn't decide what was worse—the postsight migraine his talent left him as a gift, or the fact that Belial had only told him half the story. *Headache*, he thought. Thinking that for once he was getting the straight truth out of a demon was just foolishness on his part.

And there was the object the demon had stolen from the vaults. Jack had only seen Belial afraid once, when he'd realized that Abbadon, one of the primordial beings in Hell, had escaped his prison and was about to turn Earth into his own private amusement park.

Abbadon could have easily killed Belial. He almost

had, in fact; Jack had seen the fight between the leather tosser and Belial in his true, demonic body. It wasn't something you forgot. But more than that, Jack remembered the fear in the demon's eyes. What he'd seen then was nothing compared to now.

Whoever this demon was, whatever he'd taken, Belial hadn't been kidding. This was the last act, the end of the line. And he'd trusted Jack to stop the curtain from falling.

Which makes Belial an idiot, Jack thought as he stumbled down the rickety stairs and out into the fresh air, *and me an even bigger one for agreeing to do it.*

CHAPTER 11

Margaret was playing with Lily on the floor of the sitting room when Jack made it home, and she gave him a smile before pointing out to their fire stairs. "Pete is slagged at you," she said.

"Yeah, I figured that bit out on my own, thanks," he said. He stopped to give Lily a kiss on the top of her head before he opened the window and stuck his head out. "Luv?"

"Go away." Pete had a cigarette in her hand, which told Jack exactly how black a mood she was in. She'd been much more successful at quitting than he had after she got pregnant, and now she only smoked when she was truly angry, dragging viciously so the tip of her Parliament looked like a tiny forest fire.

"Look, I'm sorry," he said. "I've had a hell of a day. Can I at least explain?"

"You know, we haven't had a fantastic day here, either," Pete snapped. "Starting with you cutting yourself and then running out of the hospital like you should be fitted for the rubber room. I had to do a lot of fucking tap-dancing to convince the doctor and the nurses you weren't a psychopath, I'll tell you."

"I was going to tell you what happened after they

fixed me up," Jack said. He felt the tight, wounded expression on Pete's face and felt it in his gut. He'd almost lost her more than once by keeping things secret—his deal with Belial, the fact that the Morrigan was after him now more than ever—and he'd be damned if it would happen this time.

He told Pete straight through, not leaving anything out, from his cut hand to the fact that his dreams weren't dreams at all, to the side trip to Belial's neck of the woods.

"Jesus," Pete said when he'd finished.

"He'd be useful right about now, what with the levitating and the rising from the dead," Jack said, "but yeah, things are fucked."

"So this demon managed to fuck up Hell with a few Fenris and something he nicked from the Princes, and Belial has no idea where he is?" Pete asked. "Fantastic outlook for the rest of us, innit?"

"Oh yeah," Jack agreed. "'M filled with hope, myself."

Pete stubbed out her fag and rolled the butt between her fingers, her brow crinkling. "Maybe it's not that bad. Who do we know who has their nose in everyone's business and could definitely tell us if there was some kind of rogue demon cult operating on British soil?"

Jack cast a look through the window at Margaret. "Pete, no," he said, the very thought of her suggestion making him want to beat his head against the wall.

"It's going to be the fastest way," she said. "Otherwise, we're just going to run around in the dark until somebody tries to destroy the world and—oh wait, that's already happening."

Jack scrubbed his hands over his face. He was exhausted, wanted nothing more than to knock back a shot of whiskey and shut his eyes for an hour or sixty, but he knew Pete was right. "Fine," he said. "I'll put on me best arse-kissing suit, and you and I will go have a talk with the Prometheus Club."

CHAPTER 12

Jack could think of few things more unpleasant than the Prometheus Club, but breaking the news to Margaret came close.

"Come with me, luv," he said. "Need to run down to the shop."

When they were on the street, Jack let Margaret lead the way, stopping here and there to examine jewelry in the street stalls, before she cocked her head and looked up at Jack. "You didn't really bring me out here to pick up some tea and fags, did you?"

Jack shook his head. "Can't put much past you, can I?"

Magaret picked up a fake purse from one of the stalls and turned it over in her hands. "You know, my dad was in jail for most of my life, and when he did come back my parents almost got me killed because they were fuckwits."

Jack figured he probably should have told Margaret that those were her parents, and for all their mistakes they did the best they could. But he wasn't that sort of parent himself, so he just nodded.

"You and Pete are the only people who ever made me feel as if things might be all right," Margaret said. "Like, you don't care that I'm weird or that my real parents are freaks. You're good to me." She put the purse back and faced Jack. "So I figure whatever it is you want from me, you can ask it. I want to help you, Jack. You're not like my dad."

"You want to be careful agreeing to help me like that," Jack said. "Good kids like you have a tendency to wind up dead when they get mixed up with bad people like me."

"You're not bad." Margaret crinkled her nose as if the very notion was ridiculous. "You're a bit rough and mean, sure, but you're good. Everyone can see it."

"Luv, if everyone could see that, I'd have been punched out a lot less in my youth," Jack said, giving her shoulder a nudge. Margaret wasn't one of those girls who flitted and darted, smiled at everything and giggled when she was nervous. She was so serious he sometimes wondered if on the inside, she was a brittle old pensioner. She had a thousand-yard stare that could back down a demon. She reminded Jack of himself at that age, when he was just starting to realize that not everyone could speak to the dead, conjure hexes, or feel the inexorable tide pulsing under the skin of everything that was safe, normal, and daylight.

"*I* can see it," Margaret said. "I can see people, and when I see you, you're good. So is Pete, and Lily. There are more good people in the world than bad, Jack. I'm sorry it's hard for you to see."

"Curse of getting older, Margaret," Jack said, the urge to joke with her gone. "Your opinion on that might change the first time some nutter comes at you with a sacrificial knife, just because you looked at him wrong."

He was stalling, and he felt a prick of disgust from the part of himself that was still the boy who thought his talent was a weapon rather than a vast cataclysm he couldn't control. The younger Jack who threw punches, drank whiskey, and dove into the pit during stage shows just because it was fun to taste his own blood.

That boy hadn't seen half the shit adult Jack had, though, so he could fuck right off. He'd never known what it was like to be a living thing in the Land of the Dead. To feel his own brain turn against him because of magic it couldn't contain. To be shivering and starving on the street in the dead of winter, needing heroin so badly that his burning blood was all that kept him moving.

Margaret moved on, out of the passage of traffic, pausing to hoist herself onto the iron fence of a council estate. "What is it you don't want to tell me, Jack?"

Jack watched a couple of hoodies kicking a half-deflated football on the graffiti-stained pavement, blowing out a lungful of air he dearly wished was nicotine. "You know those yobs that came after you when your parents got mixed up with the zombies in Herefordshire?"

"Yeah." Margaret's lip twitched in disgust. "They were lame. Totally naff."

"That they are," Jack said. "But they have something Pete and I need, only we're not exactly welcome in their little club anymore."

"And I am." Margaret's voice was flat. She wasn't a stupid child by a long shot, and Jack had wished more than once that it was easier to put things past her, to cushion her from her talent for just a little longer. He wished she didn't have to go through what he had, the birth spasms of a life no human should have to live.

"Yeah, luv," he said. "You're the Merlin."

"I'm like a nuclear bomb," Margaret said. "And they want to aim me at whoever they don't like."

"You're not wrong," Jack said. "The Prometheus Club never has anything but their own best interest at heart."

"So am I supposed to let them?" Margaret turned to face him, her eyes wide and unsure for the first time. "I'm the Merlin. Not them. You said it was my choice."

She was still a teenager, Jack reminded himself, and her mood could flip faster than a stoplight. Beyond that, she was a teenager with latent talents that would make her the most powerful mage in all of Britain, if not the world, when she came into them. The Merlin, the mage those nutters in the Prometheus Club thought would unite all the squabbling groups and sects under the banner of human magicians against . . . whoever they were slagged off at that week.

Which was complete and utter ripe bullshit, Jack knew. You could no more get mages to agree on anything than you could teach cats to do a hula dance. But for what he needed now, he was content to feed the Prometheans' delusion.

"It is," Jack said. "Say no, we'll go home, get some chips in for tea, and never speak of this again. I'm not going to force you into anything, Margaret. What you do with your talent is your choice, and that's more important than anything else, because it's a choice nobody gave me when I was your age."

She chewed on her lip for a moment, a gesture she'd adopted from Pete. "Okay," she said. "If I just have to lie to them a bit, that's fine. What do you want me to do?"

"Tell them you're not ready to come to them and be the Merlin, not yet," Jack said. "But that you do want to receive training."

Margaret wrinkled her nose. "But you and Pete are better than any of them. They're rubbish at magic."

"Of course they are," Jack said. "And like most arrogant pricks, they've got tiny talents and big egos. I just need to talk to one woman in particular, and the only way we're getting in is to show up with you."

Margaret hopped off the fence and gave him a sly smile. "Sounds fun. Sort of James Bond."

"Sure," Jack said. "If James Bond was a nutter who consorted with dark magic, that's exactly what it is."

Margaret started back toward the flat, and Jack followed her. He wasn't hungry any longer, anyway. Even though she'd agreed, there was still a chance the Prometheans could pull something and take Margaret against her will, as they'd tried to in Herefordshire, and Jack could do fuck-all on his own against a full complement of them.

The thought of Margaret living with those people turned his stomach, even more than the thought of her on her own, sleeping rough and trying to figure out what the hell this brave new world of demons and the dead was, as he had.

"So, why do you need to talk to them?" Margaret asked. "It's bad, right? You and Pete wouldn't go unless it was bad."

Jack watched the traffic, the street vendors, the usual people going about their usual lives. He tried very hard not to see the superimposed image from his visions of the burned-out hulk of Tower Hamlets and the dead roaming the streets.

"Yes," he said. He didn't believe in lying to kids. What good would that do now, at any rate? "It's about as bad as it can possibly get."

CHAPTER 13

Secret societies weren't really as secret as they all liked to claim, especially when you had something they wanted. Less than twenty minutes after Jack had Pete dial up Morwenna Morgenstern, the public face of the Prometheus Club, a car was idling at the curb in front of their flat.

Jack hadn't bothered with the suit after all—it wasn't like Morwenna had any friendly feelings toward him. Especially not after he'd done a dust-up with her little best mate, Donovan Winter. The Prometheans, and Morwenna in particular, excelled at manipulation in the way that only lifelong, dyed-in-the-wool sociopaths could. Using Jack's father to get Jack and Pete to try and rip open a seam to Purgatory was a small game, in the scheme of things.

Anyway, he wasn't there to impress Morwenna or revist his animosity toward Donovan. The hatred was there, though, a hot coal in his guts as the car sped through the West End and into wide, green, flat countryside with the occasional rise of a stately home.

He'd told Donovan that if the man interfered with his family or his life again, he'd kill him. Donovan knew he was prepared to follow through, too, so Jack hoped that would keep the father-son chatter to a minimum.

"I don't understand," Margaret said, staring out the window as they wound up an endless private road lined with beech trees toward the hulk of a brick mansion. "I thought they all lived up in Manchester."

"They've got hidey-holes all over the place," Pete said. "Rich folks like them are the greatest paranoids. Why have one secret clubhouse when you can have ten?"

Jack looked past the trees at the rolling hills, bracketed by stone walls and bracken bathed in gold as the sun went down. Absurdly, he thought of "Stairway to Heaven". *If there's a bustle in your hedgerow, don't be alarmed now. It's just a spring clean for the May queen.*

Stupid airy-fairy bullshit. If that's what most people thought real magic was all about, then they had it coming when real magic broke through the barriers, chased them down, and turned them into dinner.

Jack sighed, then looked up to find Pete's eyes on him. He was so on edge he felt like he'd snap back like a rubber band at the slightest provocation, and she could tell. They shared the gentle brush of talent against talent—it just felt like static electricity now, but when mages spent enough time together they got to know each other, how they felt when they were happy or hurt or tense or afraid. Margaret's clean energy, the bell-tone of white magic, muddled things a bit, like muffling your head with a pillow when things got loud and you had a raging hangover.

She would outdo either of them, if she lived long enough. Sure, Jack had some muddy, bloody talent the Morrigan wanted, and Pete was still stronger than him because she could take on other mages' gifts and magnify them from a stray cloud to a storm that could sweep the whole of the Black clean if she let it. But Margaret was going to be stronger still than Pete, a force unlike anything the world had seen in ten centuries. The Merlin, the hawk on high who saw everything, top of the food chain.

Jack was just glad as fuck she'd gone light-side and hadn't turned out like him. Because then the world really would be fucked, and he couldn't do a damn thing about it.

The car pulled into a round drive, gravel crunched, scary blokes in cheap suits patted them all down, and finally they were granted entrance into the Prometheans' posh den of idiocy.

It looked like any other posh country house Jack had had the misfortune to find himself in—lots of dark wood, ugly oil paintings, and hushed tones. Margaret gave everything an appraising glance, and then her high forehead crinkled. "My magic's gone."

She insisted on calling it *magic,* no matter how many times Jack told her that she'd be laughed out of any mage gathering in the UK with that sort of language.

"They keep the whole place cut off," he said. "No service in this area, luv. Sorry."

Pete fidgeted next to him. "I hate this. I fucking hate this."

"You think I feel any different?" he muttered. "Take away my talent, and what am I?"

"A man who is rather poor at following through on his promises." Morwenna Morgenstern glided from a set of double doors at the far end of the entry. She was still doing her slick City getup: slim skirts, perfect hair, and lips like a fresh wound.

"Morwenna," Jack greeted her. "You're looking particularly constipated this evening. I'd think the Prometheans all indulged in monthly group co-lonics."

Her face wasn't as pretty as she'd probably been told it was her entire life, but it wasn't bad, and she managed to give only a twitch of her cheek muscles at Jack's jab. "The last I recall, Mr. Winter, you were leveling some extremely vulgar and insubstantial accusations at me before promising never to step foot within a mile of me again."

"Oh, that wasn't a promise," Jack said. "That was a threat. I never would have let your merry band of psychopaths within spitting distance of Margaret if we weren't desperate."

Morwenna made a show of turning her back on him before she extended her hands to Margaret. He was nothing, over, a speck on her shoe. Jack tried not to feel a prick of offense, despite hating the woman's fucking guts. He could do these people some dam-age. They should at least be smart enough to treat him like he was dangerous.

"My dear, dear girl," Morwenna intoned with a voice that could have given a pixie a toothache. "I am so glad you reconsidered."

"Fuck off," Margaret said when Morwenna tried to take her hands. "I'm only here because Jack asked me to help him."

Jack gave Morwenna a wide grin when she whipped her head back around. "Sorry. Looks like you're going to have to deal with the unwashed peasants a bit longer."

Pete gave a small shoulder-shrug of a laugh, which he took as a good sign. If she was calm enough to appreciate winding up Morwenna, this all might just go the way they'd planned. Pete was his barometer for calm. She never lost her head, never wavered, until it was well and truly time to go off the rails. He didn't have that built-in stabilizer, didn't trust himself not to ignore danger signs and still, after all his fuck-ups, think he could smile and charm his way out of something. *Just one more time*.

"You seem to be laboring under the misconception that you can bargain," Morwenna said. "Let me make this very clear, Jack—you have no leverage here. Margaret is meant to be among her own kind, and by taking that from her you're making her life very difficult. If you think I'm letting her walk back out that door, to the gods know what sort of life, you must be fucking delusional."

There was the Morwenna Morgenstern he knew, all hard eyes and flashing teeth as she bit and raked at you with her words, leaving you a flayed mess too cowed to argue.

"Fine." That was Pete. "Try and keep her here, then. Ignore the fact that if we came to you voluntarily, things are already sideways and spinning into the ground. Be a stupid self-righteous cunt like always, Morwenna, because that worked out so well the last time the world was ending."

Pete ended her speech less than a foot from Morwenna's nose, between the woman and Margaret. It was Jack's turn to grin. Even-keeled and cool-headed as Pete was, it was terrifying to see her slagged off.

"We only came here because things are so bad we couldn't go anywhere else," Pete continued. "That ought to scare you, and if it doesn't, consider this: If you try to keep this girl against her will—a girl I consider *my child*—I will burn this pile of bricks to the ground with your carcass inside it, and make it my personal mission to fuck up your little club's agenda from here to kingdom come."

Morwenna swallowed hard, cheeks flushed and hands fluttering ever so slightly with nerves. Jack caught Pete's eye and nodded. Shock and awe were the only things mages like the Prometheans understood. You can think you're top of the heap, until one of your herd is ripped apart in front of you, and then you're off balance and scared.

Good, Jack thought. He wanted Morwenna Morgenstern scared.

"If you help Pete and Jack, I'll consider coming here once a month to be trained," Margaret said. They'd gone over this part carefully before the call. "But only once a month, and only if Jack or Pete is with me. And if I don't like it, I'm quitting. You lot don't have one tiny say in what I do or don't do with my talent."

Morwenna straightened her spine, a boxer shaking off a bad round, spitting out the blood and putting her defenses back up. "What sort of help do you require? A catastrophe of your own making, no doubt."

Jack tried not to let the accusation smart. It figured, the one time he hadn't backed himself into a corner with a demon deal or a slagged-off primal creature of Hell on his arse, and Morwenna assumed he'd caused the whole mess.

"The Black and the daylight world," he said. "Barrier's going to rupture unless we find the bloke who set things in motion and send him back downstairs for a spanking and no supper from the Princes."

And I'm having visions of the apocalypse that may have already been triggered. Even if I do what Belial wants, there may be no way to stop it.

He pushed the thoughts down. They weren't any that Morwenna or whatever pet mind reader she had eavesdropping needed to hear.

"And that's all you have?" Morwenna said, mouth crimping in the cruel smile of a girl who's just realized her rival came to school with her skirt tucked into her tights. "'A bloke'? Care to be a bit more specific?"

Jack thought of Belial confronting the demon, of how easily the demon had turned the Fenris, and took out his pen. "He's been kicking this symbol around," he said, grabbing up a pad from next to an old-fashioned rotary phone to sketch on. "Doesn't mean anything to me. Also, he's not a Named—he's an elemental who got too big for his britches. Thought maybe with all your vast high and mighty anointed-one mage knowledge, you might've run across the symbol somewhere."

Morwenna reached for the pad, but Jack held it back. "Uh-uh." He shook his head. "Not until you promise me—a real promise, none of that crap where you use some clever language loophole—to abide by Margaret's terms."

Margaret crossed her arms and narrowed her eyes, a pitch-perfect imitation of Pete that would have made Jack laugh, had this been anywhere else, any other time.

Morwenna's jaw bunched and relaxed, and she let out a long-suffering breath. "I promise that I shan't try to keep Margaret here against her will. I make no promises, however, about trying to persuade her to join us on our own merits, and leave you two idiots in the gutter where you belong."

"I wouldn't live here if it was raining piss and this was the only place with a roof," Margaret said. Morwenna squeezed her eyes briefly, while Margaret gave Jack a wide smile.

"I feel so terribly for what they've put in your head, child," she said. "I really do."

"Oi." Jack snapped his fingers. "Less sob-sistering, more information."

"Assuming you know anything," Pete scoffed.

Morwenna grabbed the paper from Jack and stormed back toward the double doors. "Well, come on!" she snapped when no one followed her.

Beyond the doors was a sitting room, the sort of overstuffed, flower-plagued place that old folks and the clinically depressed flocked to. Morwenna sat disdainfully on one of the threadbare velvet armchairs, touching it with as little of her slim frame as possible.

Jack stayed standing, as did Margaret and Pete, until Morwenna raised her eyes with a glare.

"I'm not going to ambush you with idiot-eating armchairs the moment you sit down," she said. "So for fuck's sake, stop hovering like a pack of wild dogs."

Jack sat, figuring he'd probably get an answer faster, and have to listen to Morwenna's store-bought plummy accent less, than if he'd pushed the issue.

"Mean anything?" he asked, pointing at the paper. The memory of the sigil was seared into him. He'd see it until he died, imprinted on his brain like a scar. Fucking Belial.

Morwenna examined the drawing under the light. Turned it, examined it again. Her lips pursed, and she gave Jack a glare as if he were a naughty schoolboy, fitting her for a wind-up.

"Let me guess," she said. "One of the Named gave this to you."

"What docs it matter?" Jack said. He was surprised she'd gone right to the consorting-with-demons place. To Morwenna, such a thing was distasteful; plus, she probably thought Jack was too stupid to do anything with a Named except get turned into a carpet.

"Because this is the sigil of Legion, an elemental demon who has many hearts and minds at once," Morwenna said.

"Wait, wait." Pete waved a hand. "Are we talking

Legion, the one Christ cast into a herd of pigs and drove off a cliff? That bloke?"

"Legion is not a name," Morwenna said. "Because he's not a Named. And he's much more than just a hive mind demon with a lot of bodies. Legion has been the boogeyman in Hell for a long time."

"Great," Jack said. "Any idea where he might vacation, were he to slip the surly bonds of that crap pool he calls a home and visit earth?"

Morwenna started to laugh—not the cool Bondian chuckle he'd expect from a woman like her, but a genuine laugh, shoulders shaking, rich and cruel. "I have no fucking idea," she said. "Because Legion is a story, Jack. He's a campfire ghost for the Named— the elemental, the *legion* member who's stronger than they are, could take over and wipe them out." She crumpled the paper, dropped it, and stepped on it with her pointy witch shoe when she rose. "Have fun chasing your apocalypse, you two," she said, opening the doors wide. "Because Legion doesn't fucking exist."

CHAPTER 14

Pete and Margaret were silent the entire length of the private lane, until the driver pulled back onto the motorway and accelerated. "I think that went well," Pete said at last.

"Don't even start," Jack muttered.

After a moment, Pete's hand closed over his in the dark car. "I believe you," she said.

"Well, you shouldn't." Shame ate at Jack's throat like stomach acid. "I bought it hook, line, and sinker. Whatever sick game Belial's playing, I walked right into it and looked like a proper fool."

He'd let the demon inside his head. Fuck, what had he done? What else had been planted there while Belial had been making his cerebral cortex a demon's playground?

"Maybe he wasn't just playing around," Pete said. "You said that Hell was in an uproar. *Something* is going on. I know plenty of spittle-flecked cult leaders who co-opt symbols to make their followers toe the line. If Legion is a scary story, maybe someone in Hell capitalized on that."

Jack felt a headache blossom behind his eyes like someone had hit him. It was too much, the visions and the demons, and he just wanted it to stop.

"Something is happening," he muttered. His sight had never acted up this way. Something was causing it, and Belial's nameless demon was involved. "But this Legion business leaves me right where I was before—holding me dick in me fist with nothing to show what might kick off the end of the world."

Pete gave him a sharp nudge and jerked her head at Margaret, sitting across from them in the car's vast rear seats.

"Sorry, luv," he said. "Don't take the filth that I spew as an example, eat your vegetables, don't skip school, etcetera."

Pete heaved a sigh. "So you're just going to give up."

Jack felt the headache multiply, spreading across the crown of his head like someone had smacked him repeatedly in the skull. "I'm not giving up, but where do you suggest we go from here? If the Prometheans say this is bunk, then I'm at a loss as to who this demon is, where he is, or what he's up to."

"Then ask the person who can tell you," Pete said. "In all the time you've known Belial, has he ever been completely straight with you? Even if the world was on the line, Belial doesn't care about humans. He only cares about himself. He's a survivor, just like you, and like you, he puts himself first."

Jack watched London growing larger in the windscreen, glittering and rising out of the blackness of the land around. Pete was right. The acid-soaked pit of hopelessness in his stomach hardened into something else, the old rage from his younger days, the thing that protected him, armored him, kept him from being fucked with by things like Belial.

"Jack?" Pete said. She withdrew her hand as a crackle of blue energy passed between them, the ambient magic that gathered when Jack let his rage or any strong emotion grow. The interior of the car was bathed in blue for a moment, and then Jack tamped it down again. He was going to save this for the target who deserved it.

"I'm fine," he said. "When we get home, though, the Prince and I are going to have a talk."

CHAPTER 15

Early, when the sun had just started to give a thought to coming up, Jack grabbed his kit and climbed to the roof of his flat. The roof was bumpy with tarpaper and disused chimney pots, covered in empty lager cans and pigeon shit, but it was quiet and private. He wasn't going to take the risk of summoning Belial in his flat, where Pete and Margaret and Lily slept.

He'd had the green canvas bag since he'd left Manchester, and in almost thirty years the color had gone from green to a vague moldy-vomit shade, the weave smoothed by thousands of hours carried on his back. The edges were frayed, and the numbers and names he'd inked on the canvas over the years were mostly rubbed out, but the contents had never varied much. Chalk, some herbs that came in handy, a flat antique mirror he'd found in a junk shop in Dublin that he used for scrying, some red thread for binding curses, and the other bits and bobs accumulated over the course of a life spent slinging hexes to get by.

Jack kicked the garbage out of the way and used the chalk to draw a circle big enough for two people to stand in. The last time he'd summoned Belial it had been an accident—he'd been either incredibly lucky or incredibly stupid, depending on who you asked. A hungry elemental could have just as easily shown up and devoured him, but instead his frantic last-ditch summoning attracted one of the Named.

Belial had saved his life, and then spent the next decade fucking it up beyond all recognition. That was the nature of dealing with demons. Nobody ever got what they wanted in a demon deal, except the demon themselves.

He'd memorized Belial's sign since that first time, the unique brand that every one of the Named carried. He drew that, dropped some herbs, and pulled out his lighter, setting them on fire. Belial's offering required blood, but Jack wasn't stupid. The demon would love to get ahold of Jack's blood. Then he would never have to ask nicely for a favor ever again. Blood magic was the sort of thing even most sorcerers didn't mess with. The last one who had, Nicholas Naughton, had snuffed himself out when the thing he'd called forth with his ritual decided the necromancer was a tasty snack.

That was what *should* happen, when you trucked with demons and black magic. You feel like the hard man for a few ticks of the universe's clock, and then something from the back of beyond snaps you up like a digestive biscuit.

The fact that he had a different sort of relationship with Belial should have scared him, Jack thought as he breathed in the smoke. It was sticky and pungent, and the scent reminded him of both church incense and high-grade marijuana, smells that wound around his senses and pitched things just slightly off. It should terrify him, should make him constantly look over his shoulder, knowing that sooner or later his luck would run out and Belial would have no more use for him.

Then he'd be dead. He might not owe Belial his soul to torment any longer, but Jack had never kidded himself on that score—when he finally kicked it for good, he was Hell-bound no matter who snuffed him.

Or bound for something much worse.

The tattoos on his arms and chest fluttered, as if a wind had passed through him, raking over his blood and bones. The feathers shifted and re-settled in a new pattern, like the flight of ravens just before he'd slashed his hand.

"What do you think you're playing at?" Belial appeared across the chalk marks from him, face twisted in fury.

Jack sucked in a hot, singed lungful of smoke, feeling his feet slam back to the ground. The time for messing about with the thing that had marked him could come later. Now he had to be sharp, because Belial was well and truly slagged.

"Did you really think you'd feed me that fat pack of lies and I wouldn't take exception?" He folded his arms, and even though every impulse in his hindbrain screamed not to, he stepped into Belial's space, forcing the demon's heels against the chalk circle. If Jack broke it, the demon would be free and he'd be lunch meat. If Belial broke it, he'd get a one-way express ticket back to Hell, courtesy of magic that was stronger than either of them.

"I'm confused, Jack," Belial said. "See, I thought

we had an agreement, an arrangement even. Quid pro quo, Clarice. But now you seem upset." He placed a hand on Jack's cheek, black nails digging in ever so slightly. "Do tell me what's troubling you, Jackie boy."

Jack slapped the demon's hand away. "Careful, Belial. I'm not your bitch anymore. My soul is my own."

"That's highly debatable." Belial snorted. "But fine, I'm not the man holding the pink slip, so what's twisted up your panties this time?"

"Legion," Jack said. He watched the demon's face, but looking for Belial's tell was about as useful as looking for a unicorn to give him a lift down to Brighton.

"So you already found out his name," Belial purred. "Quick work for you, Jack. I think our dear Petunia would have figured that out in about half the time, but then again, you never were a star pupil."

"I know that Legion is a load of shit," Jack said. "I know he's not real. So why don't you quit wanking and be honest with me for a change?" He leaned even closer to the demon, close enough so that instead of herbs, he smelled the sharp, burnt stench of the demon's body, the tickle of good whiskey and cigars, the tinge of some kind of colonge that was as thick and heavy as the scent of rot.

"Jack, I've always been honest with you," Belial said. "I may occasionally say things that you don't want to hear, but lying isn't good business."

"I'll send you back to the Pit so fast your head

will spin off," Jack growled. "So either you answer me or I'm giving you a shove over that line there."

"Jack, Jack," Belial sighed, then shoved Jack back so hard his ankle twisted and he went down on his arse. "You really think I'd answer your page if I didn't feel like it?" Belial snarled. He towered over Jack, blocking out the infant sun, his shadow falling cool across Jack's face. "You didn't even give me a proper blood sacrifice. Because that's you, Jack—always making it halfway and expecting someone else to finish up for you." Belial leaned in, and Jack forced himself to look into the demon's coal-fire eyes, not blinking, not flinching, just staying still and feeling the pulse in his neck flutter as his heart primed him for flight.

"What do you think you know that gives you the right to toe up to me?" the demon hissed. "Because it's not nerve, Jackie, nor is it conviction. You forget—I've had my hands around your heart. I've seen your guts spill onto the floor. I've tasted your blood and heard you scream for mercy, you stain upon my boot, so just because I came to you for help don't think for a *moment* that I won't crush you if you become inconvenient."

Jack held his breath. It was the only way to keep from shaking under the onslaught of Belial's rage. "I think you're a fucking liar," he said softly.

Belial blinked, twin spots of color rising in his pale fish-belly cheeks. "Excuse me?"

"I think you do need me," Jack said. "Because I'm the only one who'll help you, and I think you're scared, Belial. More scared than you've ever been. Because whoever he is—Legion or someone else, doesn't matter—he's managed to excavate the one little spark of fear left in that charred lump of shit you call a heart, and he's lit it aflame."

Jack grabbed Belial by the demon's tie and shoved him, just hard enough to get the purchase to stand up. He was careful not to touch skin; getting a jolt of Belial's magic wasn't on his agenda for this day or any other. "I think you need me—not to stop him, but to make sure you still have a place in Hell when this is all over."

Going against every instinct in him, Jack turned his back on the demon and lit a cigarette, looking west toward the City. The sun was up now, the sky the stained yellow of aged wallpaper, bruise-blue clouds clinging low above the dome of the Old Bailey and St. Paul's, flirting with the spires of Victoria Bridge. "I love this city," Jack said. "I've loved it since the first time I saw it, tasted its magic, realized that I'd finally found a place I could rest my head without hearing the voices of the dead on a fucking tape loop to eternity. And since you brought me into this, I've seen it destroyed over and over again. People I love slaughtered. Nothing but ashes in the air."

He exhaled, feeling the demon creeping around the edges of the chalk, neither of them quite willing to risk breaking off the dance just yet. "I will do whatever it takes, Belial, *whatever* it takes to stop what I've seen. I don't give a shit about you, about Hell, or any of that. I'm free of you, and if I have to throw you under the bus to keep my city and my people safe, then I'll do it with a smile on my fuck-ing face."

He turned around, praying he didn't meet a slagged-off Belial out of his human skin, in full rageful glory, ready to rip Jack's nuts off.

Belial stared at him, still in the shape of a man, a shape vibrating with fury. But Belial was an old pro at this back-and-forth of threats and offers. Too much so to ever let his rage show on his face.

"So if you want me to keep you in this race," Jack said, "and you want to have a City and a cozy flat and a bevy of elementals and arse-kissing Named to go home to when it's all over, then you will be straight with me from this second on."

He crushed the cigarette, his mouth bitter with bile and fear. "You don't have to tell me the whole story, and I don't have to help you. You think you've seen me at my worst, Belial, down there in the Pit when you owned my soul, but I'm telling you now, mate: You lie to me again, and you'll learn you haven't seen anything yet." The memories rushed up at him, tinged with black and red, echoing with nothing but screams. Jack shut his eyes for a heart-beat, opened them to find Belial with his more usual expression of disgusted ennui.

"You are truly an impossible man among an al-ready trying race," he said. "I look forward to the day when I can finally be rid of you."

"Same, times two, mate," Jack said. "Talk."

"Legion—or whoever—stole something," Belial said. "From the vaults. There are things buried in them I don't know about. None of the Princes have a complete catalog, except maybe Azrael, and you know where he's gotten off to."

"And this trinket is what's going to bring the whole mess crashing down?" Jack asked. Belial nodded. Jack felt a twist in his stomach, as if he were at the top of a rollercoaster, overlooking the drop, but he shoved it down.

"You must have a guess," he said. "What is it? Weapon? The Hell-spawned equivalent of a nuclear bomb?"

"I don't *know*," Belial growled. "All we know is that he broke in, took something, and left again. There's an empty spot with no record of what filled it. From one of the very oldest rooms in the vault—a room Baal and Beelzebub didn't even see fit to tell me existed until it happened. What I showed you is the curated artifacts, Jack. The key and the eye and all that rot. But things get lost. People forget. All except him."

Jack scratched his chin. "Or somebody told him what door to open and what deposit box to pull."

Belial showed his teeth. "See, that's the sort of quick thinking that makes me glad we didn't just drown all the humans when they first started swanning around on two legs."

"Thanks for the thought," Jack said. "So Legion—or whoever—stole whatever, and buggered off to hide on earth? With not so much as a by-your-leave from you or the other Princes?"

"Jack, if I knew where a madman bent on breaking the universe was hiding, don't you think I'd be there instead of choking on this hippie crap you insist on burning on a rooftop?" Belial snapped. "I don't know, and that part was the truth. But yes, the artifact is the way he's going to bring down the walls, and that's why I'm concerned."

Jack kicked some dirt onto the pile of burning herbs and rubbed out part of the chalk line with his foot. The demon wasn't going to chew on him, for now. The circle's use was over. "You could have just told me all this to begin with."

"Unnecessary," Belial said. "You would have just wasted time trying to figure out what he stole and not focused on the real problem, that aside from being a thief he has a remarkable pull with both Hell and the Black's malcontents. He's going to turn every dispossessed nutter in the Black against the daylight world, and who do you think they'll point to as a scapegoat?"

"Harry Potter?" Jack couldn't resist needling the demon a bit. Belial had lied to him and almost set him against an unknown quantity that commanded unknown power. He was far from the mood to play nice.

"You, you tit," Belial said. "You and everyone close to you. You used to be a bad man, but now all you have a reputation for is swooping in and saving the day when nasty types try to ruin it."

"Get off my roof," Jack said. "I ended the circle what feels like an eternity ago."

"Don't take your mood out on me," Belial said. "Save it for Legion."

"He's not Legion," Jack snapped. "That's a story. Even demons have monster stories."

"Yeah," Belial said. "Ask yourself where the story started, Jack. I wager if you think about that, it'll scare you. It did me."

Belial did the trick where there was a glimmer of sunlight and a shiver of wind, and when Jack blinked he'd gone, leaving nothing but a burned smell and a throbbing in Jack's skull.

Jack sighed and bent down to shove his gear back into his kit bag. That was the thing with spells—a lot of pomp and crackling magic, and in the end you were usually no better than when you started, and sometimes considerably worse.

He preferred his comfort zone as a hex-slinger, somebody who did the dirty close-up magic that broke bones and scrambled brains. Leave the ritual and the robes to people like Morwenna Morgenstern, and eventually Margaret, people with enough training and power to command the vast forces of the universe.

Jack had spent most of his time caring less about the vast universe. Surviving was enough work, and he avoided the types who wanted to make him into one of those twats who stood at the center of a circle while the energies of the Black crashed through them like a tidal wave, sweeping away everything in their path.

The notion scared the hell out of him. It would, Jack reckoned, scare the hell out of anyone with sense.

He intended to stand up, climb down the fire escape, and go inside to talk things over with Pete. She always knew what to do. Always saw a way through.

Pete never gave up, to the point where she could be psychotically stubborn. In times such as these, Jack reasoned, he could do with some bullheadedness on his side.

Instead, the world spun sideways as he rose, and the pink sky above London bled into black, as his sight rushed up and drowned everything in a void of smoke and howling klaxons.

CHAPTER 16

Moisture dotted his cheeks, and grit and debris abraded Jack's body as he lay prone. He heard the persistent, unending wailing of emergency sirens drifting over him. Wave after wave of sound penetrated his skin, down to his bones, deep into the fear center of his brain.

Get up, it snarled, and his eyes snapped open, a breath that tasted of chemical smoke and hot ash filling his empty lungs.

The air hung heavy, like wet cotton pressed over his face, and rain plinked onto the metal sheet roofing and the pavement below.

He was on a roof, yes, but not the roof of his flat. He stood with his back to the roiling Thames, on top of a low warehouse in the Docklands, the type he'd thought had all been bulldozed in the service of gentrification.

A slim figure stood with his back to Jack, and at first he thought it was Belial. He had a moment of stinging rage knowing that he never should have given the demon an inroad into his head.

The man turned so Jack caught his profile, and Jack saw it wasn't Belial at all. This man was fully human, wearing a tan jacket and jeans, the sort of getup a bloke wore when he was trying to appear laid back and fun but only succeeded in looking like a twat.

"You can't stop me," the man said to Jack, and a smile grew on his face. The smile was as thin and nasty as a clean wound, oozing malice the way a razor cut oozes blood.

Opening his mouth to reply, Jack instead choked when he saw himself take a few steps across the roof toward the man.

This version of Jack looked like shit. Face beat to hell, one arm hanging in a makeshift sling made from his shirt, his tattoos almost obscured by soot and dirt.

More than that, Jack thought, he looked old. His eyes were sunken, and the salt-and-pepper dark of his natural hair was starting to show below the peroxide job. He favored his bad knee, and exhaustion was evident in his voice when he spoke.

"Maybe not, but that doesn't mean I'm not going to give it the old try."

This was more than a vision, Jack realized, as his head started to throb with the sort of pain normally produced only by putting a power driver to your skull. It was an echo, a direct window into something that hadn't happened yet, but would, sooner rather than later. Not a maybe future—a certain one. The psychic feedback of the event was so great that this him, this tired, beat-to-shit future version of Jack Winter, was passing it along the line, back to the Jack who could still do something about it.

Clever bastard, Jack thought. He might not have much, but he at least had that going for him.

"Jack, I admire you and I wish you'd consider the reality here," said the man. Or was it a man? Jack wasn't physically here, so his senses were muted, those neurons that lit up when another magic user was near. Was this just a demon who was far better than Belial at looking human, because he'd had more practice? Something like Legion?

"The reality is that this world isn't a play set for you to kick over whenever you have a temper fit," future-Jack snarled. His nostrils flared, crusted with dried blood. Jack winced at the thought of the beating coming down the pike at him. Always inevitable, never pleasant.

"This world is broken," Legion whispered. "Hell is broken. The Black is broken. You don't understand, Jack. They're all pieces of something that shattered, and all I'm doing is putting it back together."

"By killing great swaths of humanity and demons alike," future-Jack snarled. "You're a proper fascist, mate. Hitler and Mussolini would be proud to count you."

"Never invoke Hitler in an argument," Legion purred. "Weakens your position. And those demons, Jack? You really telling me you're going to weep for the very creatures who gave you a life full of misery and pain rather than the birthright your talent demanded?"

"Shit choices and smack got me this life," future-Jack said. "Demons were just a side effect. And right now, my life is the best it's ever been, so you bet your arse I'm going to give my last breath, my last ounce of blood, to stop you."

Legion sighed and looked back at the city. The smoke came from a few localized fires, but Jack saw a haze spreading from the north, a dark bank of thunderclouds.

Not clouds, he realized. Birds. Thousands of them, their cries cutting through the rain and the sirens.

"The bride of war comes to feast on the corpses," Legion said. "And the walls all fall down. This is how it was in the beginning, Jack. And how it shall ever be from now on."

Legion held up the piece of metal he'd stolen and it formed itself into a small, smooth globe, dark brown in color, the sort of thing a City banker would pay too much for in a gallery. "The Princes denied me, but the world won't. And if you persist in this, Jack, I'm sorry, but you're no longer useful."

Jack saw his future self work the piece of the Gates that Belial had given him out of his sling as he and Legion closed distance.

"I'm warning you," future-Jack said. "Don't do it."

"It's already done," Legion said. "I didn't even need to break down the walls, just weaken them. I've used this marvelous little thing to pop around, prying out a stone where I needed to. A whisper in the ear of a mage in the 15th century, the right grimoire in the hands of a Nazi occultist in 1941, loosening the latches just enough to give Nergal and Abbadon and them the idea of escaping and weakening the barriers around Hell . . . when you think about it as I have, Jack, it's like the world was always waiting for this. The day it stops being segmented and becomes a whole."

The birds were close now, sweeping overhead, and Jack saw the tattoos on his future arms ripple and change, the ambient witchfire around him crackling like blue fire. Raindrops sizzled off it, steam adding to the surreality of the scene on the rooftop.

It couldn't be, Jack thought. The barriers between Hell, death, the Black . . . they were porous, but they were eternal. And now Legion was saying that everything that had happened since Pete had strolled back into Jack's life was his doing, his jumping back and forth, molding events to his end. Nick Naughton, Nergal, Abbadon, his deal with Belial . . . all to break the walls. But nothing could break them down fully. Nothing in the Black could exist on the same plane as the daylight. Side by side, yes. On top of one another, no.

They'd repel each other like magnets.

They'd cause exactly what he'd seen when he'd run from the hospital.

The Morrigan had tried to warn him, and when he hadn't listened, she'd come. The Hag, the woman who watched the end of the world, who collected the dead for her army.

She'd come to see Legion's victory.

The other Jack, the one with the eyes empty of everything but rage and grief, lunged at Legion with the key. The demon shook him off, laughing.

"Sorry, Jack. Too little, too late. If you think

you're taking me back to Hell, then you'll be trapped there, same as I was."

His other self hesitated, and Jack wanted to scream at the stupid cunt to just do it, just suck them back to the Gates and be done with it. Pete and Lily were counting on them. The fucking world was coming down around their ears, and he couldn't pull the trigger when it counted.

"Oh, did your dear friend Belial not mention that?" Legion sneered. "He can pass you back and forth like you're hopping on a tube train, but if you use the key, it's a one-way trip. You're a living soul, Jack, and your ticket isn't good for a return, even if the other Princes would let you go after you'd proven yourself a loyal dog." He shrugged. "But by all means, use it if you want. If your conviction is that strong. If you really think it's the way to stop me."

Do it, Jack tried to scream, but he was just an echo, just a bloke watching television and yelling at the screen.

His arm wavered, just for a moment, and in that half a heartbeat Legion closed the distance between them, grabbed Jack by the throat, and tossed him over the side of the roof.

He heard himself scream, felt his stomach drop, watched Legion's grin spread, the grin of a small child who'd just stepped on an ant.

"Didn't think so," the demon said, and Jack heard his body hit the pavement below before his eyes shot open.

CHAPTER 17

Jack jerked upright like he'd taken a cattle prod to the balls. "Shit!" he gasped, before he saw he was alone except for a morbidly obese pigeon pecking at a crisp wrapper and an old woman in the flat across the street, watching him through a gap in her curtains.

He gave the woman a weak wave, and she waved back. The pigeon flew away, and Jack stood up, feeling all the odd bits of him that he'd broken over the years protest. He picked up his kit and climbed back down the fire escape. Small white fireworks exploded in his vision every time he moved wrong. His head was a minefield after the onslaught of sight, and he'd wrenched something in his shoulder when he'd taken a tumble.

Pete looked up from her laptop when he climbed through the window, eyebrow rising. "You all right?" she asked.

He slumped on the sofa, throwing his bag down, and closing his eyes. He wanted to buck up, not burden her with anything more, but he couldn't. He was drained. The well was dry.

He was the man who couldn't kill Legion when he had the chance.

"Not remotely," he said.

A moment later, Pete's weight sank the couch cushion next to him. She smelled like lavender perfume, baby powder, a tinge of wood smoke, the scent of magic. A tumbler pressed into his hands, and Jack tossed back the whiskey in a single gulp.

"It'll be all right," Pete said softly.

Jack opened his eyes, looking into Pete's gaze. She had green eyes, deep and dark like a pool long left undisturbed. She was beautiful, and he was going to get her killed. He was going to get all of them killed. Legion was going to steal Lily, and Pete was going to be dead.

"Not this time, luv," he said, setting the tumbler down with a clunk.

"Oh, fuck off, Jack," she said. The snap in her voice made him look up. Pete didn't look concerned any longer. She was glaring at him. "I know how bad this is," she said. "I know exactly what it means if you can't find Legion, or whoever he is, and stop him before he tries to rip a hole in Hell. I *know* that you saw me die, and if you think I haven't lain awake just as long as you have most nights then you're either stupid or fucking over-the-moon selfish. And yet, somehow, I trust it will be all right. You know why?"

"Why?" Jack said. He felt the warm burn of shame that came from being a man with his head firmly inserted into his own arse.

"Because I trust you," Pete said. "And I trust myself. And I know that while we're together, trying to keep things safe for our daughter, that no power on this earth or any other can stop us." She put her hands gently on either side of Jack's face, one thumb running down the scar on his cheek.

"You think you don't deserve trust or anything else from me," Pete said. "But that's shite. You're the only one who can stop this, Jack. *We're* the only ones who can stand up and say no, the world will keep spinning through this day, and all the days to come. It's a burden, and probably one we don't deserve, but we must do it, and I know we will." She pressed a quick kiss to his lips. "Together."

Jack grabbed her, needing to feel her warmth, her heartbeat, and pulled her against him, wrapping his arms around her body, which was so small it still fit neatly into his arms, as if they'd been meant to stand side by side from the very start. "You're a bloody amazing woman," he said into Pete's hair, "and I don't deserve you."

"No, you don't," Pete agreed. She straightened up and looked at him. "But I'm here, and I'm kicking you in the arse. Do what you have to do, Jack, to keep the world turning, and I'll always be here when you need me. Right?"

"Right," Jack said. He picked up the tumbler and went into the kitchen, pouring another generous mouthful of whiskey. He didn't have much, but he'd seen Legion's face. He knew for sure what the demon intended to do, even if he didn't believe Legion had orchestrated things to the degree he claimed. And there was someone else from the visions afflicting him who would have some answers.

"I'll be back," he told Pete when he'd fortified himself against both his headache and the sinking feeling in his stomach that told him they were all fucked. "I'm going to see a man about the apocalypse."

CHAPTER 18

Jack took the tube to Oxford Street. After the shit-storm of the last few days, he needed people, flash, normalcy. All of the things he usually hated about London—posh types pushing through the crowds, herds of ASBOs kids screeching into their mobiles, tourists blocking entire swaths of the pavement to snap photos of what, exactly, he wasn't sure—now made him feel like he could finally lower his shoulders from his ears and relax for a few breaths.

It was hard for a demon or a sorcerer to blend in among so many mundane types. With so much metal and technology, it was a dead spot for Fae as well. He was just another plonker shuffling past the wafer-thin girls going in and out of Topshop, just another middle-aged bloke paging through the New Releases rack at HMV while a pudgy employee half his age rolled his eyes at Jack's leather from behind his ironic glasses.

Jack walked as far as Tottenham Court Road, where he turned from Oxford Street to Blooms-bury Street and the honking, glittering, bleeping commerce turned into refined flats and posh antique shops. He passed the hulk of the British Museum, turned around and made it as far as Piccadilly Circus

before he was satisfied that he wasn't being followed
or watched by anything or anyone more sinister than
a herd of Swedish teenagers sitting by the fountain,
eating sandwiches and snapping photos of each other.

He turned his senses away from the crowds
around him and into the Black, which was strong in
this old part of the City. Whitechapel had so many
layers that the flow was muted, blocked by a hundred
competing channels of spirits, death, black magic,
and cold iron distorting the signal.

Here, though, things were old, and they tended to
stay the same. He was standing at the edge of a massive circle, bound on all sides by stone and with a
massive iron focus in the center. You couldn't ask
for a better thin spot between the daylight and the
Black.

Jack used the alley between the Piccadilly Water-
stones and the next building to slip the bonds of
daytime, and when he opened his eyes, he found
himself in a twilight world, sun down but light not
yet snuffed out.

A few figures drifted through the thin wisps of
fog. The temperature here was fallish, and Jack sank
inside his leather. The Black had a different flow—
different time, different season, different citizens.

The figures—a woman in a black mourning gown
circa Queen Victoria and some kind of shapeshifter
poured into racing leathers—cast long, unblinking
stares in his direction.

Jack saw the red thread binding the mouth of the
woman and the black eyes and pointed ears of the

shifter, and he shook his head. Not so long ago, a zombie and a lycanthrope would have been ripping each other to shreds. They were both children of a necromancer—one started as a corpse, one started as a man—but as with all siblings, there were certain rivalries.

True shapeshifters, living creatures that had emigrated to the Black from a dusty corner of Who-Knows-Where, were rare. The juice to bespell yourself to flip from human to bear, big cat, wolf, or other creature didn't come along very often. But leave it to a clever fleshcrafter to figure out that if you got ahold of a living subject, you could pop out their consciousness and drop in whatever you liked, augmenting their muscle and bone and blood to be your very own little Lon Chaney wannabe.

Whatever they were up to, Jack decided he wanted no part of it. It was just another symptom of how sideways things were, war making strange bedfellows and all that.

He walked on, keeping his eyes off the pair so they wouldn't think he wanted to involve himself in their business, either as a customer or an interloper, and fixed his senses on finding the familiar roads through the twilight to the one spot in the Black he could conceivably call home.

It had been a long time since he'd frequented the Lament with any regularity. Life got in the way of visiting his local. Life, demonic prison breaks, zombie armageddons . . . Jack looked up at the red door, triple-banded in iron, and felt a flutter of unease. He didn't have many friends on the twilight side since he'd put down Nergal. Fuck it, he'd never had many *friends,* just folks who tolerated him, but now even the tolerance was gone. He'd lost count of the number of "Never darken my doorway again" speeches he'd gotten in the wake of the primordial demon pulling his Hulk-smash act on London.

Strange bedfellows, he reminded himself. There were at least a few rational sorts left who'd listen to what he had to say before they tossed him out on his arse.

He hoped.

The Lament was suitably dim on the inside, the right amount of shadow tucked in between the pools of light cast by sooty ceiling fixtures and candles stuck in mounds of wax in the center of the tables. Jack tried to ignore the fact that the burble of conversation stopped when he walked in, that only the thready tune of the jukebox carried on.

He caught a few poisonous stares from a table of hedgewitches sharing a pitcher of pink cocktails, and one outright bird flip from a pair of tweedy mages he pegged as too mild-mannered to be anything but sex cultists. He ignored it all. There was a time he would have knocked over some chairs and kicked up a fuss until someone threw a punch, but he had a mission now.

The bartender was new, a petite Indian girl wearing a Neon Trees shirt, and she set him up with a pint of Newcastle with a minimum of fuss and glaring. "Anything for you?" she asked, when Jack pushed the pint to the side without tasting it.

"Don't suppose you've got a time machine back there," Jack muttered.

"Sorry," the girl said. "Left my sonic screwdriver at home." She gave him a radiant, teasing smile, and Jack thought there also would have been a time when, after the dustup was over, he would have walked out with this girl and taken her home. So what if she had a row of pointed shark's teeth where her dull human ones should be, and the oval pupils of a reptile? Lamias needed love, too.

"I like you," Jack said, returning her smile. He passed over a tenner. "Keep it," he said, when she started to reach for change. The Lament traded in a variety of currencies, not all of them corporeal, but the fact was that whether sex cultist or hedgewitch, magicians were shit tippers.

The lamia stuck his crumpled bill in the ancient cash register and slid a glass of dark, pungent whiskey his way. "You look like you need this," she said. "Good luck with whatever it is you're here to do."

Jack knocked back the whiskey, his balance and his stomach warning him that with the next tipple, he'd be on the wrong side of pissed to stay sharp. "Staving off the end of the world, defending goodness and kittens," he said. "You know, the usual shite."

He faced the room again, relieved that no one had slung a hex or tried to shank him while his back was turned. Inciting violence in the Lament meant a permanent ban, but Jack knew he'd inspired more than a few blokes to the sort of hatred that was worth being barred for the chance to crack his skull.

The table was always the same—at the back of the room, where the occupant could see without being seen, tucked into the shadows.

Jack set the pint of Newcastle on the pitted surface and took a chair. "Some things never change, eh, Ian?"

Ian Mosswood scrutinized Jack, and the glass, with his expressionless black eyes. "I don't want to ask what you need from me, Jack. Because to come here and ask it, you must be so desperate I'm wondering if I should peer outside for a rain of frogs."

He took the glass and drank, and Jack felt the tight place under his ribs unknot. Mosswood had accepted the offering, so Jack wasn't going out the door head first just yet.

"Since when do you make Biblical references, Ian?" he said.

"I read it some time ago," Mosswood said. "Absolute bunk, the lot, but they do have some amusing stories about the end of time. I like the one about the giant dragon meant to swallow up the world."

"Eh, stole that one from Norse bedtime stories," Jack said. "The Jesus and pals squad is big on plagiarism. But then again, every mage I know stole half his spells from some dead bastard's grimoire, so we're no better."

"I was worshipped," Mosswood said. "Though never in such a ridiculous fashion. I fancy myself a more practical sort of figure. Effectual, if you will."

"Ask and ye shall receive?" Jack said. "Yeah, you

Fae types are good about that. Except what humans receive is usually a great bending-over followed by an untimely death."

Mosswood spread his hands. "Can I help it if humans are venal, weak, selfish, and greedy?" he said. "No, I cannot. I am a Green Man, not a loan officer. I'm not compelled to be fair, just as they're not compelled to accept my terms."

"You're a barrel of fucking sunshine, as usual," Jack said, "but you're right. I, venal, selfish, greedy arse that I am, do have something to ask."

"You want to know about the shadow," Mosswood said. He'd drained the glass and set it on the table, folding his hands and staring at Jack without blinking.

"What shadow?" Jack's heart thumped, his danger sense and his sight sending fingers of fear running up and down his spine.

"The shadow of her wings," Mosswood said. "I see it, as do others who are very old. None of us can see the beginning, but we see the darkness that sweeps in behind it, the covering of the whole of the world with the shadow of the crows. The smoke, the darkness, and finally the end."

Jack's mouth tasted dry and sour, like the whiskey had come back up again. "Yeah, that'd be what I'm trying to stop."

Mosswood turned his empty glass between his rough palms. He was one of the oldest creatures Jack had encountered in the Black, second only to things like the Morrigan. Jack would wager he'd lasted even longer than some of the Named roaming around down in Hell. If anyone could give him a straight answer, it would be Mosswood.

"I don't think we're meant to," Mosswood said at last.

Jack felt as if someone had put a boot in his ribs. "Excuse me? You going all zen and fatalistic on me, Mosswood? *You,* of all people?"

"My roots go deep and wide," Mosswood said. "But even the oldest living thing must eventually blow away on the wind." He sighed and leaned back on his chair, rungs bumping against the pub's stained plaster walls. "I left my realm long ago, because I did not share contempt for humans with my Fae masters. I was not like them, not like the humans, but I made my home in this little slice of shadow. I always knew it was temporary. And so should you, Jack."

Jack shook his head. He felt heavy, as if he'd already taken the beating his sight had shown him, numb and exhausted, as empty as the Green Man's pint glass. "I can't accept that. I don't live in the Black, Ian. I live with people, my people, and I can't lie down until I've been put down."

"Then it's your choice." Mosswood stuck out his hand, and Jack took it almost by reflex. In all the years he'd known the Green Man, they'd never touched voluntarily. He felt the deep, wide river of power that flowed through the Green Man, a power as ancient as the dirt beneath their feet, ancient as the first man on the isle of Britain who'd lifted his head from the mud and seen the things waiting for him in the shadows and the realms beyond. It was solid power, bright, shining, but as Jack grasped Mosswood's rough hand it faded out, until he might as well have been holding a handful of sticks.

"Been happening more and more," Mosswood said. "Ever since things started to slide sideways. Old magic's draining out of the world. What'll take its place, I can't say. Nor will I be around to see it, likely."

"Take care of yourself, Ian," Jack said, barely able to hear himself over the din of the bar. Mosswood squeezed his hand and then stood.

"And you, Jack. But then you always do, don't you?"

Jack was about to tell Mosswood to wait, that he couldn't just fold his hands and accept that this was it, roll credits, but the door to the pub opened and a man dressed in an overcoat and a red cap stumbled in. He had a handful of notices and a stench rolling off him that could have stopped an oncoming rhino.

"I really wish they'd keep the bums out of here," Mosswood said as the man shuffled from table to table, passing out notices and sometimes collecting a few coins or notes in return.

"Yeah, well, as long as they're not pissing on me shoes I try to give 'em a pass," Jack said. He'd spent too many nights under motorway bridges and in doorways to turn up his nose at someone who slept rough. Even if he did wish the bloke would invest some of his change in a can of deodorant.

The homeless man shoved a handful of paper at Jack and Mosswood. The Green Man held up his hands as if the bum had offered him a plate of rat entrails, but Jack took the cheap one-sheet and smoothed it out.

When he saw the face, his stomach dropped through his feet and kept dropping until it hit the stone buried beneath the tube tunnels, covered rivers, and disused sewers below the floor.

The bartender hurried over to the man, taking him by the arm. "Now, Gerald, I told you . . . we can't have you in here passing this stuff out."

"But they need to know!" Gerald shrilled. Jack forced himself to get a better look at the bum—he was in rags and filthy, sure, but definitely human. He had the sunken-eyed look of a man who'd spent too many years struggling through some sort of debilitating illness without the benefit of either prescription or self-medication. Jack had met fellows just like him in the state mental clinics, one of the many times he'd been sectioned when the cops picked him up for roaming the street in a smack haze. The doctors were always treated to an earful of screaming about ghosts and monsters once Jack started to detox and his sight kicked him in the brain.

A mage, just like him, but one who hadn't been lucky enough to finally put a collar on his visions. Probably another psychic, if the shaking hands and uneven pupils were anything to go by.

"Gerald, behave yourself," the lamia scolded, "or I'm going to have to bar you."

"But I can do so much!" Gerald cried. "I can save so many, all the lost and everyone struggling to stay one step ahead of the darkness. They need to know about this place, about *him* . . ."

The lamia grabbed him unceremoniously by the back of the coat and propelled him toward the door. "Sorry, luv," she said. "I've given you your warning."

Jack grabbed up the wrinkled flyer that bore the grainy photo of Legion's face, and ran after her. "Oi," he said, as she slammed the door in Gerald's wake. Her mouth screwed up.

"Look, I'm sorry if he bothered you, but this ain't a high tea. Poor Gerald is just a bit confused."

"Look, it's not about the fact that he's a bum. I don't give a fuck if he pitches camp in the men's loo, frankly," Jack said, thrusting the flyer in the bartender's face. "What's this? Who is this arsehole on the one-sheet?"

The bartender blinked at him. "That's Larry Lovecraft."

Jack dropped a gaze heavy with disbelief on her, and the bartender rolled her eyes in return. "Look, I know how that sounds. I don't know who he really is, but he took over some old monastery up in the Midlands, and he's been running it as a refuge for people like Gerald. Mages who've gone a few rounds with black magic and lost, Fae creatures who've been exiled, types who can't blend in outside the Black." She pointed to her teeth. "Like me."

"You been to this . . . refuge?" Jack asked. Legion. It had to be. Calling himself by some stupid Channel 4 talk show host name, as if this were a fucking joke.

"Me? Fuck, no." The bartender snorted. "I got one of his little trust-circle pitches from the blokes that run the vans, and I about vomited my spleen. We're all children of magic, we should all love one another, nobody else understands us like he does . . . shit. The lot of it. I'd sooner have an imp piss on my head."

"I know a few who'd be happy to arrange that," Jack said. His fist was shaking, nails carving bloody circles into his palms, soaking into the flyer where he held it crumpled. "You said he has drivers?"

"Recruiters, more like." The bartender sniffed. "They cruise all over London, mostly on the daylight side, looking for poor sods like Gerald and scooping them up with the promise of a square meal and a warm bed and unending rivers of bullshit from this Larry Lovecraft bloke."

Lovecraft: the xenophobic twit who conceived of a vast, otherwordly madness coming to swallow humanity whole. Jack gritted his teeth. On top of all his other irritants, Legion clearly thought himself fucking hilarious.

"Know where they picked Gerald up?" Jack said. When the lamia hesitated, he took her by the arm. "Please. I need to talk to Larry. It's important."

"I hear they got him down in Peckham," she said. "Near one of the missions that does the free lunches on the weekends."

Jack dropped the flyer under his boot and shoved open the door of the Lament, cool air doing little to soothe the prickles of sweat working their way down his spine.

Mosswood might have given up, but he hadn't. And now he had a face, a target to focus the rage burning like stomach acid in his guts. Belial's politics inside, Legion had thrown the guantlet with the one human who might be enough of an arsehole—and an idiot—to fight back.

Jack just hoped this wasn't his worst idea yet.

CHAPTER 19

Though days were mild and all of the bad weather other places famously harassed the UK for had gone off for the impending summer, mornings were still chilly.

Jack wrapped his arms around himself inside his thin overshirt and cotton jacket with the Gate key in the pocket, sucking on his fag to keep warm as he stood in the line of other stooped, smoking, shivering men.

This was the third mission he'd tried since the sun came up, a neat little outfit that looked more like your grandmother's council flat than a homeless shelter. A hand-lettered sign in the window proclaimed *Believe in the Lord Jesus Christ and thou shalt be saved.*

Jack tried not to roll his eyes. Believing in a higher power, in his experience, just got you steamrollered. The sign might as well have encouraged the bunch around him to *Believe in the Dark Knight Batman and thou shalt receive large sacks of cheap whiskey and fags.*

There *was* no higher power. There were the beings older and hungrier than you, and there was avoiding being stepped on when they got a hair up their bum cracks. The Romans had it right, when they stepped foot on the isle—appease the old gods when you could, run when you couldn't, and drink plenty of wine always.

"Spare one a those?" The voice was thick, Scottish, and Jack turned to see a tall, skinny television aerial of a man staring down at him from under a black watch cap.

"Sure, mate," he said. His pack was empty after that, but he could always conjure more. He swept the street again with his gaze, but only a few buses and cars passed at the nearby intersection. No sinister vans, creeping to and fro looking for willing additions to Legion's army.

"Cheers." The Scot lit up with a pack of matches, brown fingers curling around the cigarette carefully, as if it were delicate and alive.

"Line always this long?" Jack asked. There were at least thirty men gathered on the pavement. "I thought this place didn't open until lunch."

"Aye, but if you turn up early sometimes the bakery up the road comes around with yesterday's stale buns," said the Scot. "And there's always a chance somebody'll hire you a day's pay to clean the garden or paint a fence."

Jack sized up the Scot. Chatty, older than him by about twenty years, skinny but enormous, wearing a military coat that probably hailed from the 1980s. "You a lifer, then?" he said. Some just liked sleeping rough. It got in your blood, and four walls never quite felt the same.

The Scot gave him a thin smile, a smile that told

Jack he'd just confirmed something. "I thought you might not be one of us."

"I was," Jack said. "Long time ago."

The Scot nodded, sticking the fag between his lips and extending one of his plate-sized hands. "Barry."

"Jack."

No prickle when they shook. Barry was as ordinary as they came.

"You a reporter?" Barry asked. "Or a blogger?"

Jack snorted. "Do I look like I blog?"

Barry shrugged. "Never can tell. I read 'em all myself. Library's on the Internet, I go in there when it rains and do the BBC breaking news, Huffington Post, that sort of thing. Keep myself informed. Check in with my old unit occasionally."

Jack cocked his head. "Falklands? Had some mates who had brothers and whatnot involved in that."

"You can't have been very old," Barry said. "But yes, I was there. Came back, suddenly didn't have much of a taste for my semi-detached and a thank-you from Her Majesty."

"She's not very popular in the patch where I grew up, either," Jack said. He swung a glance out at the street again. A white bus, of the sort used to cart seniors to and fro from activities, was parked near the corner, but not moving.

"Listen," Jack said. "You know anything about a van, been coming around picking folks up, promising them a place to live and meals and whatnot?"

Like he'd triggered a trap, Barry's genial expression shut off, and a dark anger filled his eyes.

"I think you best move along, boy," he said.

"Look," Jack held up his hands. "I'm not press and I'm not police. I just really, really need to speak to whoever's filling those vans."

Barry regarded him for a long moment, and Jack felt his heart throb. If he couldn't find Legion's gate-keepers, then he was back to square one, just a face and a bullshit name.

"That's them," he said, jerking his thumb at the bus as it started to move, curb-crawling toward the line of homeless people. "But you don't want to go with them," he said. "Blokes get on, and they never come back."

"And I'm guessing you don't believe it's because they have a great new life at a compound in the country?" Jack said.

The bus pulled to a stop. It was brand new, shiny, driven by a shaven-headed bloke in a leather coat very much like the one Jack had relunctantly left at home. He'd needed to blend in, and he felt naked without it.

"I've seen enough God-botherers to know when someone's just bending your ear and when they're a cult," Barry said. "And mark my words, Jack, these blokes are the sort who'll have you in trainers and matching outfits before a fortnight's out."

"Oi." The shaven-headed drone glared at Barry, taking a thin black police baton like the one Pete carried from his pocket. "Shut your face or I'll give you something to cry about, Nancy."

Barry ignored him, still staring at Jack. "Good luck, son," he said. "You're gonna need it."

The bald drone went down the line, picking out Jack and a pudgy kid still wearing the vestiges of his life before he'd hit the street—brand-name wind-cheater, good sneakers, prescription glasses that weren't third-hand, scratched, or broken. The kid sucked nervously on a lip piercing, and Jack leaned over to him. "You should probably stay out of this."

"Fuck off," the kid snarled. "You take your share, gramps, and leave some for the rest of us. I'm not going to piss off just because some towheaded rent boy doesn't like it."

Jack rolled his eyes. "Fine, you ruddy little ASBO. Suit yourself." If Margaret ever reached the stage where she talked like that, he was going to lose his mind.

"You two," the drone said. "You interested in taking a trip to a place with a bed and some food? In exchange, all you have to do is listen to a speech from the leader of the commune, Mr. Larry Lovecraft." The drone had said the line so many times it sounded like a draggy tape recording.

"You have no idea how interested I am," Jack said. He climbed in the bus after the kid, who practically bowled him over to be the first one up the steps.

Just a normal kid, even if he was an arse. A few scraps of latent talent, nothing he'd ever notice unless he got smacked on the forehead with a hex. Walking right into Legion's maw just because living on the streets was much rougher than it seemed on telly, and he wanted an out that didn't involve crawling back to his home life.

The coach lurched, and Jack felt sick. Legion was like a bird of prey, high on his wire, picking off the vulnerable. Thinning the herd before the real culling started.

Closing his eyes and steadying his breath, Jack told himself to stay calm. He felt the piece of the Gate in his pocket, resting against his hip. In a perfect world, he'd get close and snatch Legion, and the both of them would be back in the Pit before the lunch hour.

Oh, didn't he tell you? You're mortal. That's an express ride with no return ticket.

Jack leaned his forehead against the glass, hoping the cool vibration of the coach would still the memory of his latest vision. Demons lied, and Legion was clearly a champion at it.

Or Belial could be jerking his chain even harder than he'd thought, still lying to him. Either situtation was possible.

As the coach picked up speed and entered the M25, Jack decided he'd cross that bridge when he came to it. Right now, he was going to find Legion and do his bit to put things back where they belonged.

Or he was headed into the country to die trying.

CHAPTER 20

The coach hummed on for several hours, past Oxford, closer to Birmingham than London before it pulled off the motorway onto a B road, and from there onto something that Jack thought might have last been used to herd medieval sheep.

After what seemed like an eternity of potholes at war with both the coach's suspension and Jack's spine, they rolled to a stop in front of a low pile of stones and a slate roof that Jack supposed could have passed for a monastery at some point in the distant past.

A group of men in threadbare clothes loitered in front of the main doors, and not far off a generator buzzed, delivering power via a thick orange cable fed through a shattered window.

The whole place looked like a before shot on one of those posh makeover shows that Pete liked to watch sometimes, when she was trying to turn her brain off for sleep. Beside him, the kid sniffed.

"Looks fucking haunted."

"We should be so lucky," Jack muttered.

The bald bloke gave him a shove. "Move along. You'll be taken for a shower and delousing and then we'll see about a bed."

Jack decided to just go along—the more concrete information he could give to Belial, the better. The kid was busy goggling at everything as they passed room after room filled with decades of dust, junk, and mildew, and Jack was busy taking inventory of the sad sacks floating about the place.

There were mages, and he caught a few markings of orders like the Stygian Brothers—black magic to the core. The usual mix of shapeshifters and other dark-dwelling creatures of the Black. Even a few zombies stood around, one staring out the window at a far-off field dotted with the modern relatives of the sheep who'd made the road, the other in an alcove off the long hallway banging his head repeatedly against a wall.

They came into a thin, high room that Jack supposed had been the chapel at one point, and he started as a gray shape drifted down from above the altar. The *bean-sidhe* glared at him, her eyes as black and glassy as rock chips, before drifting away, the blood dribbling from her mouth leaving cold, hissing droplets on the stone floor.

If Legion was taking in Fae creatures, particularly nasty attack dogs like those, this was a serious coup against Hell indeed. Fae stayed away from the rest of them, whether they checked the human, demon, or "other" box. Pete had dealt with them once, just one of their many ruling bodies, and that once had been enough for her.

Jack didn't like Fae, didn't trust them. They were alien in a way demons weren't. You couldn't suss out their motives—and on a personal level, it had been a pack of *bean-sidhe* that a vengeful sorcerer had once sent to kill him.

Fae rulers kept a tight hold over their subjects—Mosswood was one of the few who'd managed to carve a life for himself outside their realm. If Legion had the power to attract followers even at the risk of what their rulers would do, Jack decided he was going to start having second thoughts pretty fucking quickly about meeting him.

A large room that Jack guessed had once been some sort of stable attached to the monastery proper held a cistern and a collection of makeshift hose showers that dribbled cold water, contributing to the damp stench rolling out from the falling-down space.

"Take your clothes off," said the drone, and Jack looked over at a trio of naked men who were having their heads shaved at the other end of the room.

"Fun as this looks," he said to the bald bloke, "I think I'll just see Legion now."

The drone blinked at him. "Eh?"

"Larry, Love Doctor, whatever he's calling himself here," Jack said. "I admit that I'm not really ready to don the mouse ears and be part of the club, mate. I told a little white lie so I could talk to your fearless leader. I know, it was awful of me, but there you have it. Probably best I'm not indoctrinated. I have a terrible problem following orders, and I look like shite in a jump suit."

The drone reached for the police baton again, but the same lilting voice Jack remembered from his vision stopped him.

"It's all right, Terrance."

Jack expected his first glimpse of the demon to be worse, somehow. He thought there should be some recognition, at least—this was the bastard who haunted his dreams, after all.

But there was nothing but a flat sense of disappointment. Legion's human body was small and ordinary, and his voice had an almost teenage cast.

"Mr. Winter did come here to talk to me," the demon said. "I invited him."

Jack watched the gears that ran Terrance's brainbox grind and smoke for a moment, and then he jerked his thumb at the kid. "What about this one?"

Legion came over, looking the fat kid up and down. Legion wasn't much bigger than Pete, in height or frame, but that started the first inkling of fear in Jack. The less care demons put into making their human forms large and scary, the more punch they usually packed. Belial was a prime example—that bastard was practically a midget, and he had enough magic to flatten London and put up a new Wizarding World of Harry Potter in its place, if he felt like it.

"Clean him up and put him to work feeding people," Legion said, inhaling a sharp whiff of the boy's scent. The kid recoiled.

Good lad, Jack thought. *Finally got that survival instinct working. Too bad it'll do you fuck-all good in this place.*

"Come with me, Jack," Legion said. He clapped Jack on the shoulder, but Jack had a lot of practice not flinching. It took all the fun out of it for bullies if you didn't react.

"After you, Larry," was all he said, knocking the demon's small, soft white hand off him.

"Oh, come on now," Legion said. "Is that any way to treat a new friend?"

"You and I aren't friends," Jack said, giving the demon a sharp smile. "So let's just have that understood right at minute one, shall we? Save both of us a lot of tears shed into our pints later on."

Legion didn't alter his expression in the slightest. The face was a mask, Jack realized, even more than Belial's was. Absolutely no relationship to what was going on beneath the surface. The perfect poker face.

"Have it your way, Jack," was all he said before he opened the door to the monastery and ushered Jack in.

"After you," Jack said. If Legion thought Jack would show his back, the fresh air in the country had driven him stark raving mad.

Legion pulled a pout. "Jack. You don't trust me."

Jack tilted his head. He was having a damn hard time watching this plastic life-sized doll being ridden hard by a demon whose true form he couldn't get a handle on, but he was going to keep this nice and civil until the screaming started if it killed him. Abbadon hadn't rattled him, the Princes hadn't made him shake—he was damned if some little pipsqueak with an ill-fitting human suit was going to get him there.

"Should I, Larry?" he said at last.

Legion grinned wide, so wide that the skin of his face creaked. "Probably not."

The key weighed in Jack's pocket, but he left it alone. Legion wasn't stupid, and neither was he. "You want to do this right here, in front of the true believers?"

Legion winked at him, and Jack felt a yank in his guts, like he'd missed a step and started to fall. When he blinked, they stood in a small turret room overlooking the fields and the grounds, the figures below them moving around, pushing wheelbarrows, trimming bushes, or carting loads of laundry to and from an outbuilding.

"Neat trick," Jack said.

"One of my best," Legion said. " 'Course, I got a lot more I could show you if you slag me off, Jack."

"Belial told me about your little *Doctor Who* gadget," Jack said. "So cut out the stage show. If you want to impress me . . . well, you can't."

"Poor Belial." Legion sat on the sill and looked down at the people below. "He believes in the Princes as much as those creatures down there believe in me. How disappointed was he when he had to tell you I'd yanked the most precious artifact in Hell's vaults out from under his nose?"

"No so much disappointed as gunning for your balls," Jack said. "I'd watch it with him, were I you. Belial's trickier than he seems."

"To you maybe," Legion said. "You're human."

"And what are you?" Jack asked. If he was going to get a hold on Legion, it was going to have to happen soon. "A demon with delusions of grandeur? Because I know the whole Legion thing is bunk, mate. I'm not some starry-eyed nincompoop fresh off a turnip lorry."

He knew he'd made a tactical error the minute the words left his lips. Legion closed the distance and shoved him into the wall, the plaster cracking under Jack's skull. "I *am* Legion," the demon hissed. "I am the undoing of this world."

Letting go of Jack, he began to laugh, a sound that didn't match the movement of his lips, that sounded more like wind screaming down a tube tunnel than any sound produced by a human mouth.

"All right, all right," he said. "So that was a bit dramatic, but seriously, Jack . . . I am the thing that the demons fear. I'm the thing they kept locked up beside what I took from them. And now, they've fucked up and I'm free. I've got the humans, the Fae, and soon there won't even *be* a Hell any longer to stand against me. So tell me, Jack, what grand plan do you have?"

"I don't believe you, first of all," Jack said. "A few stray Fae doesn't mean you've got any sort of influence."

Legion shrugged. "All right," he said. "See for yourself."

Jack felt the top-of-the-rollercoaster sensation again, and when he opened his eyes they were in the woods he'd seen from the turret, grass wet under his boots and Legion grinning at him like he'd just pulled two naked succubi out of a hat.

"Told you that was my best one," he said.

Jack ignored him. His senses prickled at the

encroachment of something that cut a wide swath through the Black—not quite the hammer fall of a demon's magic, but something bigger and badder than him all the same.

He swallowed the dry lump that grew in his throat as six Fae stepped from the trees—not creatures, but actual Fae, tall and black-eyed, with blue veins creeping under their pale skin. They regarded Jack as he stared at them. He'd never been this close to a Fae, by choice, and he decided it had been a smart decision. They felt like being covered in snakes, like cold water pouring down his throat and burning every last bit of air from his lungs.

"Jack," the demon purred. "These lovely, very pale fellows would like to show you the error of your assumption. Interested?"

"All right," Jack said. "So you and the Fae are cozy. How long you think that'll last when they find out you're gunning for top chair in Hell?"

Legion began to laugh again, slinging his arm around Jack and walking with him down the slope back toward the monastery.

"Jack, I don't care about Hell. I hate that place and I'd gladly see it burn. Hell gave me the means to come here, to this place, and what did I see? More misery. More suffering. More creatures stranded where they shouldn't be. Begs the question . . . why?"

Just tag him and use the key, Jack's mind screamed at him, but Legion's fingers clamped down on his shoulder, so hard he felt the bone creak.

"I swear if you reach for that pig-sticker Belial kitted you up with I'll rip your arm off and feed you the fingers one by one before I mail the rest of you to your wife," Legion hissed. "There's so much misery in this world, Jack. All the worlds. I'm going to take it all away."

Jack dug in his heels. He believed that Legion would hurt him, but he wasn't going to be led around like a toy poodle. "If I had a tenner for every speech from every twat who had plans for the apocalypse, I'd have enough for a holiday in Spain with a personal bikini-clad waitress to pour sangria directly into my mouth and then change my daughter's diapers, so why don't you just get it all out of your system and then we can get on with what you really want."

Legion blinked at him. All of his reflexes were slightly out of sync, Jack realized, like he was being remote-controlled. "But that is what I want," the demon said. "And it's what I'm going to do. You know and I know that the Black has been rattled to its core. Hell is cracking. One more shake, and the whole thing is going to fall over in a pile. I aim to be the thing that flattens it all. Then there will be no more Black. No more daylight. No more Hell. All together, Jack. Just like we are here."

"I'm sure you know that if the barriers come down, everything will collapse under its own weight like an overloaded footie stadium."

"I'm counting on that bit, yes," Legion purred. "Jack, I appreciate your moxie. I love the human spirit and all the stupid shit it makes you lot do. But rest assured, this will happen. I've spent a lot of time moving about, setting this up just so, so the person who would try and ruin it for me, well . . . let's just say it would be regrettable for this person to have a wife or a baby daughter that I could access."

Jack had sworn he was going to stay calm. He was going to play this right, use what his visions had given him to his advantage and not let fear take over. He hadn't considered rage, though, and it threw a wrench into the entire thing.

He moved for Legion, and the demon blinked out of existence, coming back with a shimmer a few dozens yards away, laughing that nails-on-metal laugh again.

Jack looked down at his palm, the key clutched in it, rough sides biting into his hand and causing dark blood to well up.

"That's good," Legion said. "Use that rage, Jack. I know you won't, but I'll offer to let you come along with me. Stand on this side of the equation for a change, the side without the bloodshed and heartbreak. You don't have any friends in the Black and precious few out of it. You have nothing to lose if everyone is forced to live in the same miserable pit of existence."

"You think you're special?" Jack had landed in mud and could taste earth and grit on his tongue. He spat them out. "You think you're unlike anything the world has seen before? I've got news for you, Legion." Jack pulled himself to his feet. Maybe this was it—this was the great arse-kicking he'd seen himself take. Well, so be it. He wasn't going to just stand here and let the maniac bang on about ripping the universe a new arse.

"You're nothing," Jack ground out. "You're a petty little demon with a god complex, and I've seen a dozen of you in my lifetime. My *human* lifetime. That should tell you exactly how often somebody gets that bright idea down in the Pit. If you want a dick-measuring contest with the Princes, then have at it. But you leave the rest of us alone, because if you keep up this nonsense, collecting followers and making life hard for humanity in general, then I am going to put an end to you, and you won't end up in one of Belial's cozy little torture chambers."

Jack took a step toward Legion, even though it was probably the exact opposite of an appropriate reaction, which was to run the fuck away, fast as he could. He never had much common sense when he got really angry, which is why he only got really angry about once a decade or so. He could see blue fire at the edges of his vision, as his magic gathered and he didn't give a rat's arse in that moment whether or not he walked away. If this shit-stain moved on him, they were both going to bleed.

"You'll just be dead," he snarled at the demon. "Dead as every other twit who rolled the dice with the apocalypse and lost. Don't fuck with me, Legion, because I'm not like other humans. I am capable of making your life exceedingly fucking difficult, and if you cross me or my family my last breath will be spent shoving you face-first through the Bleak Gates and into the Land of the Dead."

Legion blinked again, and had him by the throat. Pete would have been furious, Jack thought, letting his anger get a leg up like that. Making him sloppy and grandiose instead of clever, which was what the situation called for. Any twit could shout and wave his arms. Nobody was going to stop a mad demon by cursing him out.

"Oh, I like you, Jack," Legion said. "I think I'll keep you alive just long enough to see what becomes of this world you love so much. And then, once I've systematically broken you and everyone you care about, you'll die hearing the screams of your family." The demon tightened his grip, and as he did his skin rippled and changed. Jack caught a glimpse of the face behind the mild mask the demon wore. It was all sharp edges, the chitinous shell of an insect, with eyes that were gold and depthless, twin suns that you couldn't look at without burning.

"But not yet," Legion whispered, lips brushing Jack's ear. "We both still have our work to do."

Jack opened his mouth—to scream or curse more, he wasn't sure—but gravity kicked him in the ribs again and he stood at a service station on the motorway, a group of coach tourists staring at him with frowns.

"*Konnichiwa*," he said, waving them off.

He made his way around the back of the service center, pulling a stray piece of chalk out of the pocket of his homeless getup. Belial glared at him after Jack had blinked and the demon had shown up, straightening his tie.

"What now? Can't you just phone, like a normal person?"

"I found Legion," Jack managed. His hand was on fire, the gash deeper than he'd initially thought.

The key rested in his pocket, still humming with the power of the Gates. He'd been so close. So close, and he'd fucked it up.

That was a better lie than admitting Legion was never going to let him get close in the first place. A sucker punch from Jack and a quick trip back to Hell had never been in the cards.

"Well, I don't hear a celebration going on downstairs," Belial said. "So I'm guessing he handed you your arse and sent you on your way."

"We need to talk," Jack told him. "That thing he stole, the bit that puts space and time in a blender— he's gotten very fucking proficient with it. He has bigger plans than Hell, and I think he's fully capable of executing them. He's insane, Belial. You lot are going to need a bigger boat."

Belial grimaced. "I was afraid of this. That's what comes of nobody bothering to find out how the one piece of junk we have lying around that could really do some damage actually works. Always too afraid of it getting into the wrong hands."

"I hate to break it to you," Jack said. "It's in the wrong fucking hands. Has been for some time. He's claiming that he used it to set up Nergal, Abbadon's jail break, all of it. Could he be telling even the slightest bit of truth, Belial?" Saying it out loud made Jack's throat constrict. That much power was beyond anything any living creature was supposed to carry. Even Abbadon, the first citizen of Hell, the thing that predated demons by millennia, hadn't carried that much juice.

"He could be," Belial said after a silence that was

entirely too long for him to be speaking the truth when it ended. "He could also be fucking with your head. He's rather good at that."

"You gave me a rock and a pat on the back, and that's not going to do it anymore," Jack said. He fished the key out of his pocket and held it up. "We need to see the Princes."

Belial shook his head, but Jack chopped the air with his hand. "No excuses. No fucking gatekeepers. Take me there or I'm using this and showing up in their parlor myself. Going to start shouting and putting my feet all over the furniture."

"I hate you sometimes, you know that?" Belial growled, grabbing Jack's arm.

"I hate you all the time," Jack said as the walls of the world fell away. "So we're even."

CHAPTER 21

There were no frills this time, no buttering him up before they bent him over. Belial stormed ahead of Jack into the meeting room, the Princes sitting at the round bone table with their heads bent.

Baal looked up, eyes narrowing. "What's the meaning of this?"

Belial shot Jack a black look. "This was your idea, princess. Speak up."

Jack wondered what his life was coming to when speaking to Baal and Beelzebub didn't rank as the most likely to make him piss himself in the course of a day.

He told them about Legion, about his visions. He laid everything out, feeling the eyes of two of the oldest demons in Hell boring into him as he did. It was the same feeling as when he'd go with his mum and watch her beg for yet another extension on their rent from the council when he was a boy. The feeling of knowing that the whole performance was getting booed before you even began.

"Tell me, crow-mage." Beelzebub folded his delicate, multi-jointed fingers. "What makes you think you're such an expert on this Legion problem?"

"I dunno," Jack said. "Maybe because you set me

up as your hard man and used me to track him down, and now my arse is on the line while you're sitting tucked up here in your magical pitchfork palace?"

Belial coughed, letting him know he'd gone too far, but Jack rolled on. He was beyond caring what the Princes might do to him. They'd ceased to be the boogeyman under his bed long ago.

"Look," Jack said. "According to him, he's lined up at least one of the rulers of Faerie on his side. He's got enough mages to turn all of London into tinder. He's got zombies, lycanthropes, tinker, tailor, soldier, spy. What more do you need to realize that this entire thing is fucked and you need to take drastic action?"

Baal flared his nostrils. "If what you say is true, that drastic action could provoke a war with Faerie. Or with the human necromancers. Hell's numbers are diminished, as Legion counts so many among his followers. Would you see Hell fall, crow-mage? Is your game revenge for what was done to you at Belial's hand?"

The demon cleared his throat at Jack's shoulder. "Baal, I assure you . . ."

"Shut up, Belial," Baal snapped. "The offensive was your plan, and it hasn't worked. Now it's down to us. The fact is, Legion commands the artificer, and so we are at a disadvantage. If you were not so young you would see that."

"Nice name for something that can flip the cosmos like a pancake," Jack said. "Why on earth would you even leave something like that lying around?"

"Azrael was the only one who knew of it," Baal

sighed. "He had many secrets. This one, he shared with the wrong demon."

"Yeah, about that," Jack said. "Who *is* Legion? I mean, I heard the stories. But who is he, really? How can a regular bloke grab the one thing in all of Hell guaranteed to twist the Triumvirate's panties and run off with it?"

"Because they all trusted Azrael to keep them safe from the bad men," Belial said, acid eating at each word. "But when Daddy turned out to be a twat who'd fiddle while Abbadon and his pals turned us into sausage meat, they were left scrambling, and now they're a bit red in the face."

Beelzebub shot to his feet, chair knocking backward. "You never did know when to just *shut up,* did you?"

"Oi!" Jack stuck his fingers in his mouth and whistled. The sound cut through the small space, taking the wind out of Beelzebub's sails. "Look, you don't want to tell me who Legion really is, fine. Guarantee I'll find out before this is all over. The point is, he's got this artificer, he's using it to reenact the plot of every shit episode of *Doctor Who* there is, and we need to do something about it." He folded his arms and bestowed the Princes with the same look he gave Margaret when she was being a brat. "So what's that going to be? Because the dragging him to Hell bit is off the table, I'll tell you right now. No way am I getting within spitting distance of that bastard again."

Legion's face, his real one, crept into Jack's mind, and he shivered. There was something alien about it—as if Legion were not just a creature of Hell but a black hole, consuming all it touched.

"That won't be necessary," Baal said. "We are going to take over the operation from here, crow-mage, and rest assured, Legion will no longer be your problem."

Jack had expected some threats, maybe a kick to the ribs or a slam in the skull, or perhaps just the invitation from the Princes to jump up his own arse, but this wasn't right. Demons never gave up, never smoothed things over and told you everything was going to be all right. Demons lived to get the upper hand, and to watch you squirm while they did it.

And he'd failed, rather spectacularly. That should at least merit a few pokes verbally or with a hot poker.

"Oh, fuck me," Jack said as the truth slammed into him like a lorry. "You're going to make a deal with him, aren't you?"

Belial gave a grunt from beside him, but the two other Princes remained unmoved. Beelzebub spread his hands. "Bargains are what built Hell, and they are what will continue to keep it running. Legion will be given certain . . . concessions in return for giving back the artificer."

"And by concessions, you mean Earth as his merry stomping ground," Jack said. The rage was boiling again, hot and fast up his throat. "You bastards," he whispered. "He doesn't want a consolation prize. He doesn't want anything except to watch you burn. Let me give you a tip: When he kills you, and you're rotting in the Land of the Dead, and you feel a drip on your head, that'll be Legion, pissing on your graves."

Belial shoved him aside, gripping the edge of the table with his black-nailed hands. "You two geriatric morons can't be serious."

"Way to go," Jack said. "That'll win 'em to your side."

"You got a seat at this table by subterfuge and backstabbing," Baal told Belial. "Don't act so shocked that you lost it the same way."

"I've *seen* what this bastard can do," Belial growled. "Much as it pains me to agree with anything that comes out of Jack Winter's mouth, the little bastard is right. Legion won't bargain with you. He'll use you to tear down Hell, and then it'll be so long and thanks for all the Hellspawn for the both of you. Are you mad?"

The Princes stood in unison, monsters in slick black undertaker suits, and Jack instinctively backed off a step. If Belial was about to lose his head, he didn't want the spatter on him.

"Your services as the third in this Triumvirate are no longer required," Beelzebub said. "I suggest you get the fuck out of Hell before our good mood turns sour."

"I hope the two of you end up just like Azrael," Belial snarled. "You deserve it, both of you."

Jack put his hand on Belial's shoulder, scarcely believing he was touching a demon voluntarily. "Come on, mate," he said. "Before they call security to cart your stuff out in a box."

Belial came with him as far as the door before he wheeled around. "Legion may have stolen the artificer and started this war, but the two of you brought down the walls of Hell. Soon, there will be nothing left, and you'll be kings of the wasteland. So fucking enjoy it, the both of you. I always thought you were twats."

He threw the doors wide, knocking one of the Fenris on guard off balance with the violence of the swing.

"Good luck with that whole deal-with-the-devil thing," Jack told the Princes. "Hope it bites you right on the arse."

He turned without waiting for the Princes' reaction, and ran after Belial before anyone in Hell could decide they wanted to keep him there.

CHAPTER 22

They emerged back into the daylight in Kensington, not far from the City Line stop, and Belial sat down on the curb and pulled out a black cigarette, sucking on the foul smoke until he'd completely enveloped his head in the cloud.

Jack waited and watched, not wanting to be the one who set the demon off.

"You know, I put in my time," Belial snarled. "I was small change for a thousand years, collecting souls and doing deals and keeping my legions in order. I kissed the boot of plenty of Named jockeying for position with the Princes. Watched them eat each other. Then one day I pop up because some idiot mage has cast a summoning and wants to trade his soul for thirteen more years of life, and after a millennium of careful watching and waiting for my time, you fuck everything up in thirteen short years."

Belial exhaled. "Life was so simple before I met you, Jack. You're poison to anyone who plans to have things go their way."

"Sorry I fucked up your winning streak of torture and mayhem there, mate," Jack said. "Now how are we going to kill Legion?"

Belial glared at him, a look so withering Jack felt

sure that his head should be catching on fire. "*I* can't do anything, you twat. *I* have no more connection to Hell. All of my talents, all of my power, it's cut off. My credit's no good anymore. I can't even shift out of this wretched two-legged body."

The petty, cruel part of Jack, the part of him that kept him from staying entirely in the white light of untainted magic, the kind that whispered that if he'd just let go he could sweep away so many of his problems, whispered that there was never going to be a better time than this one to hand Belial some payback.

Jack shut it up. That side of him was the one that went looking for power, and trouble, the one that got him wrapped up with demons in the first place. That side of him was a fucking coward that could only be counted on to look out for itself.

"Do you want to cry, or do you want to figure out how to get back in the driver's seat?" he asked.

Belial viciously ground out his foul cigarette and stood up. "I want you to leave me alone, Jack. I'm not your friend. Just because I can't turn you to vapor any longer doesn't mean I need your help. You're done enough."

"Hey!" Jack scrambled up as well. "You were the one who pulled me into this. You can't just crawl off to lick your wounds and leave the entire world to be Legion's buffet."

"I wish it were different," Belial said. "But I'm in no shape to do anything. Don't you have any other friends, Jack? Anyone who hates you, even, who hates demons more? Because I am no longer your sensei. I do not have all the answers, or even any of the fucking answers, so I wish you good luck, but I'm well and truly out of it."

Jack started to yell at him, but Belial walked through a patch of shadow and was gone. "Of course," Jack shouted at the spot. "You lose every trick except that one, don't you, you fucking knob?"

People had started staring, so Jack reined himself in and found a phone to call Pete. He was seething over what Belial had said. As if the demon had ever been anything but a pain in his arse at best, and a shadow over his entire life the rest of the time. They weren't friends. They were different species, and for Belial to prove it, cutting and running to survive like demons always did, made Jack so angry he could barely think straight.

He had to, though, because if Belial was checked out, then it was up to him and Pete to do something about Legion.

Pete picked him up in the Mini before too long, and she had the grace not to ask what had happened since he'd gone out to see Mosswood.

"I fucked up," Jack finally said.

Pete gave him a wan smile. "I figured when there was no victory dance maybe things didn't go as planned."

"About as far opposite as you can get," Jack said.

Pete tapped her fingers on the wheel as they waited at a stoplight. "So what next?"

Jack shrugged, and she reached over and gave him a light shove. "Come on. This didn't work—what's your next idea? Legion is still roaming around out there, and you and I are going to shut him down, so even if it's unpleasant, tell me what you're going to do next, and 'I dunno' is going to get you such a smack, I'm warning you now."

Jack grimaced. "You always did know how to motivate a bloke."

"One of my many talents," Pete said. "Now start thinking like you've got a brain instead of just a pickled mess between your ears."

Jack watched the parade of posh row houses, pocket parks, and high-end shops that made up Kensington roll past, and then frowned as Pete turned her car toward the river, crossing at Vauxhall Road and finally pulling into Battersea Park.

"What's this?" Jack said. The morning crowd of joggers, walkers, and bird feeders had turned out, and Pete got out of the car and motioned to him to follow.

"I used to come here a lot," she said. "When I had a case I couldn't unstick, or I'd had a bad day, was missing my dad. Things like that."

Jack stayed quiet. Pete didn't talk much about her father, a formidable police detective who'd never met a villain he couldn't pin with his hard green stare. Connor Caldecott had found a mass in his left lung and was gone inside a year.

Pete led Jack away from the noise, down one of the bridle paths that wound a leisurely route back toward the Thames. "I came here when I was trying to decide if I was going to help you or run the other way, actually. Right after we met up again."

Jack shouldn't have been surprised, but he didn't feel angry at the revelation Pete had considered leaving him and his problems in the lurch. She was smart, and you'd have to have been a simpering fool to think he was a good bet when Pete had found him again.

He found a patch of ground that didn't look overly damp and sat down, looking across the river at the Chelsea embankment. On days like this, with just a few clouds, the sun glittering off the towers of the City, it was hard to imagine that he'd ever glimpsed a future like the one his sight had shown him.

"I'm glad you stuck around," he told Pete, who sat next to him, legs stretched in front of her.

"Me, too, most days," she said, leaning her head on his shoulder. "Now, my question still stands. What are we going to do about all this?"

Jack stroked her hair absently, the dark strands rippling through his fingers. "I burned most of my contacts in the Black during that mess with Nergal. Your copper friends will get shredded if they try to shut down Legion's little foster home for sorcerers through daylight channels, and he's got the Fae on his side, as well as a fuck-ton of elemental demons just waiting to boil up out of Hell like someone chucking up a bad curry."

He looked back at the river as a cloud passed over the City, shadowing everything on the north side for a moment. Beside him, Pete stiffened. "What the fuck is that?"

Jack looked up and saw that the cloud was not a cloud but the gang of crows and ravens he'd seen when Legion had walloped his sight. They were real, though, no doubt about it. Tourists standing on the terrace overlooking the Thames cried out, and groups of people ran for the pagoda to get under cover.

Pete yanked at his arm. "Up," she snapped, and Jack stood, but he shook her off when she tried to drag him to cover. There were so many birds, more than he would have thought existed in the whole of the British Isles.

The darkness, Mosswood whispered in his memory. *The darkness that's coming to cover everything.*

"Jack!" Pete screamed in his ear, close enough to rattle his skull, but she was too late. Jack could feel his sight gripping him, all the meters of his senses screaming into the red. Something was here, something that wasn't demon or Fae, the figure that walked in the wake of the darkness to collect the dead it left behind.

You've been avoiding me, Jack.

The Morrigan glided across the grass, leaving a trail of blackened, dead earth in her wake that oozed blood as she came toward him.

There was a time when his brain gave up and recognized that the fight or flight instinct was useless—that no matter what he did, the predator had her jaws around him. Jack felt himself go limp as everything real faded, and he had a sense that he'd probably fallen, back in his body, and would wake up with a lump on his head the size of the Twickenham pitch.

"Like the plague, luv," he said. There might be no escape for him, but that didn't mean he had to go the crying, begging route.

I'm not here for pleasantries, the Morrigan said. He didn't know how she talked, as she had a mouth full of bloody fangs, hair made of feathers, and the eyes of a bird. Feathers sprouted from her body, and she was wrapped in the shredded ends of a shroud, soaked in the blood, so the tales said, of the first man to raise his sword against another.

"Just dropping in to ask after the kids, then? They're fine, thanks. Can't chat, love to your mum, see you later," Jack said.

The Morrigan closed the space between them. Her breath was cold and oily on his face, and it smelled of turned earth with a tinge of rotting meat. The scent of battlefields and mass graves, the cold of a tomb closed up so long only the dead remembered it.

Your games are diverting, but not today. Today, we speak of grave matters.

"I know the world's a tip," Jack said, "and that things are sideways. I've gotten this speech about five times now. Legion is the hammer, we're the nail, and all of us are scrambling to convince him he doesn't really want to shatter the world into a million pieces."

I care nothing for the creature of mud who would break the world, the Morrigan snarled. *I care only to maintain the balance as it must be.*

"Funny, coming from a hag who was ready to wipe humans off the map to raise her zombie army when she had the chance," Jack said. "You're not on the side of the angels here. Don't think I'll forget that."

I have my motives, the Morrigan said. *In the end, death will be the only resident of this lonely planet. But I was foolish, and I contributed to a fissure that will become a fracture, and if it cracks there will be no world to inhabit.*

This was the first time, in all the decades he'd been seeing her, that Jack had heard the Morrigan utter anything except threats. She'd appeared to him, to Pete, and every time it was the same litany. *I'll own your soul, Jackie-boy, so know that every breath you have in you is just a temporary reprieve.*

But now, she'd said it. She'd admitted a mistake. After everything he'd seen since Belial had popped up, this was the first time Jack had felt genuine fear take up residence in his belly. The Morrigan was ancient, one of the old gods worshipped by the old races, things millennia older than humans. Only the proto-demons like Nergal and Abbadon were her contemporaries, and even that was debatable.

"What are you saying?" Jack said. "That you're actually requesting my help for once, instead of flapping in here to throw your weight around? What makes you think I'd listen to you for one second longer than I listen to something like Belial?"

Because you consort with demons, the Morrigan hissed. *But they cannot stem the tide. Only death can combat death, Jack. I am not asking. I am telling. If you wish to stop the march of Legion's soldiers across the face of the universe, you will do what you were born to do and stand at my side.*

"There it is," Jack muttered. "Carrot and fucking stick."

I cannot force you, the Morrigan said. *If I could, I would have claimed you as my avatar long ago, Jack Winter. But now, the enemy of my enemy is my friend. The demons are sad, sulfur-born bastards. The Fae are too wrapped in tradition to see what their actions have wrought. Only I, and my legions of the dead, stand ready.*

"And to get them free of the Bleak Gates, you need me," Jack said. "Once Legion is down, what then? Full-tilt zombieland all across the earth, I suppose?"

Every victory has a price, the Morrigan purred. *Every war has casualties. At least, when you join with me, there will be a world to mourn. If you thrash and scream as you are now, things will vanish as so much cosmic dust borne away on a hurricane.*

"I won't thrash *or* scream," Jack said, trying not to flinch at the proximity of something so ancient and rife with magic. It was like kissing up to a cockroach, making your skin crawl no matter how good your self-control was. "So that you're very, very clear on my answer: There is no way in hell or any other world that I will ever trust you, or allow you to use me to unlock your own particular brand of apocalypse. You can keep trying, but I'll be dead before I help you."

So be it, the Morrigan said. *Dead, I can live with. You are mine, Jack. You belong to me, you wear my marks. By the end of this affair, you'll beg me to accept you into my embrace.*

"I'll be holding my breath," Jack snarled, shoving away from her. "Or rather, I won't, because you'll still be stuck in the Land of the Dead and I'll be here, where you can't touch me."

The Morrigan ran her talons along his tattoos,

which flared and responded with blinding pain. *Don't be so sure.*

He came back to himself in a flood of cold and wet, as Pete poured a bottle of water over his head.

"Fuck me!" he shouted, swiping the droplets out of his nose and eyes. "Did you have to go and do that?"

"You were twitching and moaning," Pete said. "It was that or someone calling 999 about the nutter rolling around on the grass frightening the children."

She pulled him to his feet. A wave of nausea passed over him, and Jack fought it down. Somebody among the law-abiding citizens of London had already called the police, and he didn't need to waste time while Pete talked her way out of trouble using her copper connections.

"You going to tell me what that was all about?" she asked when they were sitting in the Mini again.

"The usual," Jack said. "The Hag wants me to fall in line."

"Jesus," Pete said. "You'd think at a time like this even she'd change the fucking record for a few minutes."

Jack shifted in the tiny seat. He always felt wrung out after his sight had been plaguing him, and this was no exception. He'd lost track of how many hours he'd been awake, how many times he'd been shifted between the barriers of worlds. It wore on you, tore you down bit by bit, crawled inside your head until you had a hard time telling what was real and what was just a shadow.

"She did make me think of something, though," he said. "Speaking of folks I'd rather never see again."

Pete nodded. "I'm listening."

"There is one mage sect I know Legion would never get his hooks into," Jack said. "Bastards bigger than even him."

Pete swallowed hard, putting a hand on his leg. "I know what you're talking about, and you don't have to do it."

"That's the thing," Jack said. "It's them or the Morrigan, so I do have to do it. In fact, the only choice I have is to go to them, or sit back right in this park with a picnic basket while we watch London burn."

CHAPTER 23

As much as he hated flying, Jack passed the flight to Dublin unconscious, snapping awake when the plane touched down. It was only a little over two hours from Heathrow, but he felt like a new man when he and Pete cleared customs. Lily was in the care of his mate Lawrence, Margaret had gone to stay with Morwenna, and they were both safe for now. He could focus on the task at hand.

"Haven't been here in so long," Pete said. "Not since I was thirteen or fourteen. Last summer we spent with my grandmother before she died."

"You in the country," Jack said. "That must have been something."

"*I* handled it fine," Pete said. "My sister spent the entire summer sneaking off down to the pub and sobbing to her boyfriend at the pay phone at the end of the road leading up to our gran's farm. She never could deal with solitude."

Pete's sister was a terror in heavy eyeliner, the sort of girl who floated around the fringes of real magic without knowing exactly what she was toying with. Pete had never been that way. She'd been painfully, acutely aware that there was another world out there from the moment he met her.

"I haven't been back since I was twenty or so," he offered. After the emergency workers had scraped him off the floor of a flea-ridden hotel room, he'd been sectioned for a few months. Time in the mental ward, with no way to pass it except chatting with the ghosts he saw with more clarity than the living, had made him realize what utter shit all the training he'd received from his old mage order had been. Nothing could control his sight. Nothing could change the fact that he was marked by an old god, the kind of creature that could reach him no matter how far he ran.

He'd gone back to England, and he'd met Pete. Then he'd died, briefly, crawled inside a smack syringe, and never looked back.

Dublin didn't hold a lot of fond memories, that was for sure. And he wanted to be here even less than he had the first time, as a scared fourteen-year-old kid with nowhere else to go.

Pete stayed quiet most of the way into the city from the airport, but she spoke up when they got off the train. "What do you need me to do?"

"Stay close," Jack said. "Seth and I didn't exactly part on good terms, and he didn't leave the brothers on ones that were any better."

"Brothers," Pete snorted. "Never had any use for those stodgy boys' clubs. Just an excuse to sit around, smoking and whingeing even though your lives are bought and paid for."

Jack laughed. The idea of the crow brothers as some sort of gentleman's establishment was funny enough; the idea of Seth McBride, the mage who'd trained him to use his sight, as a member of one even more so.

"Seth and them are more the pie and a pint, kick you in the teeth if you cross them, loose collection of vagrants types."

Pete wrinkled her nose. "They sound lovely."

"Oh, they'll hex you into next week first chance they get if they think there's a few euros and a decent bottle of whiskey in it for 'em," Jack said. "The crow brothers don't exactly follow the white hat system. They're suspicious and dangerous, and they're not big on loyalty."

"Then why should we trust them at all?" Pete said.

"Because the crow brothers, above all else, teach their number to be survivors," Jack said. "And they're all so petty and backstabbing that they know the nasty tricks no other human mages do. If we want to find a way to knock down Legion without a demon's help, then they're our best bet." He lit a cigarette, careful to keep the smoke away from Pete. "Now I just have to reintroduce myself without getting knocked on my arse."

There was a pub tucked away in the warren of streets around Trinity College where Seth had taken him when they'd first come to Ireland. Jack had considered running back then. No adult ever took an interest in him unless they wanted something. And he was out of England, away from the grasp of his mother and anyone else who might have a use for a teenage boy with a talent for magic and nobody to look out for him. He could disappear, go back to roughing it and stealing to get by.

"You'll be sleeping upstairs." Seth favored black jackets and skinny ties, and he had the nervous tic of a former smoker, tapping his fingers on whatever flat surface was handy.

Jack narrowed his eyes. "With you?"

Seth sighed. "We've been over this. I'm not into rough trade, and even if I was, you're not my type. I'm trying to help you, the way nobody helped me when I was like you. So, you'll be sleeping upstairs, *on your own,* and during the day you'll help Wallace run the pub."

Wallace had been about a thousand years old, a grizzled veteran who hated the fact that Jack was English almost as much as he hated his hair and his music and everything else about him. It was 1985, the Troubles were still a long shadow over everyone's day, and Jack had adopted an Irish accent as quickly as he could.

Seth hadn't reappeared for weeks, and when he did, he sat down at a table near the back and started doing sleight of hand tricks. "Quickness of the hand is quickness of the mind, boyo," he said. "Have a seat."

That was how it went, for two long years of pushing a mop and listening to Wallace scream at footie matches on the pub's single, miniature black and white television. Jack worked and tried to keep the psychic episodes to a minimum, and Seth would show up with weeks or months between visits, show him card tricks and simple hexes, talk to him about things like necromancy and scrying and what to do if you ran afoul of either, always at the same table in the corner.

It was still there, still covered in the same sticky varnish, the same wrinkled Guinness coasters. The telly was new, flatscreen and gleaming above the bar, but everything else could have been exactly as Jack had left it when he walked out the door twenty years ago.

Pete sniffed. Jack felt the scent of bleach and stale alcohol tickle his nostrils. "It grows on you," he said, easing the door shut behind him.

"We're closed!"

Jack started at the voice, more a rumble of lorry tires over rocks than a sound made by a human throat. "Wallace?" he said.

The old man grumped from behind the bar, clutching a cane in one hand and a cricket bat in the other. "Who the fuck wants to know?"

Jack blinked. Wallace had been old when Jack had come to Dublin—now, he looked rather like a walking, talking, slagged-off mummy, a few strands of white hair clinging to his spotted scalp. Still, the hand holding the bat never wavered.

"It's Jack Winter," he said. "Put that down before you break a hip, old man."

Wallace sneered. "Jack fucking Winter. Now I want to hit you more than ever."

"Oh look, a man after my own heart," Pete said. Wallace glared at her. One eye was cloudy with cataracts, but the effect was still rather like being stared down by a bridge troll.

"And you might be, Miss Posh? Come down from Blighty to gaze at the peasants, have we?"

"I've done plenty of gazing," Pete said. "My father

came over from Galway when he was a boy. Spent every summer as a girl with my grandmother Megan, listening to her tell stories of the old Irish heroes and the indepedence war in 1915. Still, it's stupendous to meet somebody who was actually there to witness it firsthand."

Jack flinched. If Wallace had ever had a sense of humor, he'd lost it when he'd started doing favors for the *Fiach Dubh*.

Wallace's face flushed, but he started croaking and lowered the bat. "I like her, Jack," he said. "Much more than I ever liked you." He sank into the nearest chair, the cane creaking under the weight it supported. "Why the fuck did you come back here?"

"Desperate times and all that," Jack said. "I need to talk to the brothers, Wallace. The ones still in good standing, that is, still with access to the archives."

Wallace jerked his head at the other chairs around his table. "Sit yourselves down, then. Can't very well have you standing there with your thumb in your arse, can I?"

Jack had hated Wallace—the old sod had never liked him, never even tolerated him for most of the time he'd slept in the attic, on a military cot sandwiched between cases of whiskey and the spare odds and ends of Wallace's life before the pub. Wallace had made no secret that he thought Jack was a piss stain, and Jack supposed he'd done a poor job hiding what he, arrogant English bastard that he was, thought of a worn-out old Irishman who still teared up at the strains of "Danny Boy."

He guessed that people really could change. He,

at least, wasn't nearly as arrogant as he'd been. Death had a way of taking the wind out of your sails.

"You look like hammered shit," Wallace said.

Then again, maybe they didn't ever change as much as you hoped they would. "You want to flap your gums, or you want to call the brothers and get me out of your hair?" he said.

"Already called," Wallace said. "Minute you tripped the protection hexes around my establishment. Sloppy of you, Jack."

Pete gave Jack a black look. He rubbed his face with his hands, feeling the tiredness creep back behind his eyes. Wallace was right, that was sloppy. There was a time he would have at least noticed that the same musty old hexes from twenty years ago were still in place.

This was what he wanted—to see the crow brothers. Why, then, was his stomach flipping as if he'd just swallowed a fifth of tequila and chased it with a questionable curry?

Pete's head snaked around as a shadow passed between the pub's window and the streetlamp outside. "Somebody's watching us," she said.

"More than somebody," Jack said. The Black pulsed, just a bit, as if someone had thrown a stone into a pond.

"They're outside," Wallace said, standing again. "Don't make a mess in my establishment, you hear? I'll be upstairs."

"Are we okay?" Pete asked as Wallace stumped away. Jack turned to watch the pub door swing open.

"Doubt it," he said.

Three mages, two men and one woman. None of them looked happy to see him, but on the bright side there was no one he recognized, either. The chance of any of the crow brothers he'd slagged off directly being in the pack was low, but he had exactly that sort of shit luck.

"Well, well," Pete murmured. "I see they're not just brothers any longer."

"Yeah, that is new." Jack stood, extending his hand to the female mage. "Hello, sweetheart. Jack Winter. I don't believe we've met."

"Keep that paw to yourself, 'fore I snap it off," the woman growled. Jack dropped his hand back to his side.

Pete gave a small giggle as she stood up and came to rest just behind Jack's shoulder. "The more I meet of your old friends, Jack, the more I like them."

"We are not friends with this bastard," the bigger of the two men growled. He was rangy, with narrow eyes and a crooked nose, the epitome of Black Irish good looks that Jack was sure had the ladies all aflutter. It was the other mage that grabbed his attention, though—small and stocky, quiet, glaring at Jack like a dog aching to be let off the chain. If this went into the shit, that was the one he'd need to take down first. One good leg-locker hex to make sure he couldn't pound Jack's skull into powder should do the trick.

"Nor do I have any desire to lock hands with you in the bonds of brotherhood," Jack said. "Just need to ask you lot a favor." He looked the tall mage up and down. The man's leather jacket bulged at the ribs, as did the right ankle of his ill-fitting trousers. Mages going about like it was the Wild West was new—the *Fiach Dubh* Jack had known would have laughed themselves sick at the idea of toting around a gun.

"You're not in any position to ask for anything," the woman said. "You turned your back on the brotherhood a long time ago, Jack Winter. Now fuck off back to England before we decide to get unfriendly."

Witchfire, green and hazy, crackled around the woman's fists. Jack held up his own hands. It was three against two, but he'd at least get the big bastard before he went down. "I don't give a shit about what happened twenty years ago, and neither should you. I doubt you were even out of diapers when I had my falling out with your colleagues," he said. The woman's nostrils flared.

"But," Jack continued, "you lot taught me to be a survivor, and I wouldn't come back here unless this was truly life and death. Not just for me, for all of us."

"Not interested," said the tall mage. "And since you can't seem to follow directions, I'm going to have Moira here show you out."

"You move one hair on your head and you're going to be one very sorry girl," Pete said from behind him. Jack glanced around to see a small black box in her hands, her fingers curled around the stubby butt and yellow trigger.

Moira bared her teeth. "What do you think you're going to do with that? I command magic, girl."

"And this is a stun gun," Pete said. "Metropolitan Police riot gear, standard issue, brought through the hell of airport security just because I know not to trust you. As to what I'm going to do with it, if you try to hex either me or Jack, I'm going to shoot you with it, watch as you twitch around, pee yourself, and pass out, and then I may well take a few photos for posterity, just because I don't particularly like you."

She raised the stun gun to bear between Moira's eyes. "Let's all be civil adults," Pete said. "Or at least pretend we're capable of such behavior."

Moira dropped her hand after a moment and kicked the nearest chair over. "Why'd you have to come back here?" she snapped. "Bad enough the way things have been going without Jack Winter in the mix."

"Let me guess." Jack took a seat. If he wasn't in immediate danger of being hexed, he was going to save his energy. "Upsets, critters popping up where they shouldn't, necromancers wreaking havoc on decent folks just trying to sell a few ancient demonic grimoires and make a semihonest living?"

Seth had kept a rare book shop as a nominal profession when Jack had known him. Seth had also run off after Jack's suicide attempt, chucked in his contacts and reputation in Dublin, and gone to wait out his lifespan and destroy his liver in the slums of Bangkok. Jack didn't blame him. At the time, it had sounded like an excellent idea. He tried to quash the idea that always popped up when he thought of Seth that he'd ruined his only friend's life right along with his own by trying to top himself. Seth had vouched for him to the bigwig brothers, and Jack had flamed out in spectacular fashion. Seth wasn't any more welcome here, now.

"Same as everywhere else," said the stocky mage. "Same as it ever was." His voice was as rough as the rest of him, more Belfast than a local boy, and he had the short haircut, steel-toed boots, and aggressive set to his shoulders of ex-military. SAS, Jack guessed, the type of bloke who was used to being ready to kill the man across the table from him.

"You know," Jack said. "Knew another crow brother who loved the Talking Heads, insufferable bloke by the name of Jimmy Donelly, had one of those half-and-half haircuts. Looked like a Shetland pony."

The stocky mage glared. "Jimmy Donelly was my father."

"Ah," Jack said. "Lovely that you two have so much in common."

"What do you want?" the tall mage asked. "You wouldn't be here unless you wanted something, so get to it."

"I have a problem for you, but a solution, too," Jack said. "The things you've been seeing, the storm that's shaking things up all over the Black, that's the work of a demon named Legion. He's a villain, hard to kill, has the Fae on his side, and I figure if anyone in the wide world knows how to even the pitch with this bloke, it's you lot. I just need a peek at the goodies, and then I'll leave you well enough alone."

"Can't do it," said the tall mage. Jack favored him with a narrow glare.

"And who died and left you in charge?"

"My brother," the tall mage said evenly. "His name was Roger McAmmon. I'm Keith. He was the one who'd been in the longest. Most of the old guard is retired or dead, except for Wallace. It's been a rough couple of decades on this side of the pond. Turf wars with the necromancers, a lycanthropy outbreak, a smartarse trying to raise an army of golems from bits and bobs in the local graveyards . . ."

Jack held up his hand. "I get it. So you're telling me no."

"I'm telling you we've got our own problems, Jack, and we don't need your particular brand of trouble muddying things up."

"Listen," Pete said. "I know that you and Jack aren't on good terms. I've heard that song from every dirty secret in his past that I've run across. But this isn't about him. For once, he's trying to do right, stop something that's worse than any of your local concerns, and I'd consider it a real favor if you'd just let him do what he needs to do."

"We know who you are, too, you know," said the stocky mage. "Petunia Caldecott, the Weir."

"Now you've done it," Jack said. "No one calls her Petunia and lives to tell the tale."

"I'm glad you know who I am, because it means you know what I can do," Pete said. "I'd consider it a personal kindness if you'd just help Jack out."

Jack waited, watching the three mages. They were

young, but they were battle-hard and suspicious, and territorial as hell. If their positions were flipped, he wouldn't be keen on some dinosaur with a penchant for demon trouble stomping all over his city, either.

Keith McAmmon sighed. "I can't let you look at the archives."

"Why—" Jack started, but Keith cut him off.

"The archives were destroyed. About eight years ago, there was a dustup with a sect of necromancers trying to raise hungry ghosts on our turf, and they burned our archive as retaliation."

"I thought a brother's—sister's—whatever's books were his own," Jack said. "Whose bright idea was it to centralize the lot?"

"My brother's." Keith coughed, and Jack was gratified to see Jimmy the younger and Moira shift their glares to him.

"Then no offense to your dead brother, but he was a great bloody idiot," Jack said.

"All that's left is Declan," said Moira.

Pete lifted an eyebrow. "And Declan is?"

"A psychic, like you," Keith said. "He's just, um, a bit more involved in his talent than you seem to be."

"Translation: He's off his rocker," Jack said to Pete. This had been a thin idea to start with, really just a hope that maybe something from the time he'd spent with Seth, the few short years when things had started to look up for him, would be the key to kicking Legion in the arse.

"Sounds like fun," Pete said. "I always did enjoy talking to a crazy mage."

Moira shrugged. "We can take you over to his flat, but you're not going to get a word of sense out of him. He's been deep under for at least a decade."

"Trust me," Jack said, pushing back from the table. "Crazed ramblings and I are old friends. It'll be like coming home."

CHAPTER 24

Declan lived in a bedsit over a closed-down chip shop, and the odor of stale cooking oil and fish permeated the plaster and the narrow staircase. A naked bulb swayed as Jack and Pete mounted the stairs. "We'll wait here," Keith said. "Declan doesn't like too many people in at once, and he gets on best with Moira. Any sign of trouble, though, and you're done. I'll see your carcass on a boat back to England myself."

"Yeah, yeah, shaking in me boots, rest assured," Jack said, following Moira up the stairs. Pete brought up the rear.

"I don't like this," she murmured. "It's a bottleneck if anything goes wrong."

"Things have already gone wrong," Jack said in an undertone. "But this is going to turn out all right, I promise. Just let me talk to this Declan and we'll see if he can help us."

"I wouldn't expect too much," Moira said. "He doesn't make any sense on a good day, and on a bad day, good luck getting a word in edgewise."

She knocked on the single door at the top of the stairs, soft and unthreatening. "Declan? It's Moira. I've brought visitors, if that's all right."

They waited for a long minute, Jack listening to the buzzing of the light, and then the door rattled with the sound of half a dozen bolts being undone. "Moira?" The voice was small and hesitant, sounding more like a scared kid than a full-grown psychic.

"Yes, luv," she said. "Do you think you might let us in?"

Declan peered around the doorframe. He had owlish eyes behind black-rimmed glasses and a shock of dark hair that looked as if he spent most of his time sleeping on the left side of it. His face was soft, rounded, and covered in dark stubble. He blinked shyly when he saw Pete and Jack.

"Why Moira," he said. "You've brought the storm with you."

"These nice folks just have some questions," Moira said. She reached in through the crack and laid a hand on Declan's arm. Jack expected the psychic to kick up a fuss, but instead he smiled at her and pulled the door open.

"Then you bring the wind and rain inside, yes?" His voice had the singsong quality that Jack had encountered in quite a few folks he'd met in the mental ward, the kind of dreamy voice that was focused on things only the owner could see.

"Thank you," Pete said, as Declan stepped back to allow them in. "This means a lot to us, truly."

Declan frowned at her. "You are a hole, full of light. You are the sun exploding. I can't look at you. You burn me."

Pete gave Jack a raised eyebrow, but she shrugged. "I suppose that's fair."

"What about me, Declan?" Jack said. He tried to keep his tone soothing and even, though that had rarely worked on the psychics and schizophrenics he knew. You just had to play in their world, go along with what they saw, until you learned what you needed and could drop back into reality.

Often enough, he'd been the one off in dreamland, and so he didn't begrudge going along with Declan.

"You?" Declan examined Jack, through his glasses and then closer, lifting the lenses and bringing their noses almost to touching. "Your wings are lifted by the storm. You are in the dark but you are not the darkness."

"No?" Jack tilted his head. Declan blinked, then shook his head to and fro hard enough to give himself whiplash.

"No. Not yet."

"Declan," Jack said, as gently as he could manage. "What else do you see around me?"

Declan cocked his head, as if he were listening to a dog whistle, and then he reached out quicker than a cobra and grabbed Jack's chin between his pudgy fingers.

Jack stayed still. Dealing with psychics was tricky, especially one in the throes of a severe break from reality. As if there were any other kind, when you could see things that would drive the average plod on the street screaming into the nearest nuthouse.

Declan breathed, eyes screwed up behind his streaky glasses, and Jack glanced around the man's one-room flat, seeing what his options were if this little trust exercise didn't go his way.

One corner was taken up by a bed, just a mattress and box spring up on cement blocks, covered in a rumpled sleeping bag and more crisp wrappers than Jack had previously believed one man could generate.

The wall opposite the bed was entirely taken up with televisions—small, large, old, new, all square old-fashioned sets that buzzed quietly, tuned to a dozen different channels. They heated the room to a temperature that made sweat roll down Jack's spine, and he saw Pete wipe at her forehead.

The ceiling of the flat was plastered with newspapers, which also covered the windows in layers thick enough that even the streetlight outside didn't penetrate. The four corners of the room were strung with dusty herb bundles, red thread, all the trappings of every sort of protection hex Jack could think of.

"You scared of something, Declan?" he asked, keeping his voice even and low. "Worried about something getting in here?"

"Oh," Declan breathed, turning Jack's head to and fro in his vise grip. "He's already inside. He's in my head. He's in your head, too."

Jack frowned, and Declan mirrored his expression. "Don't be sad, Jack," he said. "Soon he'll be everywhere, and then you and I won't feel so lonely, seeing his shadow falling across our footsteps."

"Yeah," Jack said, easing out of Declan's grip. "That can't happen. Do you see anything else? A way that Legion doesn't end up with the world in his hands?"

Declan sat down in a rickety rolling chair arranged in front of the TV screens and spun around. "Nope," he singsonged. "Nothing. Nothing but the darkness, the storm, and then when he comes, you'll all be like me."

Jack fought the urge to slam his fist through one of the screens. "So you're telling me to just lie down. That there's not a damn thing anyone can do to stop this?"

"Ashes, ashes," Declan whispered. "We all fall down."

Jack did bang his fist into the wall, rattling the detritus littering the shelves and the floor. Moira started toward him, her hand raised. "Enough. He did as you asked. He gets tired."

Jack watched the look that passed between Declan and Moira. He gave her a sweet smile, before crossing his eyes and sticking out his tongue.

"You two together long before he went off the deep end?" he asked. Moira went to Declan and stroked the sweaty strands of dark hair away from his forehead.

"Five years," she said. "Then, about eighteen months back, things got really bad. Got so he couldn't sleep, because he'd wake up screaming, and when he was awake he couldn't tell the difference between me and one of his visions."

"Nergal," Pete murmured. "Hate that ancient bastard a little more with each passing day."

"There's nothing here," Jack said. "Sorry to have troubled you and Declan, Moira." He rubbed his forehead, throbbing from the buzz of the screens. The *Fiach Dubh* weren't what he remembered. Hell, not much was what he remembered in these strange times. Seth never would have lain down and accepted the end of the world.

But Seth wasn't here. He was probably sloshed in some karaoke bar halfway around the world, if he wasn't dead in the gutter outside it.

The crow brothers couldn't help him. He was on his own.

"Don't be sad," Declan said. "Don't cry out loud, the lady says. That's not thunder you hear. That's the wings, the wings beating the drums, and the drums are the heartbeat of the dead." He looked up again and pointed at Jack. "I know you hear it, crow-mage. I know you. . . ."

Something skittered outside the window, flashing across the paper cover, almost too fast for the eye. Moira and Pete both wheeled around, hands dropping inside their coats, Pete's for her stun gun and Moira's for a small leather-wrapped bundle. A focus for some sort of hex, Jack wagered, something strong enough to blow a hole in the wall of the flat.

He would have liked Moira and Declan if he'd met them under different conditions. They reminded him of himself and Pete, if things had just gone a bit differently, and he'd replaced his penchant for smack with one for greasy snack foods.

"What the fuck was that?" Moira said.

Declan wrapped his arm around himself and started to rock. "All around," he said. "Cold and fire, all around, muddy blood and black eyes, staring at me . . . stop staring at me . . . stop stop stop stop . . ."

His voice rose into an incoherent scream, and

Moira grabbed his arm as more shadows filled up the window frame, scratching and chittering as they tried to find a way in.

Jack heard a pane shatter, and he jerked his head at Pete. "We need to go."

They thundered down the rickety staircase, Declan clinging to Moira and babbling. At the door, Keith met them with a frown. "What's happening?"

"I don't know," Jack said. "But your boy here has gone full throttle around the bend, so whatever it is, I assume it's not here to cuddle."

Jimmy pointed into the close shadows around them as the street lamp blinked out under the onslaught of the small, chittering creatures. "They're everywhere. Those flying bastards are just the start."

Jack saw the three pale figures fold out of the shadows. He saw the Fae's arm come up, too late. By the time he'd figured out what they were, it was already far, far too late.

Keith went down first, the black glass blade embedded in his throat so he couldn't even scream, Jimmy lasted a bit longer, firing off a hex that spat currents of electricity all over the street, striking one of the Fae assassins in the chest and knocking him to the ground.

The swarm with them, though, was relentless; tiny bodies with oily, translucent wings covered Jimmy, stripping his flesh even before he fell to the pavement, writhing in agony.

Pete yanked Jack back inside and slammed the door as the swarm landed against it, the sound of a thousand tiny nails on the wood like sandpaper against Jack's ears. Pete wheeled on Moira. "Is there another way out of here?"

"There's a basement," Moira managed. "But I'm not leaving him."

Declan sat curled in a ball, staring at the door with wide eyes. Jack stooped in front of him and repeated the gesture of grabbing the man's chin in his fingers. "Oi. Listen. I've been where you are, mate. Those are Fae soldiers outside, cold-blooded killers, and I know they're playing hell with your sight right now. But forget them, mate. Moira's not leaving without you, and if we don't move, she dies. Even you can't be so far gone, yeah?"

Declan swallowed hard, blinked, and stared up at Jack. "Your fingers are cold."

Jack helped Moira sling the pudgy psychic to his feet, and together they got Declan down to the basement. Moira pointed at a grate in the floor. "That goes down to the storm drains. Lots of iron—they'll have a hard time following us."

Pete flipped the grate off and gestured at Moira and Declan. "You two first."

She grabbed Jack's arm after the pair dropped into the wet, dank black space below. "What is going on? What do the Fae want?"

"Damned if I know," Jack said. "But they seem pretty insistent on getting it, so let's keep moving."

He dropped and grabbed Pete around the waist so she wouldn't break her ankle in the drop. She landed hard and cursed. "I hate being short."

"But you're so adorable," Jack said.

Pete shot him a look that he could tell, even in the near pitch dark, was poisonous. A green glow lit the way ahead of them, and Jack saw Moira standing at the junction of the drain and a larger pipe, gesturing them along while witchfire writhed around her.

"These drains let out down at the piers," she said. "From there, we can make it out to sea."

"Fae hate salt water," Jack told Pete. "If we can get to a boat we'll be safe."

"I know that," Pete hissed as they walked single file, hugging the wall to stay out of the worst of the waste water. "I have spent almost five years tagging after you now, you know."

Footsteps rattled in the tunnel behind them, and Moira waved her hand. "Keep it down," she said.

They walked in silence for another few hundred yards, and then Moira breathed a sigh of relief. "I think that's done it. If I never see another Fae again it'll be too soon—"

She choked, and her knees buckled. Moira went face-first into the water, her red hair spreading around her head like a billow of blood. The witchfire she'd conjured flickered and went out.

Declan gave a wail, the sound of an animal in excruciating pain, crumpling against the tunnel wall.

Jack conjured a light of his own, and the harsh blue glow illuminated the blade in Moira's back. A good hit, jammed squarely into the center of her back, next to the spine. A nick of the heart, a near-instant bleeding out.

"Jack," Pete said softly. He looked up to meet the eyes of one of the Fae, who leaned down and retrieved his knife from Moira's body.

"I track warm-blooded things like you," the Fae said. His voice was musical and low, like listening to a snake try to speak English. "No matter how far underground you burrow."

Pete pulled her stun gun, but Jack waved her off. "Don't bother, luv. He's an experienced killer, and he'll have a blade between your eyes before you can pull that trigger."

"Yeah," Pete said. "But at least I'll give him something to think about."

"Try to harm me," the Fae said. "I would relish the kill of a Weir. It would be very good to return home with such a trophy."

"You don't want to do this," Pete said. She was using her copper voice, the voice designed to calm killers and free hostages. "I'm a friend to the Queen. I—"

"I serve no Queen," the Fae snarled. "My King follows the path of war and conquest, and so that is the path I follow." He pointed at Declan. "Now stand aside. My blade still wants for blood."

Jack didn't feel anything—not the cold water rushing past his ankles; not the cold, foreign magic of the Fae assassin; not the panic-stricken heartbeat driving the blood through his ears at a thousand miles an hour. At the stage where he knew he was about to either die or do something so monumentally stupid he'd wish he were dead, his brain shut down all the but the essentials.

So.

He could hex the Fae, but some of them resisted magic. The *bean sidhe* who'd tried to kill him wouldn't be dented by anything less than an incendiary hex, and down here he'd suck out all the oxygen and crisp-fry Pete, Declan, and himself along with the Fae.

He could try to take the knife, but the only way that would work out would be when the Fae voluntarily planted it in his spleen.

Everything snapped back—Declan's screaming, the freezing water, the cold magic rolling off the Fae.

Jack looked at Pete, who spared him only a glance, stun gun still pointed at the Fae. "Don't use that on him, luv," he said softly. "Shooting him wouldn't do a bit of good."

Pete caught his meaning as he lifted his feet from the water, bracing on a narrow ledge above the spill. She was brilliant like that. He was damn glad she was there.

"Declan," he said, making sure to shift his body between the Fae and his new psychic mate, "might want to get those feet out of the water."

Declan curled himself into an even tighter ball, and as the Fae lifted his hand to use his knife again, Pete pointed the stun gun down and shot into the water.

The leads sparked, and the entire gun blew up with a pop, shards of plastic flying in every direction. Acrid chemical smoke filled the tunnel as the Fae was lifted off his feet by the charge and went flying backward, smashing against the bricks, his blade falling into the water.

Jack slung the hex before the Fae could recover, the leg locker making the creature go stiff, snarling like a dog who wanted to chew his leg off.

Making sure to keep his distance, Jack came over and looked down at the creature. He didn't look so tough after ten thousand volts had run through him, but still, the black eyes, the veiny face, and the pointed teeth would be enough to make anyone keep their distance.

"Right," Jack said. "Either I leave that hex on and by the time I'm far enough away for you to slip it, you drown, or you tell me what I want to know."

The Fae spat at him, a black glob of saliva hitting Jack's pantleg.

"I'll take that as a sign you're happy to chat," Jack said. "Why're you trying to kill me?"

The Fae's lip curled. "I wouldn't dirty my blade. You consort with demons."

"I hate to be the bearer of bad news, but your ruler is consorting with the king bastard of all Hell-spawn," Jack said. "So that sort of makes us even. Except not at all, because you just murdered three mages."

"I follow orders," the Fae said.

"And Legion ordered you to kill me?" Jack snapped. "Warning you, mate, I'm getting bored, and leaving you to drown would alleviate that pretty quickly."

"Legion ordered me to kill all remaining members of the *Fiach Dubh* I could locate," the Fae grumbled. "He left orders to leave you and the Weir alive. That's the only reason I didn't stick a blade in your lovely bride back there."

Jack shut his eyes for a brief second, trying not to slam the Fae's head inside out against the bricks. "Of course not. Because he used me to find them and wanted me to know it."

The Fae gave him a nasty, razor-edged grin. "That sounds about right."

Pete came to his shoulder. "I think we need to get Declan away from this bastard before he has a stroke."

"But I have so much more to tell you," the Fae purred. "How you led me right to your old order. How that old man, Wallace, put up such a fight when we came for him. His blood will be in the plaster and wood of that pub forever. Fitting, if you think about it . . ."

"You listen to me." Jack's voice didn't shake, and he was glad of that, because he wanted to make sure the message got through. "You tell Legion that there is nothing I will not do to see him dead at my feet. Nothing he can leverage against me, because if it comes down to me or him, I'll ride the both of us straight down to Hell."

"He's counting on it," the Fae said, starting to laugh again. "He wants you alive, you stupid sack of meat. He wants you to be a witness to his glory, to watch every last thing you care about burn. And you will, mark my words. Your crow brothers, your loves, your *daughter* . . ."

Pete's boot connected with the side of the Fae's

head, snapping it to the side. He slumped. She stood back, clenching and unclenching her fists. "Prop him up so he doesn't drown if you like. I don't give a fuck."

She turned around to help Declan, and Jack nudged the Fae with his toe until he sat upright again. "More than you deserve, you bastard," he said. The Fae moaned, and Jack bent over, so his lips almost touched the creature's ears. "If you get out of here, you tell Legion I'm coming for him," Jack whispered. "No more games and empty threats. Him or me."

"Jack!" Pete called. Declan sagged against her, but he looked a bit less green around the gills, and he accepted Jack's arm when he offered it.

Pete scouted ahead, but they made it to the piers without further incident. Jack found Declan some dry clothes in a crane operator's shed, while Pete sat with him, her hand over his, listening as he rocked back and forth, a few tears dribbling down his pale cheeks.

"We should get on the ferry back to the UK," Jack told Pete. "Just in case any more visitors from fairyland show their faces."

Pete frowned. "What about Declan? We can't just leave him here."

Jack looked down at the psychic, who sniffed and shook his head. "It's all right. I'll just wait here until they gut me like a pig. Or like a fish, now. I always wanted to live near the ocean. It sings to me. Quiets down the sight."

"Don't be ridiculous," Jack said. "Just come with us, and we'll make sure nothing happens to you."

"Moira," Declan said, rubbing his temples. "Moira could tell me what was real and what wasn't. Now what will I do?"

"We'll figure it out," Jack said. "Look, I don't have any answers, Declan. My bright idea was to get blitzed on heroin to keep the sight at bay. But I know what you're going through, and Pete and I just want to help you."

"Liar," Declan said. "You want me to tell you how to keep the storm away. Well, I don't have an umbrella. We're all going to die. Except you. You'll be alive, your body, but you're just as dead as the rest of us, once he takes his place."

"You can doomsay all you like if you just get on the bloody ferry," Jack said. "Come on, mate. Humor me."

"If you ride on the storm, if you don't hide, then you can fly," Declan whispered. "Let the wings lift you. Don't rip out the feathers. Put the blood in the air, blood he can use to water the earth of his new world, his new graveyard, ashes of the dead raining down on your tongue."

Pete looked up at him, and Jack couldn't meet her eyes. "What is he saying?"

Jack felt a headache spike behind his eyes, and he rubbed his forehead viciously. "Nothing. It's nothing that can help." He was not taking up the mantle of the Morrigan. Because if he did, he wouldn't stop the end—he would be directly responsible for it.

A different apocalypse was still an apocalypse, wasn't it?

"Ashes, ashes," Declan singsonged sadly. "We all fall down."

CHAPTER 25

The ferry ride was almost nine hours, but if it meant a reprieve from the threat of a Fae attack, Jack would have gladly made the crossing of the Irish Sea in a leaky rowboat.

Pete managed to get Declan to quiet down and sleep with the application of hot tea laced with one of the Valium pills Jack kept on him in case he got beaten up or had to put himself under—trance states were remarkably easy when you had the best opiates the black market had to offer.

Pete offered Jack a paper cup of black coffee, and shoved it into his hands when he tried to wave it off. "You need it. You feel awake now, but the adrenaline is going to wear off and you'll crash."

Jack emptied the cup down his throat. His stomach growled at the influx of bitterness, but it couldn't make him feel any worse than he already did. "Legion used me to get to them. He had them slaughtered just to make a point."

"He's *trying* to get to you," Pete said. "If he's trying to get to you, it means you can actually hurt him. You have something, and he's doing his damndest to put you off the scent."

"By killing four innocent people?" Jack said.

"That's a hell of a distraction." He didn't think Legion was afraid. He thought the demon was having fun, batting him around with his paw before he went in for the kill.

"I'm sorry about them," Pete said. "Really. I know they helped you a lot when you were younger."

"Yeah, it was a long time ago," Jack muttered. "I don't even recognize the order anymore. They didn't used to be that fatalistic. Two fingers up at the rest of the world was more their style."

"End times make a lot of folks doom and gloom," Pete said. "I saw it all the time when I was with the Met. Any time something in the world got bad—economy, elections, terrorists, volcanoes—the nutters would come out of the woodwork, shooting up their corner off-license and putting their heads in the oven. Thinking about the future drives some people over the edge."

"Try *seeing* the future," Jack muttered. Pete jerked her thumb at Declan.

"If you end up like that, please don't expect me to wipe up your drool and change your diapers."

"Luv, don't be silly," Jack said. "You know you'd never get me to wear a diaper."

Pete reached out and patted his knee. "You'll figure it out. You do have your clever moments."

Jack let the silence fall. Pete was good at calming people down, getting them to focus on the moment and think things through. She'd spent a good chunk of her adult life meeting people on the worst day of theirs, getting them to describe their attackers, talk about the moments when they thought they might die. Her greatest gift, though, was knowing when to be quiet and let people work things through for themselves.

He tried to think like Pete. He had no allies, nobody who would help him. There was no way to simply deport Legion back to the Pit. So why was the demon even bothering with him, other than pure spite? Even Belial had walked away from him as a bad job when the Princes turned on them.

Jack stared up at the buzzing light fixture above his head. "I'll be back," he told Pete, standing and fumbling in his pocket for a piece of chalk.

She pointed at the salt-streaked windows. Morning sun turned the horizon gold, but the waves of the Irish Sea were still deep gray.

"Where are you going? We're in the middle of the fucking ocean."

Jack pushed open the door to the car deck. "Just going to get some air."

He went up the steps rather than down, ignoring the CREW ONLY sign painted on the heavy watertight door. The top deck of the ferry was small, damp, and freezing. Wind slicked his hair back against his skull and wrung tears from the corner of his eyes as soon as he stepped out.

Jack ignored the elements as best he could—it was poor form to conduct summonings where just anyone could pop in. Besides, he wanted Belial off-balance and listening when he said what he had to say.

A wash of spray passed over the deck, filling Jack's eyes with salt, and when he swiped at them Belial stood in front of him, arms folded. The rolling of the ship didn't move him in the slightest, and his black eyes bored into Jack with all the force and intensity of a hurricane.

"You know, twice is pushing it," Belial said. "Three times in less than a week, I'm thinking you *want* me to kick your arse from here to Liverpool and back."

"They do say the third time's the charm," Jack said. Belial scowled.

"They can kiss my lily white arse. What do you want from me, Jack? I don't have any more bright shiny favors to do you, no more deals to make. I told you I'm out."

"I know," Jack said. "And I wanted to say, for my part in it, I'm sorry." In all his life, he never would have imagined he'd be standing in front of the demon who'd taken his soul, apologizing. Then again, he'd never imagined that he'd ever have the upper hand with Belial, either.

Belial gave a weary sigh. "I'm not going to kiss your bum and make it all better. Stop bothering me. I just want to spend what little time this miserable human world has left in peace, and preferably very drunk."

"It doesn't have to be this way," Jack said. "You and I both know that Legion is only one demon, one pissant with a big mouth and a bigger ego. You had an idea how to get rid of him when you brought me into this, and I know you, Belial. You always have a plan B."

Belial sat down on a container of life vests and sighed. "He's a lot more than that, Jack. Fuck me, I don't know *what* he is. I'm not even certain he's a demon; he's got a demon's name, but you and I both know there's no way an elemental could pull off this kind of thing. And the ancients are locked down—they only made a finite number of those, fortunately."

"Whatever he is—demon, old god, unicorn," Jack said. "You're a survivor, Belial. Survivors always cover their own, and they always know everyone's weak spot. You knew mine. You knew I was a coward and that I'd do anything to stay alive and out of Hell. You manipulated me for close to ten years with that. So what's Legion's sticking point?"

"You said it," Belial said. "He's as arrogant and vain as Lucifer supposedly was. Thinks the sun sets and the moon rises out of his bum. He thinks he's unkillable, and I've been around long enough to know that's just not true."

Jack felt for the first time in days like there wasn't a hundred pound weight sitting on his chest. "And?"

"And there's plenty of things in the vaults back home that will kill things in ways that keep them dead," Belial said. "Azrael supposedly had a blade taken from the Morrigan herself—the hand of death. I'd imagine that'll put down anything that draws breath."

"Azrael had a lot of toys, didn't he?" Jack muttered.

"It's beside the point," Belial said. "I can't go back there, and even if I could, I wouldn't even know where in the vaults to look. Azrael wasn't exactly the warm, welcoming type even before he started making back-room deals with things like Abbadon."

"He must've talked to someone," Jack said. Belial shrugged.

"Azrael didn't have a fondness for human conversation like I do. He did, however, have a fondness for torture and classical music, so there's that."

"There is something in those vaults that could find the blade," Jack said, remembering the things creeping about in the cases that Belial had shown him. "That eye."

"To use the Allfather's Eye requires a capacity for magic that even I don't have," Belial said. "And forget you, scarecrow. You'd turn into tinder if you so much as touched that thing."

Jack rubbed out the chalk line with his foot. "Then it's a good job I know somebody who can handle it just fine."

CHAPTER 26

"You've got to be joking," Pete said. She, Jack, and Belial were gathered in an empty sleeping cabin, the demon sitting on the bed, tapping one toe of his pointed leather shoe against the deck, Jack facing him, and Pete blocking the door. He didn't miss the signal there. She wasn't happy with either of them, and they weren't getting out of this.

"I wish I was, but I've tried everything else, including this one's asinine plan to stab Legion with a bit of stone like we're back in the caveman days," Jack said. Belial gave him a grunt and bestowed another baleful glare.

"I fail to understand, then, why he's here," Pete said. "In fact, I really don't know why he's here, since I still owe him a kick in the teeth for involving us in this in the first place."

"My dear, you're a human being living in the world," Belial said. "Once Legion is done cementing his base, *that* will make you involved."

"From what I saw," Jack said, "we don't have very much more time before he spins his little globe one last time and drops the barriers between the Black and everything else. It was still spring in my vision.

Trees were still green. You know, the ones that hadn't been burned down."

Pete passed her hands over her face. "If we live through this, I'm going to slap the both of you into next week," she said to Belial. "Just so we're clear."

"If we live through this, I'm going to be back in Hell, far from the grating sound of your voice," Belial grumbled. "But do your worst, by all means."

"Oi," Jack said. This new Belial kept throwing him off—he could almost forget for a few moments at a time that Belial was a demon, a predator, and that made him even more dangerous. "You speak to her like that, *I'll* feed you your own teeth."

"Are we going through with this idiotic plan or not?" Belial snapped. "Because I tell you, I'd much rather go back to what I was doing when your chicken scratch got me here. It was brunette. Her name was Candi, with an *I*."

"You're so charming I may vomit," Pete said. "I'll be sure to aim for your shoes if I do."

"Just tell Pete what you told me," Jack said. He would never say out loud that the demon was right—this was a desperate idea, the last gasp of his attempt to avert what he'd seen in his vision. Then again, if it didn't work, they were fucked anyway. Might as well go down, as Bon Jovi said, in a blaze of glory.

"The Princes won't let me stroll into the vault, so the first problem is that it's guarded by a fuckton of Fenris, who'd like nothing more than to rip my legs off and make them into appetizers," Belial said. "Then, you need a blood key."

"Is that what it sounds like?" Pete said, wrinkling her nose.

Belial nodded at her. "A Named demon's blood. If anything goes wrong, we're locked in the vault for good. Once we get access to the eye, the girl wonder here will have to keep it from melting her face off long enough to scry for the location of the blade. Then it's a simple matter of somehow getting out of there before the wrath of 665 of my brethren rains down on your head."

"Well, once we get through the hard bits, I'm sure it'll be no trick at all to have Scotty beam us back to the *Enterprise*," Jack said. Belial huffed.

"If I'm going to get it from both sides I'm leaving right now."

"You're sure this blade can really kill Legion?" Pete asked Belial, even though she looked at Jack when she asked it.

"I'm sure of nothing except that I have a hangover and you two are the most irritating human beings I've run across in a thousand years of existence," Belial said. "So shall we kick on, or are the two of you going to live out your short remaining days annoying each other to death?"

Pete spread her hands. "I'm ready. What do you need from me?"

Jack rubbed his chin. Now that there was a direction, something for him to focus on other than the pounding in his head from his visions and his brush with the Fae, he was starting to think again. That had always been his only asset—cleverness. Cleverness had gotten him out of Manchester, cleverness had told him that going with Seth was the right move, and cleverness kept him one step ahead of the Morrigan, even now.

He could be clever one more time. That was going to be the easy part.

"You've got your part down," he told Pete. "I don't want to tax your talent if you're going to be handling an artifact with as much voltage as that thing in the vaults."

"Consider me a tour guide," said Belial. "Even if I wanted to do the heavy lifting, I don't exactly have a full bag of tricks these days. A demon exiled from his home is about as useful as a bum pissing in the gutter while it's raining." He stood, straightening his tie. "Have fun, kiddies. Give me a shout when our little Wild Bunch is ready to ride."

CHAPTER 27

Pete called Ollie Heath, her old partner in the Met, and had him take charge of Declan. Until this was over, sectioning was the safest place for the poor nutter, Jack thought.

"All right," he said when it was just the two of them. "You were the police. What makes for a successful robbery?"

"Not getting caught, for a start, which we most certainly will," Pete said. Jack found the whiskey bottle and poured them both a glass.

"At least try to pretend for a second we have any hope of doing this," he said. It had to work. Or it had to kill him. He'd decided after that first encounter with Legion that he wouldn't end up like the Jack in his vision, alone and half insane, searching for his stolen daughter and mourning his dead wife.

"Okay, good heists usually have a couple of components," Pete said, rolling her glass between her hands. "A front man, a driver, and an expert. You know, safe cracker, expert in stolen Nazi art, that sort of thing. Somebody to pin down what's of real value, get it, and get out. The front man handles the rough stuff, and the driver is self explanatory."

"We've none of those things," Jack said. "What now?"

Pete shrugged. "You get caught, do a hitch in prison, mend your evil ways. Except, wait, this is Hell, and we're robbing a vault full of demonic artifacts, not the corner off-license, so we'll probably all roast for eternity with pokers up our arses."

"The Fenris are no joke, but they're not hard to manage," Jack said. "They really just want to be let off the chain. If we gave them something to direct all that pent-up demon rage at . . ."

"I pity the bloke, but all right," Pete said. "A distraction. Belial provides the Hellspawn blood, and I find the blade. All that's left is getting out of there."

"I guess we're relying on Belial for that, too," Jack said. "And before you chime in, no, I don't like it either, but I have to trust that he wants to live more than he wants to watch the Princes peel off my skin."

Pete drained her glass, giving him a look over the rim that said she knew he was full of it, that they couldn't trust anyone, including Belial, but she had the grace not to call him out on it to his face. "Distraction, then. Somehow I doubt setting off a few firecrackers outside the front door is going to do the trick with these types."

Jack went to his shelf of grimoires and ran his hand over the spines, the smooth slither of old leather and vellum worn shiny with time familiar as his own fingerprint. "Used to be so simple," he said. "Summon what you need, sling a few hexes, and you were riding high."

"Yeah, I remember the first time you summoned

a demon around me," Pete said. "Worst fucking experience of my life."

"You did almost burn down my flat," Jack reminded her. "Not a walk in the park for me, either." That day had been when he'd known for sure. That Pete was the Weir, that she could destroy him and everything around her, and that he had to stay by her, because without him they were both going to end up dead inside the year.

He pulled one of his go-to grimoires off the shelf. "That gives me an idea, actually."

"Burning down the flat?" Pete said. "You almost did that enough by leaving the kettle on and your fucking cigarettes burning on every flat surface, thanks."

Jack flipped the pages. The grimoire had come across Seth's desk at the bookshop, and even though it was full of useful—and no doubt valuable— information for summoning and hexing, he'd handed it over to Jack. Of course, most of it was written in Sumerian, so that had been Seth's own version of a little joke.

"Do we have any ketchup?" he asked Pete. She frowned at him.

"That's your bright idea? Condiments?"

Jack dropped the grimoire on their ottoman, open to the relevant page, and hunted up some fresh chalk, salt, and a few herbs to speed things along. That was all you needed for most spells, and if you had the talent to back it up, you didn't need anything at all except a few words of power. The more elements you mixed in, the higher the chance of fucking up and having whatever you were trying to conjure snap back and slap you in the face.

"I'm surprised you don't remember," he said, digging through their ancient icebox for the nearly empty bottle.

Pete watched him as he chalked out the proper signs inside the circle, sprinkled some salt for extra hold, and dumped a puddle of ketchup on the sitting room floor, and then she gave a dry laugh. "Him? Seriously?"

"Honestly, I've never been sure if it's him, her, or other," Jack said. He lit the herbs, which snapped and fizzed.

"Hrathetoth!" Jack snapped, and the little demon emerged out of the smoke, blinking its large gold eyes at him.

"Crow-mage!" it squealed. "Never again you call me! I warned you!"

"Calm down and stuff your face," Jack said. "Then you and I need to talk."

This was a risk. Hrathetoth might have been small and furry, with a tail longer than its body, but it was still a Named demon, and if it was among the number loyal to Legion, it would go running straight back to him.

The demon wiped the last of the ketchup off its face and pricked its pointed ears, furry black tufts bristling out of them like an antenna array. "Talk, talk, talk," it groused. "All the meat sausages do is talk."

"Yeah, and you're going to listen to me," Jack

said. "I summoned you and gave you an offering, so it won't kill you."

"Not you," Hrathetoth cooed. "But when the rain comes, umbrella keeps you from getting wet. And when it's dark, too late for talking. Shhhh." Hrathetoth stuck one of its small webbed fingers to its lips. "If he hears the talk, out come our tongues!"

"So I take it you're not a fan of Legion," Jack said.

"Muddy man. Leaving his footprints all over the nice clean world." Hrathetoth sniffed.

"I don't deny he's slimy," Jack said. "How'd you like to help get rid of him?"

"Not slimy, greasy," Hrathetoth said. "Greasy like a meat sausage. You, too. All of you." He wrinkled his button nose at Jack. "Meat goes bad if it stays too long. We'll throw this one out, yes yes?"

"Well, that was easy," Pete said from outside the circle. Hrathetoth hopped to face her.

"Hello, pretty black hole," he said. "I can't look at you. You make my brain feel tingly."

Pete gave Jack a look, eyebrow arching to its maximum disapproval. "Really?" she said. "This is your big idea?"

"Listen," Jack said to Hrathetoth, "all you have to do is go to the Princes' vaults and keep a couple of Fenris busy long enough for me to liberate something inside. Think you can do that?"

Hrathetoth thumped its tail against the floor like a heartbeat, and then grinned, revealing a truly impressive array of needlelike teeth in three straight rows. "Fenris stink almost as bad. Wet doggies, tiny brains." It stuck out its paw. "I'll help the crow-mage. Shake!"

"You must be insane," Jack said. "I'm not touching you."

"Shake or no deal, meat puppet!" Hrathetoth shrieked. The sound pierced Jack's eardrums like an air horn, and Pete winced.

"For the love of all that's holy, just shake the thing's paw. Hand. Whatever." Pete said. Jack sighed, but he took Hrathetoth's paw between his fingers and shook it. The shock of magic felt like taking a stun gun to the chest. The demon was small, but it had power boiling through it all the same. Jack just hoped it would be enough to keep the Fenris from ripping him, Pete, and Belial to shreds.

"Hooray!" Hrathetoth shrieked. "Blood and guts and guts and blood! See you soon!"

"Can't wait," Jack muttered. He rubbed out the chalk line. "Return no more until you are called, et cetera." A noxious puff of smoke rolled across the flat, and when Jack's eyes stopped tearing Hrathetoth was gone.

Pete slumped back on the sofa. "Have I mentioned yet today that I despise demons?"

"Get it out of your system," Jack said, getting a rag to wipe up the ketchup. "Because we're going right down the Yellow Brick Road into their home sweet home."

CHAPTER 28

There was no adequate way to prepare someone for a visit to Hell, so Jack didn't even try. Pete had seen things that few mages even dreamed of—places like the Land of the Dead, the white nothing comprising the slivers of space between the worlds, a purgatory where things lived that most people couldn't even have nightmares about. She'd seen things through the eyes of the Morrigan and the Hecate, had even brushed up face to face with Nergal. Jack figured she was a lot better prepared to handle Hell than he had ever been.

Still, her expression when Belial brought them to the waiting room outside the vault wasn't pleased.

"What in the holy fuck," she said, "is that *smell*?"

"Crematory furnaces," Jack said. "They feed the damned into them, burn them to ash, and mix it with blood to feed the elementals."

Pete paled, breathing through her mouth. "I am never eating a hamburger ever again."

Belial took a deep breath. "Smells like fresh air to me, sweetheart."

The demon tried to hide it, but Jack saw the beads of sweat working down from his hairline, staining the collar of his pristine white shirt. If they were

caught, he and Pete would merely be dead meat.
Belial would be at the mercy of the Princes, and
Legion, for the rest of his demonic lifespan.

Belial glared at him. "You feeling sentimental,
Jackie?"

Jack shook his head, gazing around a corner
down the long hall leading to the vault. It was the
same featureless steel bulkhead as the inside, the
only hint that this wasn't some boring bunker back
in the daylight world the three Fenris standing guard
over the vault door.

"Where's your distraction, crow-mage?" Belial
grumbled. "About time to start throwing fireballs,
don't you think?"

Jack gave Belial a wounded look. "Come on. I *am*
capable of being subtle sometimes." He was starting
to feel the sweat creeping over his own flesh. It was
Hell, it was hot, and they had about three more
heartbeats before the Fenris realized they weren't
supposed to be hanging around and ate them for an
early lunch.

"Do something, Jack," Belial snarled in his ear,
"or I'm going to."

Jack was about to turn around, clock Belial in the
jaw, and make a run for it when a pop sounded at the
far end of the tunnel and one of the Fenris cried out,
swatting at his eyes.

Hrathetoth appeared in midair, bouncing from
the head of one Fenris to the next, digging its claws
into their eyeballs, yanking their hair out by the
roots and peeling their skin off in strips.

Three more pops sounded, and Jack saw a trio of

smaller, furrier, toothier versions of Hrathetoth appear, setting on the Fenris like piranhas on a prime cut of filet mignon.

"Look at that," he said to Pete. "He brought friends."

"He really hates sausage, I guess," Pete muttered.

The tiny demons took off running, climbing the walls, skittering along the ceiling, laughing and cackling in their demonic dialect. Jack didn't speak it, but he could tell by the way the Fenris reacted that Hrathetoth had called their parentage, and quite probably their genitalia, into question.

The Fenris pounded after Hrathetoth and its friends, completely ignoring Pete, Jack, and Belial. Jack plastered himself against the tunnel wall until they passed, then hurried to the main doors.

"Big, scary, and dumb as posts," Belial said when he caught up with him. "You have to love Baal's best and brightest."

"Blood." Jack pointed at the row of three spikes set into the doors at chest level. Belial bared his teeth.

"I'm aware of my part in this." He rolled up his sleeve and pressed his forearm into the spikes. "You know, you could be a little more grateful. I am spilling my blood for anyone who cares to collect it."

"You'd also sell me to the Princes in a heartbeat if we get caught, so cut out the martyr song," Jack said. "I've heard it before, and it's second verse, same as the first."

The doors groaned open. Jack heard the Fenris howling in the distance, and his chest didn't unknot until the vault doors had sealed behind them.

"You two have fun," Belial said, rolling his sleeve down. The punctures had already healed to black spots, Belial's blood bubbling against his pale sharkbelly skin. "I'll be right here when you're through."

"I don't think so," Jack said. "How do I know you're not directing me right into a booby trap?"

"One, because we want the same thing, and if we don't get it we're all fucked right up the arse with a pole the size of the O2 Arena," Belial said. "And two, you don't. Your choice is to trust me, and get this done, or not trust me like you always have before, and watch things get progressively worse until you're in shit up to your ears. Again, as always."

Pete plucked at Jack's sleeve, which was good, because the rage was coming on again and he was finding it difficult not to take a swing at Belial. Not because the demon was wrong, but because he was right. Belial was a survivor, and Jack had a decent hunch they were on the same side, but he also remembered Belial's face when Jack had been his prisoner, tortured beyond all endurance.

Belial had enjoyed that. It was a truth Jack could never quite slip away from, no matter how much history had built up between him and the demon since then.

Because it meant he'd never fully put his trust in the demon, no matter how desperate the circumstances.

"Fine," he said. "But if you try to fuck us, Belial, when I have the blade I'm finding you and using you as a practice run for Legion."

"I never tire of these little chats we share," Belial said. "They make me positively glow inside."

Pete tugged at Jack again, sharper. "Come on," she said. "Clock's running."

Jack turned around. It was the only thing he could do—turn his back on the demon and hope he didn't end up with a knife in it. He followed Pete down the narrow hall inside the vault, but he still felt the demon's eyes on his back, and he knew if he turned around he'd see Belial's mocking grin.

CHAPTER 29

Jack didn't waste time trying to get the case holding the eye open, just picked up a scarred metal mace hanging on the wall in a weapons array and smashed through the glass. Pete gave him a crooked smile.

"Direct. I like that in a man."

Jack brushed the glass away from the stand, careful not to touch the eye. Even being this close to it without a barrier was running wires through his sight, charging them with the electricity of magic so old and inhuman it would be like stepping into a vacuum without an air supply. A few seconds to be shocked and in agony, and then nothing.

He looked back at Pete. "You know, you don't have to do this."

She shrugged, stripping off her jacket and fishing out her billfold. " 'Course I do." She handed the billfold and the coat to Jack. "If I start to have a seizure, don't let me swallow my tongue, and roll that up to put under my head."

"Pete . . . ," Jack started, but then sighed. "All right." He'd done plenty of things to make her worry, make her wonder if he was going to open his eyes again. The least he could do was not baby her when it was her turn, and be standing by in case things went pear-shaped.

Pete reached out and picked up the eye. Her talent worked as a channel, a wide-open frequency for whatever magic the subject on the other end possessed. If she took too much, her talent would burn her from the inside out. Or the magic would roll outward, wild and uncontrolled, and burn not just Pete but everything in her path.

Jack waited, not breathing, and for a moment everything seemed fine. Pete let out a small shiver, her eyes rolling back in her head. "I can see . . . ," she breathed. "I can see so much, Jack. It's beautiful. . . ."

Then she cried out, falling to the ground and clutching at her skull. "It's too much," she moaned. "Too much . . . I can see it . . . I can see *everything.*"

Jack dropped to his knees, reaching out before he had time to realize what a royally bad idea that was. He just wanted to make the sounds stop, the moans and the whimpers that quickly built to screams. He touched Pete, and she was still touching the eye.

The shock was worse than electricity, worse than anything he'd ever felt. It was like being struck by lightning and plunging into ice cold water all at once.

He thought he might have screamed, but he wasn't sure. All he could see for a moment was darkness, and then a million dots of light filled his vision. They weren't dots, he realized. They were worlds, entire realms, places like the Black and Hell and the world he lived in, all strung across the blackness like diamonds scattered on velvet.

There were so many. Jack felt his eyes fill with

tears. The pain was indescribable, the feeling that his brain would burst from the onslaught of information.

This was what Pete was seeing. Her Weir talent was running off the chain and she was channeling him as well as the eye, feeding into his sight like Belial's memory trick had.

He tried to find her, find any sign that they were still attached to their physical bodies—that they were still alive, and the feedback from Pete's talent hadn't turned them both into ash.

Ashes, ashes, Declan whispered in his ear, *we all fall down*.

The million dots parted, leaving a hundred and then half of that and then less than a dozen, spiralling down until there was only one glowing orb in Jack's vision, and then it brightened and blinded him, until he saw the vaults of Hell before him.

They were much different than the boring, sterile museum basement that Belial had brought them to. These were old, more ossuary than vault, lined with the skulls and bones of elemental demons, horned and spiked, the long-toothed skulls of wolves mixed in with the ones that looked more human.

A single demon, wrapped only in a black loincloth and the trailing pinion feathers of his black wings, stood before a simple wooden box. He held a blade in his hand. It was broken off halfway down the shaft, coated in sticky black blood and feathers. The demon himself was covered in deep slashes and cuts, like he'd tangled with a giant bird.

"Azrael," Jack whispered. It was only a memory,

what he was seeing, an event the eye had observed impassively. Azrael smiled to himself as he put the knife in the box.

"And if that bitch ever tries anything, we'll stick the rest of this where the other half went," he said to someone that Jack couldn't see. He tried to turn a bit and caught a glimpse of Pete out of the corner of his eye. He tried not to choke, or scream.

Pete had human features, looked like herself, but where her eyes should be was a bright void, a screaming well so deep and wide that it could have consumed every one of the worlds that he'd seen when the eye hooked on to his talent.

It was the most terrifying sight he'd ever witnessed, bar none. His talent was a part of him, in his bone and his blood, but it was a *part,* just one of the things that made him Jack Winter, like his crooked nose or his bum knee or his complete inability to appreciate music produced after 1994.

Pete's talent, though—it *was* her. It was in every atom of her, lived inside her like she was a vessel. That much power shouldn't be possible for a human body to contain, and yet she did it, without even trying.

The glow grew brighter, and Jack only caught a glimpse of the tall, human-looking figure Azrael had spoken to before he realized the much more urgent problem. Pete's talent was burning them both up, and he had no way to break the connection.

"What about me?" the figure whispered. "If she finds me . . ."

"She won't," Azrael said, caressing the blade once

more before he shut the box and moved to the iron door of the vault. "No one will. Oh, and if you think you're going to use your little body-hopping trick to get out of here, this place only has one purpose."

"You wouldn't . . . ," the figure started, but Azrael smiled.

"It dampens all magic. Mine, too, which is why I didn't tell you until just now. Wouldn't do to have you get it into your head to attack me."

Blackness started to creep in on Jack as he watched, not the spooky metaphorical darkness he'd heard so much about but the kind of blackness that came with any of the half-dozen times he'd overdosed or lost his air slowly. The first sign from his body that he was on the way. *Don't worry about your eyesight, mate,* it whispered to him. *You won't be needing it for much longer.*

Jack tried to pull back from what he'd seen of Pete, what the eye had shown him. They were in a room, on a floor, him clutching Pete and her clutching the eye, surrounded by steel and broken glass. . . .

"No!" the tall figure howled as Azrael slammed the door. "Don't you leave me here! I swear if you do I'll find you!"

Azrael gave a laugh that echoed even through the half-inch of iron. "Promises, promises," the demon's voice echoed, and then there was silence, except for the raging screams of the thing trapped inside the vault.

Jack used every trick he'd ever tried for breaking the hold of his sight—he had tattoos that were supposed to help, Pete's idea, and he thought of those, of the sting of the needle when he'd gotten them inked. He still had a body, provided it wasn't burned to a crisp.

Reaching out with the hand that wasn't on Pete's forehead, he felt the cold shards of the smashed glass on the floor all around them. The eye was going ballistic, showing him things in quick succession—the cold stone palaces of the Fae realm, carved from the rocks beneath like living creatures emerging from hibernation, a cold wasteland where things without eyes crawled across a glacier toward a sea filled with frothy blood, the white nothingness between each of the points of light where the worms that had almost been unleashed on the daylight lived, still waiting for the moment when the barriers fell.

Jack grabbed the glass, squeezing it tight and slicing into his palm. The sting helped, causing the visions to flicker like a bad signal, but it wasn't enough. Only real, immediate physical pain could break through the grip of his talent.

He sucked in a breath, than raised the glass and jammed it deep into his thigh, biting into his jeans and the flesh underneath. He tried to miss the major artery running up the inside of his leg, but at this point, there wasn't a great deal of difference between letting Pete's talent devour him and bleeding out.

The lights of the vault room shocked his eyes, and he screwed up his brow against the jolt of pain. Pete lay on the floor, very still, and Jack used the handle of the mace to nudge the eye out of her grasp.

She shuddered, ever so slightly, and her entire

body started to glow as white witchfire wreathed it. Whatever power she'd absorbed from the eye was inside her, just waiting to be redirected against whomever got in the way. Which right now, was him.

Jack leaned down next to her mouth, careful not to touch her, and his stomach flipped when she didn't breathe. His leg hurt like a bastard, but he wasn't bleeding much as long as he kept the shard embedded in the wound.

"Pete," he said. The witchfire flickered and then, like mist falling into the hills and valleys of the countryside where Seth had kept his summer cottage back in Ireland, it faded back into her body. It didn't dissipate, as extra power should. It crawled back inside her and took up residence, just waiting.

"Pete?" he said again. If he touched her, he was going to get vaporized. Not that he cared, if it woke her up.

She jolted upright, and Jack gave an involuntary yell, scrabbling backward and causing a fresh font of blood from his leg.

For a moment her eyes were pure white, and then they faded as he watched, back to the usual dark green. He'd never forgotten that color, since the first time he'd seen her face to face. She had eyes you could drown in. Human eyes.

"Fuck me," he said, flopping back onto the hard floor. "Don't you ever scare me like that again."

Pete examined her hands in response, touched her face and hair lightly. "I don't feel well," she told Jack.

"You sucked down enough magic to light up all

of Wales," he said. "That'll give anyone a tummy rumble."

"Jack." Pete stared at him, her pupils wide with fear. "I don't know if I can hold it down."

"Look." He levered himself up and crawled across the floor to her. "Just wait until we get to the vault. You saw what I did, yeah?"

Pete nodded, her cheeks coloring. "This is really bad. This is worse than anything I've ever channeled."

"I know," Jack said. "Listen, luv, I wouldn't lie to you—this is bad. But that room can hold in anything—you saw who Azrael left down there. So either he's *still* there and you can use your death ray on him, or the room will keep the wave in."

Pete blinked, and Jack saw her press her hands together to stop them shaking. "What happened to your leg?" she asked abruptly.

"Oh, you know." Jack grabbed a stick, wider at one end than the other, from the weapons array and used it to prop himself up. "Stabbed my own leg to break out of a psychic vision that was going to leave me brain damaged. The usual."

He offered Pete a hand, but she shrank away. "Don't. If you touch me, I'm going to drain you. The Weir just wants more, Jack. It always wants more."

"It'll be all right," he said, with a conviction that he didn't feel. He couldn't shake what he'd seen when the eye had gripped him. "You just have to get us to that room, and everything will be all right."

Pete got to her feet. She moved slowly, keeping her arms close to her, like if she touched anything she'd shatter. "Promise?" she said, her voice sounding more like Margaret's than her own. Young, scared, looking for any shred of reassurance she could find.

"I do," Jack lied. "Just walk, Pete, and everything will be fine."

CHAPTER 30

Pete had no trouble with the myriad twists and turns of the inner vaults, leading them through dozens of hallways, lifts, and stairwells, ever deeper and ever downward once they left the display room. Jack wondered how many hundreds of feet below Hell they were. How many thousands of years it had been since any eye—demon, damned, or human—had rested on the stone walls and dripping, rusted iron doors of the inner sanctum.

"I saw it, you know," Pete said after a time. Her voice echoed into the upper reaches of the vault, and they both jumped. They were walking along a narrow corridor lined on both sides with vault rooms, dozens of catwalks crisscrossing above their heads like an iron spider web.

"What did you see?" Jack whispered. His own voice taunted him, echoing from the curved walls and ceilings so high above their heads they were invisible in the dark. *See, see, see.*

"This place," Pete said. "It's a circle, a maze really. To build it must have taken hundreds of years. I doubt anyone knows what's at the center of this thing."

"Yeah, and I don't want to find out," Jack said. "I

just want to get the Morrigan's blade and get out of here."

Pete stumbled, and Jack fought against his urge to help her up. She grimaced as she stood, pressing her fingers to her temples. "We have to hurry," she said. "It's talking to me, trying to convince me to just unleash it, destroy this place. I don't have much longer before it turns."

"Fight it," Jack said. "Just listen to me. Talk to me about anything while we walk, all right?"

Pete moved faster, her gait hitching with pain, but she was still quicker than Jack, whose leg had started to bleed enough to soak his jeans all the way down to his ankle. His vision spun just a bit, but he kept going. He'd be fine. He'd had worse injuries. He wasn't the one in danger of burning alive.

"Do you know," she said, "I bought myself a funeral plot. A while ago, my first year in the Met."

Jack swiped a hand over his face, finding cool droplets of sweat. "Maybe this isn't the best subject for us."

"Most officers run a higher risk of dying on the job in their first few years," Pete said. "They're inexperienced and arrogant and think they're untouchable. It was next to my dad's. Lovely little spot. Knowing it was there kept me sharp, kept me from doing stupid shite that would have gotten me killed."

"Pete . . . ," Jack said, as they started down a narrow flight of stone stairs, a spiral carved into the earth like the passage of a great worm.

"I sold it when I found out I was pregnant," Pete said. "Because I knew then that I was never going to need that plot. I'm not going to die on the street, Jack, because I stopped the wrong plod with a grudge and a black-market gun."

"Of course not . . . ," Jack started, but Pete held up her hand.

"I'm not going to die in my bed, either, because if I've learned one thing from being with you, it's that we're all just specks compared to what's out there in the universe. And seeing what that thing had to show me confirmed it. I bought that cemetery plot because I was afraid, Jack. I was afraid that I'd see death coming and have no way to stop it, just like my father."

Jack liked to think he'd learned to keep his mouth shut at the right times over his tenure living with Pete, so he focused on walking without falling over, limping heavily as they moved down a low hall lit with a string of hissing, fizzing Edison bulbs. The iron doors looked familiar, and he hoped they were close.

"I figured out that it's not about dying," Pete said. "It's about living with the time we have, doing what we can to look at ourselves in the mirror, and not being afraid. I made myself look at my death, Jack. I've done it a dozen times, and this is the closest I've come."

She stopped in front of the last door in the row, the iron blistered with rust and green fingers of oxidization. "I'm not afraid," she said. "I'll never be afraid again. So don't worry about me, all right?"

Jack couldn't look at her. "I can't help it," he managed. "I *am* afraid, Pete. Why do you think I made that deal with Belial?"

"You bought your plot," Pete said. "Big fucking deal. You were the one who taught me how to not be afraid, Jack. Of anything. You're not brave because you don't have any fear. You're brave because you do what needs to be done."

She rapped her knuckles against the iron. "Now get this door open, because if you don't, we're both getting up close and personal with the Land of the Dead."

Jack exhaled. It felt as if he had a load of stones in his pocket, and somebody had just reached in and snatched out the heaviest one. Just a small piece, but now he felt like whatever happened next, he could probably come out the other side without breaking down into the sort of mess who'd sell his soul and scramble over everyone else in the world to save his own life.

"Yeah, okay," he said. "No problem, luv." He dropped the crutch and put his hands on the door. The lock was pretty rudimentary—he guessed the real power of the room came from whatever hexes Azrael had put in place.

No time to worry about that now; the hexes wouldn't reach out and bite him. Pete was counting on him. Jack pressed his fingers against the lock. Locks had never been difficult for him, even when he'd had a go at picking them the old-fashioned way, without any magic.

The lock clicked, and the door swung open a few inches, the waft of air shut in for a thousand years dry and stale in his face.

Jack flinched for a split second, waiting for who-

ever Azrael had screwed over to come screaming
out of the vault and rip his face off.

Pete moved past him, the white witchfire rising
from her skin again. "Come on!" she rasped. "I'm
going to nuke whatever's in here—you better get the
blade."

Jack flipped his lighter open. He didn't want to
risk any conjuring this close to Pete and her run-
away talent. The small flame illuminated the stone
table where the wooden box lay, covered in a millennium of dust and the webbing of a creature that
Jack didn't care to imagine.

His light also caught the bones embedded in the
walls—whether they were here for burial or more of
Azrael's victims, he guessed he'd never know.

"Jack!" Pete's voice held the kind of sharp urgency reserved for diffusing bombs, or going into
labor. "Get out," she said.

Jack started to shake his head as he grabbed the
box and stuffed it into his coat. "I'm not leaving you
here."

Pete stared at him, the white overtaking her eyes
again. "Get . . . out . . . ," she groaned, her voice echoing off the walls of the vault. "We can't both turn to
ash down here, so *go*."

She was right. Pete was always right. One of them
had to make it out of here, for Lily and Margaret,
so they would have a world to go back to.

"I love you," he said, running for the door. Pete
managed a thin, pain-filled smile.

"I know."

Jack bolted from the vault, slamming the door

behind him. The iron was thick. It had blocked out everything but darkness for a thousand years, but it couldn't block out Pete's screams.

Jack had never been one to pray, even when he was a small boy and his mother had dragged him off to church every Sunday to look good for the neighbors, until the vicar kindly suggested that until she could stop taking hits off a gin flask during the service, the Winter family should probably just stay home.

What was the point? There was nothing out there that would help him out of the goodness of their heart. The gods weren't altruistic—they were the most selfish, scheming ones of all. There was no magical sky grandfather who would swoop in and make everything all right if he really, really wanted it. Faith was for people who didn't know better. It was for the small boy he'd been, keeping the faith that someday his life would be more than a council flat, a mother who only made it to the bathroom half the time when chasing her gin with a handful of benzos made her puke her guts up, and a mind full of dead people only he could see, who wouldn't stop talking no matter what he did.

Faith was bullshit of the highest order.

But he still covered his head as the ground shook and dust rained down, and he let himself believe, for just a moment, that Pete was all right. If he was going to have faith in anyone, Pete made more sense than any fairy tale humans made up to feel better about not being able to see what was waiting out there in the dark beyond the campfire.

The miniature earthquake trailed off, and Jack watched the door, which had come loose and hung crookedly off its hinges. Blood rushed through his ears, but after a moment the door fell and drowned it out with a *clang*, narrowly missing the toes of his boots.

Pete supported herself against the wall, her thin arm shaking. "Did you get it?" she asked. Her voice was hoarse from screaming, and she was as pale as a corpse, but she straightened up and swiped the dust off her cheeks, leaving dark runnels from her sweat and tears.

Jack pulled the box from his coat. "Got it," he said. "Are you . . ."

Pete waved her hands. "Later. They must have felt that from their head to their arse—we have to go. Now."

Jack didn't say anything, but he did reach out and shoulder her weight, even though his leg twinged like he'd taken to it with a cattle prod. "You know the way back?" he said.

Pete nodded. Her hair was lank with sweat, but her breathing had calmed down and she was no longer emanating magic like a loose high-tension cable, snapping sparks at anyone unfortunate enough to get close.

"Wait," she said as they started to move. "Check the box. Make sure Belial's not fucking with us."

Jack pulled out the box with his free hand and flipped the latch, his stomach doing a somersault. It could so easily be empty. Then he'd be right back where he was when the whole mess started.

The blade sat on a nest of black straw, a film of dried blood still resting in the groove. The broken edge shimmered as Jack tilted the box for Pete to see. "Looks like you could stab someone with it," he said.

Pete nodded. "Good. I've got someone in mind."

CHAPTER 31

Jack had half expected Belial to be gone when they reached the main vault doors, but the demon was leaning against the doors, examining his nails. The only sign he'd even been a part of the break-in was the trickle of blood staining the cuff of his shirt.

"You two don't know the meaning of the word *subtle*, do you?" he drawled when they limped into sight. "Discretion is a foreign fucking country."

"Shut up," Jack said, giving Belial a glare that he hoped would make the demon's head explode in a puff of smoke. "Just shut up and get us out of here."

Belial twitched at his tie and his cuffs, making sure his tie pin was straightened just so.

"Hey!" Jack shouted, loud enough to rattle his own eardrums. "You do realize that when the Princes get down here, they're going to find you as well?"

Belial rolled his eyes upward, tapping one finger against his teeth. "Give me the blade, and I'll see what I can do."

Jack narrowed his eyes. "I knew it. I knew you had some other angle."

Belial shrugged. "I said I'd help you get the blade. I didn't mention anything about free rides back to London."

"What do you think you're going to do with the blade?" Pete spoke up. She still clung to Jack, one hand on his ribs inside his coat, one around his waist. He tightened his grip on her in response, trying to signal in a small way that somehow, this would be all right.

"Oh, I thought I'd donate it to the British Museum and take a nice little break on my taxes while simultaneously swelling with generosity toward my fellow man," Belial said. "I'm going to kill Legion, you little twit. What do you think?"

"You really think the Princes will welcome you back with open arms if you're the one to off him?" Jack said.

Belial curled his lip at Jack. "Let me think about this: yes. Yes, I do. I wager they'll be so grateful, in fact, that when this is all over there will only be one Prince of Hell. Who will be me, in case that was too cryptic for your small mammal brain."

"You're an idiot," Jack said. "But fine, here." He passed over the box, despite Pete's murmur of protest. "Now that I've bought and paid for it, I *do* want my ride back to London."

Belial gave him a wide grin as he stuck the box in the inside pocket of his suit coat. "Anything for a satisfied customer."

CHAPTER 32

They emerged into London near the pavilion opposite the Victoria and Albert Museum. Pete sat down
heavily on the carved steps, and Jack's body decided
that sounded like a wonderful idea and followed
suit. He didn't fight it.

Belial took the box from his jacket and used it to
give Jack a salute. "I do like you, Jack. Much as I
like anything made of meat. I'll be in touch. Knowing a Prince is going to be a good thing in the long
run. You'll see."

He turned and walked away into the shadows,
and Pete nudged Jack. "You're not even going to try
to hex him?"

"First off, any hex I can sling is going to bounce
right off that beast's scaly hide," Jack said. He could
barely keep his eyes open, and his leg had started
hurting in earnest, each beat of his heart sending a
fresh throb of molten fire through his thigh. "Second,
I'm too tired to go after him for a petty squabble."

Pete snorted. "I almost died, and he stole the
blade from you. That's not exactly petty."

"I'm truly sorry for what you had to do," Jack
said. "But as to the second part . . ." He reached into
Pete's jacket and drew forth the blade, which looked

smaller and older, less threatening, out in the fading sunlight of the real world.

Pete's mouth opened, then shut again, and she managed a grin. "Dammit, Jack Winter. Just when I think I've seen all your tricks."

"That one's nothing special," Jack said. "Seth and I practiced lift and drop about ten thousand times when he took me in. Bought me dinner and a roof over my head more than a few times when things were thin."

"And now it's got us a way to kill Legion," Pete said. She looked down at his leg and grimaced. "After we get that looked at, of course."

"I'm fine," Jack said, although the pain in his leg insisted differently. "Just run by a pharmacy with me and grab some first aid, then we need to find out where Legion is and how we can get to him."

Pete stood. She was already steadier, and her color was coming back. Jack was glad that at least one of them didn't look like they were two steps from kicking off. "I don't believe you," she said.

Jack clambered up and tried to reply, but his leg sent such an electric charge through him that his chest seized up and his words came out as a moan.

He tried to tell Pete he was fine, some disinfectant and a pressure bandage would make him right as rain, but that blackness came up again, the one that had nothing to do with his sight, and he passed out before he hit the pavement.

CHAPTER 33

Usually when his sight was so bothered, Jack dreamed—vivid, terrible dreams informed by the psychic residue of whatever space he was in when he blacked out. This time, though, he had a real dream. Seth had taken him to his summer cottage when he was fifteen, the night before his birthday.

"Thought we might spend the weekend here, and I could show you a few hexes," he said. "You don't need to spend your birthday listening to Wallace yell at the news channel."

It was August, and the green lay over the countryside like a fog, making everything appear smeared and unreal, bringing the heavy scent of cut grass and sheep manure, tinged with the nearby ocean spray, to his nostrils.

Seth looked at Jack sideways while he regarded the mage's small tumbledown cottage. "You ever had a proper birthday before?"

"Once," he said. "When I was five, me mum got a clown."

"Christ, that's horrible," Seth said. "Had I known, I would have bought you a few sessions on the couch as a gift for this particular anniversary."

Jack watched as one crow, and then another,

landed on the ridgeline of Seth's thatched roof. "I think I'm way beyond that," he said, getting out of the car. Seth did as well, also watching the birds. Nothing escaped his gaze. He took the cigarette from behind his ear, making it disappear in his right hand and reappear in his left.

Jack remembered thinking that was odd. Seth only did his sleight of hand tricks when he was nervous.

"Listen, kiddo," he said. "You're going to hear this sooner or later, so I'm just going to tell you. One day soon, you're going to hear some things about yourself that are going to be hard to take. I don't want you to get upset, though. I want you to know how I saw you when we met, and know that won't change."

Jack watched another crow join the two staring at him. They seemed awfully tame, but he'd spent his entire life in cities, surrounded by nothing but pigeons. What did he know about wild birds?

Seth thumped the top of the car. "You listening to me, boyo?"

"Yeah, yeah," Jack said. He could hear the sea roaring at the foot of the cliffs beyond Seth's front yard. It was the only sound aside from their voices. He'd never been anywhere so quiet.

"You're a good lad," Seth said. "Whatever happens, don't you go and forget that."

The crows took flight, screaming, and Seth didn't move until they were out of sight, black dots on the gray sky that eventually faded away into nothing.

The light of the sky turned into the bare bulb of a

hanging lamp glowering down at him, and Jack squinted into it. "If this is the afterlife, the ambience is shit," he said to whomever might be listening.

Pete's face slid into his vision, slightly blurred at the edges. Jack took inventory of his parts and felt slow and dopey, the warm caress of opiates warming his bloodstream.

"I'm sorry," Pete said. Her voice was full of vibration, and it came to him as if through a pane of wavy glass, distorted and high. "You were screaming. They had to give you a shot."

"They?" Jack said. His throat was sore when he talked, and he could barely make out his own words.

"Relax, Mr. Winter," said Morwenna Morgenstern, coming to stand next to Pete. "You're in good hands."

"Fuck me," Jack groaned at the sight of her. "Pete, what'd you do?"

"Called some people who could help," she said. "Now, relax. They didn't undress you or anything. They're just giving us a safe place to fix you up."

Even in his excessively drugged state, Jack picked up the signal. The Prometheans hadn't searched him. They didn't have the blade.

That helped the screaming inside his mind quiet down a bit. To come this far, only to be foiled by the Dudley Do-Rights of the Black, would sting more than any betrayal from Belial.

Which made him remember that he owed Belial a kick in the balls, and he tried to sit up and get off the table.

"Whoa, whoa," Morwenna said, shoving him back

down. "You're in no condition to go anywhere, Mr. Winter." She turned away, out of Jack's line of sight. "Victor, we need another shot over here! Now."

"Bad girl," Jack said, a giggle bubbling out of him unbidden. "You know I was a drug addict?"

"Believe me, Mr. Winter," Morwenna sighed. "I know more about you than I ever wanted to."

"You lie," Jack said, giving her a wide smile. "You know you can't get enough of me, luv. Uptight broads like you always fall for the dark, dangerous types. . . ."

"All *right,*" Pete said as Morwenna's shambling horror, Victor, came into view with a syringe. "If you don't knock him out with that I'm going to do it with my foot."

"Calm down," Morwenna said. "He'll be dreaming, Ms. Caldecott. Don't you worry."

CHAPTER 34

Seth had tried to keep him calm before the initiation, but Jack remembered feeling his heart slam like it hadn't since he'd come to Ireland and stopped sleeping rough and looking over his shoulder. He'd been in plenty of bad situations since, thanks either to his own penchant for finding trouble or because of messes that Seth brought upon them.

Seth never fled, though. He was always there, always had a plan and a backup to the plan. When Jack fucked up, Seth got him out of it. When Jack couldn't con or fight his way out of a bad situation with the numerous enemies the *Fiach Dubh* counted, Seth always had a bright idea.

But now Seth stood in the door of the caravan, staring out into the field, toward the orange glow of the torchlight.

"Just remember, Jack . . . whatever happens . . ."

"I promise not to make you look bad," Jack said. "I've got it, all right? It's an initiation, not a party. I will conduct myself with the utmost dignity."

"Please." Seth conjured a lit cigarette and dragged on it. "You wouldn't know dignity if it jumped up and bit you on the testes, boy." He passed the cigarette, and Jack took a pull, blue smoke filling the small interior of the caravan.

"I promise," he said, softer. "I know I fuck up a lot, Seth, but I won't tonight. I get that this is important to you."

He was eighteen, and he could join Seth as a full member of the crow brothers, privy to their archives, their secrets, and the bad blood with most other mage sects.

If Jack was honest, he couldn't fucking wait. He could sling hexes and do simple spells and summonings, but this was the big show. He could learn real showstoppers, have real power. Maybe even find a way to keep his sight from hitting him upside the skull whenever he got within spitting distance of a ghost.

"Not me," Seth said, gesturing Jack out of the caravan, where a knot of other crow brothers waited. "You, Jack. This night is all about you."

The brothers stripped him to the waist and painted his torso with blue woad, the symbols signifying that he belonged to the *Fiach Dubh,* skin and bone and everything in between. Seth had told him to expect a lot of bullshit druid pomp and ceremony, but he'd also warned him that things went wrong all the time at these things. The patron goddess of the crow brothers was mercurial, to say the least, and if she took a dislike to an initiate, they were hamburger.

The brothers led him to the stone circle, into the ring of torchlight. Jack lay on the stone slab in the center, trying to ignore the blood grooves and the stained earth around the altar.

He turned his head and caught sight of Seth, standing outside the circle, his white shirt gleaming in the low light.

The crow bothers circled him. Their robes were cascades of gleaming black feathers, their hoods crowned with silver beaks that hung low, shadowing their brows.

The smoke from the torches was pungent, and that was how he explained it later. A bad trip, brought on by nerves and fear and too much hallucinogenic smoke.

Because behind the crow brothers, a figure moved. Golden-eyed, mouth dripping blood. The Morrigan approached him, and Jack remembered from Seth's pep talk that she'd either accept or reject him, and that rejection was very fucking bad indeed.

He wasn't sure how it worked—if she'd drink his blood, look into his head, or ask him the airspeed velocity of an unladen swallow.

What she did, though, he couldn't have planned for. She came to him, climbed the altar, and stood over him. Then she reached into his chest with her talons, his blood spurting far enough to hit some of the crow brothers, putting her hand around his heart. Putting her mark on him, on the inside where he would always feel it, even if no one could see.

She marked him as her own, and when he woke it was daylight and everyone except Seth had gone. He sat at the base of a stone pillar, surrounded by fagends and the ash from the torches, shaking, his eyes sunken and his fingers twitching.

He stood up and came over to Jack, putting a

hand on Jack's shoulder as he examined his bare chest. The blue paint was smeared, but his body was intact, heart beating, ribs where they should be. There was no sign of anything he'd experienced in the night.

"What the fuck was that?" he asked Seth, and the mage shook his head.

"You belong to her now, Jack," he said, lighting the last cigarette in his pack. He dragged hard on it, the cherry flaring, and he didn't offer to share. "I guess in a way I should have known—with that talent of yours, and all that power you can pull on command, you were never long for this world."

"Seth . . . ," Jack started, trying to stand. It didn't work out so well, and he slid to the muddy ground.

"I'm sorry," Seth said, backing away from him. "But you're the crow-mage now. You've gone beyond my pay grade. I stay away from the Hag, and she stays away from me."

"Seth, please . . ." It hurt to talk. Jack felt as if his limbs were no longer his own, as if there had been some fundamental violation of his body and mind, something he couldn't remember in detail but felt all the same, right down to his bones.

"I'm sorry," Seth said again, with more urgency. "But I can never see you again."

He walked away, Jack would always remember, without any hesitation. Straight back to his car, never once turning back. And he did see Seth again, after his suicide attempt, after he understood what being the crow-mage meant. Saw him more than once, but it was never the same. The Seth McBride he trusted, thought of as a brother, walked away from him that morning, and Jack had never met him again.

That Seth had walked away and left Jack there, broken and alone.

When he woke again it was gentler, floating back down into his mind on the puffy cloud of copious amounts of prescription drugs.

"Whatever they're giving me, see if you can get some to go," he said when he saw Pete sitting next to his bed. "Be great to bring out at parties."

"It's just some Percocet to tide you over," Pete said. She pointed at his leg, which was swathed in tight, bloody bandages. More lay in a trash bin near the foot of his bed. "Morwenna says you're lucky. Your leg looked like the zombie apocalypse after their doctor got the glass out."

"Doctor? More like some fly-by-night veterinarian, based on how these stitches feel," he said. The wound felt hot and jagged, and he hoped that Morwenna's pet surgeon had slipped in some antibiotics along with the good drugs.

"Whoever he was, you're alive," Pete said. "And because I asked so nicely, I got Morwenna to send someone to check on Legion without us having to lift a finger."

Jack groaned. "What did we end up owing her for that, I wonder?"

Pete offered him a paper cup of water. "I'm thinking that's one of those bridges we cross after we avert the apocalypse, myself."

Jack swallowed the water in one go. The inside of

his mouth felt like a gravel pit, and his throat was swollen and hot. Going through surgery was somewhere on his list of fun Friday nights after getting hit by a taxi and listening to chamber music while sober.

"Thank you," he rasped to Pete. "Even if you did give these posh twats something to hold over our heads."

Pete moved herself to lie down next to him, putting her hand on his unbandaged leg. "At least you still have a head for them to threaten, thanks to me. You owe me big time, Mr. Winter."

Jack grinned at her. "As soon as I'm mobile again, I'll express me gratitude in numerous anatomically improbable ways, don't you worry."

Pete gave him a jab. "You're higher than a pigeon with a jetpack, so I'll let that one slide."

Jack pouted at her. "You're horribly mean to me."

Pete nodded, nestling her head into his shoulder. "Yeah. And that's why you love me."

Jack was going to suggest they express their love with a well-deserved lie-in when the door opened and Morwenna strode into the room. "Am I interrupting?" she asked, with an expression that any bitter old nun would have killed to mimic.

Pete sat up, keeping her hand on Jack. "You found something," she said. "At that monastery."

Morwenna exhaled, tapping her fingers against her leg. "How much do you know about this, really? And I warn you, don't play dumb with me. I'm going to be very upset."

"You know that scary story you tossed us out for

telling you?" Jack said. "Well, that's where the scary story is currently holed up, with half the kingdom of Faerie as backup, plus enough elemental demons to turn every person in London into their very own beans on toast."

"It's considerably more serious than a gathering of ragtag interests," Morwenna said. "Our sources say the Faerie king himself is there, and that this demon has Fenris guarding him along with a host of lesser elementals. Egregors are patrolling the perimeter and the monastery itself is hemmed in by Fae assassins."

Pete let out a long breath. "Shit."

"I don't know what your ulterior motive is," Morwenna said. "But going near that place is suicide." She went to the door and opened it again. "I'm not going to tell you your business, but I assume you do want to stay alive. If you have some idiotic notion about going out like a superhero . . . please don't drag the Prometheans into it."

"I can hardly gad about in a cape like this, can I?" Jack snapped. Morwenna gave a delicate sniff.

"You have until sunset to get yourself together and leave," she said. "The Prometheans don't need the kind of trouble you're bringing."

Pete gave Morwenna a poisonous glare. "The Prometheans are going to be sipping tea on the ashes of the world if they keep this up," she said.

"We have endured for a thousand years," Morwenna said. "The prophecies have us existing for many more."

Jack managed to sit up, feeling around for his

coat and his pants on the floor next to the bed. The weight of the blade was still in his pocket, and he breathed a sigh of relief. "The Prometheans are going to vanish under what's coming just like me and Pete," he said. "The difference is, we're willing to adapt enough to fight back."

He struggled into his pants. Thanks to the drugs, his leg only twinged a bit. "I think you and I are done, Morwenna. The Prometheans no longer have any claim over Margaret, or us. I wouldn't be eager to meet us again if I were you."

"Just goes to show," Morwenna said. "You do someone of your class a favor, and they repay you with insults."

"You can send us a fruit basket after we kill Legion for you," Pete said. "Then you can consider us even."

CHAPTER 35

Jack sat down on a small stone bench outside the gates of the Prometheans' country estate, watching the empty road. "What exactly are we going to do now?"

Pete massaged her forehead. "I have no idea. I just didn't want that bitch to think she got the upper hand."

"She's right, though," Jack said. "Much as I thought those words would never march across my lips. If Legion has a full complement of elementals and Fae, he'll liquidate us the minute we land within a mile of that monastery."

Pete pulled out her mobile and dialed up a local cab company. "So what do we do?" she asked while they had her on hold. "I mean, aside from getting hold of a teleport spell. Do those even exist?"

"I met somebody once, in Amsterdam, who said he did it," Jack said. "Turns out he just ate too many hash brownies and thought he'd walked through a wall. Tried to do it in front of me and knocked himself out."

"Maybe we could summon him," Pete said. Jack felt the ache in his bones start up again at the very thought.

"Do we really want to summon Legion? He's going to be one angry little cult leader when we zap him out of his cozy compound and into our sitting room."

"When you want to take down a target you have to separate him from the herd and run him to ground," Pete said. "And I think that's our best hope." She frowned at Jack. "If you're up for it."

"I could not be less up for anything," he said. "But sure, why the fuck not? The worst he can do is kill us and burn London to the ground, and wait, that's already happening."

He thought about watching Seth vanish in his dream, and rubbed a hand over his face to dispel the cobwebs from his brain. If he was going to work a summoning on this scale, he needed to be sharp.

Pete gave the cab their address and shut her mobile. "Good," she said. "Tell me what you need from me so we can nail this bastard to the wall."

CHAPTER 36

Jack put the word out to Mosswood for the materials he couldn't pick up from his own supplies, and he and Pete stopped at the flat just long enough to grab his kit. The clock was running on when Belial would figure out that Jack hadn't given over the blade, and the last thing he wanted was not one slagged-off demon but a pair, both gunning for him.

"We need a place to do this other than a flat in the middle of a block with a thousand people," he said to Pete as they packed up a pair of canvas bags.

Pete pulled out her mobile. "I can probably find a place. I need to check on Margaret and Lily anyway."

She walked away while she called Ollie Heath, and Jack took a moment to make sure he hadn't forgotten anything he couldn't live without.

The flat wasn't much, but it had been home ever since he'd come back from Ireland. Sure, he'd gotten the deed by convincing a senile sorcerer to sign it over, the walls were stained, the windows let in every draft that blew by, and the furniture was mostly picked off various surburban curbs in early mornings before the trash brigade came along, but it was as much a home as any place he'd ever slept.

Pete was here, Lily was here. Most of the good memories of his life wound back to here.

He sat down on their rickety sofa for a moment and looked out the sooty windows, over the rooftop of the place next door. The sky was already fading into dawn. Putting together supplies for the summoning had taken most of the night, but he didn't feel tired anymore. He found the last of the Percocet that Pete had cadged from Morwenna and dry-swallowed the pills. Just a few more hours, and one way or the other, this would all be over.

He wasn't sure if the thought was a comfort or a terror.

Pete came in from the kitchen, holding out her mobile so he could see mapped directions to an address. "Ollie says this place is still in limbo with the city government," she said. "We shouldn't have any company, and all that's around it are warehouses and self-storage setups. Nobody in range if something happens."

Jack nodded. "Good enough," he said. Pete hefted her bag.

"Ready?"

"No, but that's never stopped me before," Jack told her. Pete went out, and he looked around the flat one more time, acutely aware that it might be the last time he did so, then he shut the door behind him.

CHAPTER 37

The warehouse Ollie sent them to had been used as an illegal casino by the Russians, and Jack felt a heavy stone settle in his guts as the Mini crunched over gravel to the wide oversized doors.

"Of course," he murmured, looking up at the broken-down four-story building.

"Something wrong?" Pete said. "Ollie said attorneys and the city are still fighting over this place after the seizure, and they're too cheap to send a detail around to check on it. Quiet, out of the way . . . I thought it was what you wanted."

"No," Jack said, climbing out of the Mini and trying to work the stiffness out of his wounded leg. "It's perfect."

The warehouse looked just as it had in his vision, except that the sun wasn't yet up. It was close, though. Close to the time when Legion would stride to the roof and bring everything crashing down.

Jack started for the door. "We need to move," he said to Pete. "Legion's going to make his play soon."

Pete didn't question him. She pulled the ragged yellow Met tape off the door. The padlock had already been clipped by hoodies looking for a place to loot or shoot up in, and the interior loading bay blossomed with graffiti.

Jack hopped onto the platform and surveyed the vast interior space. The floor was rough boards covered in decades of dust, and light beamed in from lacy holes in glass skylights. A few crates and boxes had tumbled on their sides, spilling their straw innards, but the contents were gone. In the far corner of the warehouse, a pair of dirty mattresses and a craps table turned on its side didn't bear closer inspection.

Jack set down his kit bag and turned in a slow circle. Plenty of iron to keep out interference, and plenty of space to keep himself at arm's length from Legion.

"All right," he said to Pete. "Let's get started."

They chalked a wide circle, at least twenty feet in circumference. He needed to be able to move in any direction without breaking the lines. Jack sprinkled salt as an extra bit of electric fence, then set all the barrier sigils he knew around the edges. He held off sketching the symbol Belial had planted in his mind. No need to start the party early.

"None of these barriers will do fuck-all, likely" he told Pete. "So stay sharp. Won't be easy to contain him."

Pete sat on her heels, brushing chalk dust from her palms. "It's no fun if it's easy. We need anything else?"

Jack looked back toward the double doors. "Just some herbs and one particular extra I asked Mosswood to bring."

Pete stepped carefully, so as not to disturb the chalk and salt line, and went to her own bag, taking out her collapsible metal baton. "Brought my own extras," she said. "Just in case Legion decides he wants to make this physical."

Jack thought about his tenderized state he'd seen in his vision. "I think that's a distinct possibility."

He jumped when the booming knock sounded at the door, his heart giving a painful thud. He was doing all right hiding his nerves from Pete, but he was doing a shit job of making himself believe he didn't have them.

"I hope you know you've gone insane," Mosswood said when Jack peered through the gap in the door.

"You would be far from the first to think that," Jack said. Mosswood passed over a canvas-wrapped package, and then a glass vial carefully cushioned inside a small box.

"I know what these herbs are for, so I'm going to skip the foreplay of *You don't know what you're doing* and *Are you bloody stupid*? and just say that I hope I'm wrong. I hope you come out of this in one piece."

Jack felt the electric shock of his fear and his own gnawing doubts subside a bit. "Thanks, Ian. That actually means something coming from you."

"I'll say goodbye," Mosswood said. "And though it's probably futile, I'll hope it's not for the last time."

"Oh, come on," Jack said, giving Mosswood's tweed-clad shoulder a slap. "How many times have you seen the world end, Ian? This is nothing."

"Even so," Mosswood said sadly. "I think my

time here among mortals is at an end. I will be going home, Jack. If we pass one another in the mist some day, I probably won't know your name. Fae-lands have that effect." He pressed his hand briefly on Jack's shoulder. "We were good friends, but that is past, and as Hartley says, 'The past is a foreign country.'"

Jack felt a sharp, sudden sensation just behind his eyes. He would be sad when the Green Man was gone, he realized. Sad in the way you're sad to lose a favorite teacher or a really top-notch bartender. "Well, they also say 'Don't know what you've got till it's gone,'" he said, pushing down the prickle. Moping around was a luxury he didn't have right now. Later, he could think about exactly what Legion had taken from him—his fellow crow brothers, Mosswood, his own sense of security—but now he had to kick the bastard's arse.

"Very poetic," Mosswood said. "Dostoyevsky?"

"Cinderella," Jack said. "The band, not the princess. You take care of yourself, Mosswood."

The Green Man nodded and backed away, and Jack shut the door. He gave Pete the herbs to start burning, and he turned the vial in his hands.

"Do I want to know?" Pete said.

"It's blood," Jack said. "I somehow doubt Legion has a handy little call button like Hrathetoth, and blood is the most powerful conductor there is for ritual."

Pete wrinkled her nose at the vial. "Please tell me that's not human."

"No," Jack said. "Demon." He uncorked the vial

and poured the sticky black substance into the metal bowl he kept in his kit, placing it at the center of the circle. "And before you ask, I don't know where Mosswood got it, and I know enough not to pry."

"You know, there was a time when this sort of thing would make my skin crawl," Pete said. "How things change, eh?"

Jack rolled his shoulders and his neck. It had been a while since he'd been in a stand-up fight, but he had no illusion that this summoning would be anything but. No room to be clever, no way to cut and run. Either he or Legion wouldn't be leaving this circle.

He was going to prove his vision wrong, or he was going to die trying.

Looking over at Pete, standing just outside the circle, stun gun at the ready, he gave her a smile. "It'll be all right," he said.

"Liar," she said.

Jack turned back into the center of the circle, pulling on the deep well of the Black that lay beneath London. It rushed up at him faster than it ever had before. The barriers were thin everywhere, thin as wet paper, and the tide of magic rushed up and covered him. Witchfire blossomed not just from his body but all around the warehouse, sparking off every surface and racing between the rafters like lightning jumping from cloud to cloud.

He touched the Morrigan's blade once more for reassurance, and then started talking.

Words didn't matter so much as intent with magic. Keep it simple, Seth always said. Simple is best.

That way there's no mistaking your intention to perform some feat of power.

Jack usually came up with a little phrase, something designed to tickle the frequencies of whatever or whoever he was trying to cast or summon for or against. This time, though, he only had one intent. Only needed one word.

"Legion," he whispered. "Legion, Legion, Legion . . ."

He took all the power, all of the witchfire running off him like a flood, and he dipped deep down into the well, pushing the power into the circle, through the demon's blood. That was his link to Legion. That was what made him strong.

"Legion," he said. "Come here, you bastard. You and I haven't finished yet."

When he called up demons, there was always a moment of contact, a sense of presence when you'd latched on to the other side of the equation, wherever the demon happened to be. Demons weren't human, and they felt a certain way. He could almost see their outlines wrought on the very fabric of the Black, their own personal magic signature that granted them enough power to flatten any human mage, but also made it possible to pull their body and magic into summoning circles.

But with Legion, there was nothing.

No spark, no sense of tapping into the demon's feed. The Black was on, roaring through Jack like a turbine pushing on full power, screaming through the summoning circle so that the herbs withered into ash and the blood in the metal bowl started to boil before the vessel melted into slag and sent liquid metal and demon blood running across the wood floor.

"What's wrong?" Pete shouted, and Jack realized he was pulling down so much power he'd kicked up his very own whirlwind, the witchfire racing in a cyclone around the warehouse, whipping Pete's hair and Jack's coat but leaving the salt and the summoning tools untouched.

"I don't know!" he shouted back. "I've never had this happen with a demon before!"

"That's because I'm not a demon," Legion said. His shadow loomed up, his body filling Jack's vision, and then Jack was flying through the air, feeling wind and grit on his face before he smashed through the crates and hit a steel girder holding up the wall behind it.

Jack's field of vision turned into a flashbulb, and Pete screamed, but Legion ignored her and started for Jack, crossing the circle with no more trouble than a human would have stepping off a curb.

Jack felt a hammer blow land on his chest when he tried to breathe. One of his lungs was done for, and he'd felt ribs give way when he'd hit the girder.

"Well *done,* Jack," Legion said. "Made some rookie mistakes, though."

Breathing was agony, a thousand razor blades scraping against his breastbone, but Jack managed to get out a sentence. "Like . . . what?"

Legion crouched down and knotted his fingers in Jack's hair, tugging Jack to face him with a sharp sting to his scalp. "If you wanted to summon me, you should have used human blood."

Jack felt as if he'd been hit all over again. He didn't bother trying to talk anymore. His face was clearly telling a story, because Legion started to laugh. "That a bit hard to swallow? Imagine how I must have felt."

He lifted Jack up by the hair until Jack stood. Legion pressed him against the wall, one hand pressing down on Jack's collarbone until it gave a crack.

Jack found the air for sound, then, and he screamed until it echoed off the rafters. His entire world was red, and black started to spiral up as Legion kept laughing. "Imagine my life in Azrael's torture vault, all that magic, that new wild magic he plucked out of this miserable mud-pit you call a world, and nothing to use it on. Imagine knowing that you are not a demon, that you are new. That you are an abomination. That things like the Morrigan wished to enslave me. Imagine how lonely that was."

He spun abruptly, dropping Jack to the ground again, and Jack curled around himself just like he was seven fucking years old again and trying to defend himself against his mum's boyfriends' boots and fists.

"I'll thank you not to insult my intelligence by trying to sneak up on me, Ms. Caldecott," Legion snarled.

Pete stood a few feet from Legion, brandishing her baton. "Leave him be."

"I don't want to harm him." Legion spread his hands. "I asked your husband to join me, Petunia. I don't want to harm anyone. I just want them all to have the chance I never did. Equal footing. No more demons above mages, mages above humans . . ."

"You know what?" Pete said. "I could not give less of a shit what you want, mate."

She swung and Legion held up his hands, baton glancing off his forearm. They bit into his flesh. He laughed and laughed until it was all Jack could hear beyond the erratic thumping of his own heartbeat.

Legion jerked the baton from Pete's grip, and then advanced on her. Pete backpedaled, tried to get out of his way, but Legion had speed that no human could match and he grabbed her, tossing her like she weighed less than a suitcase. She landed at the edge of the loading dock and slid over the edge, disappearing from Jack's view.

Legion turned back to Jack. "Alone at last."

Jack tried to get up, but any movement started the agony afresh. He didn't even care that Legion was in front of him anymore. He just had to make sure that Pete was all right.

"Relax, Jack," Legion said. "I didn't kill her. I want her to see this, just like you."

He grabbed Jack by his ankle and dragged him to a wire-frame lift, tugging the door shut after them. The ride to the rooftop was an agony of bumps and jostles that told Jack he had at least three broken bones and some truly spectacular internal injuries that were probably hemorrhaging even as Legion hummed, stopping the lift at the roof and dragging Jack outside.

Gravel scraped at his cuts, but he was done fighting. His body wouldn't sustain any more punishment.

He was at Legion's mercy.

Legion reached into the pocket of his coat and

brought out the small orb Jack had seen in his vision. "Azrael made so many things," Legion sighed. "I'd like to think I was the best, but this . . . this truly is it."

He stepped up onto the low ledge at the edge of the roof. The sun was up, and London turned gold under the rising rays. Legion was a black smudge, a shadow against the light that made Jack screw up his eyes. He hoped the demon would keep talking until he could stop feeling like he was going to vomit or pass out, and think of something actually useful.

"This made it all worthwhile," Legion said softly. "I was in the dark for so long, but this let me go everywhere. I saw so many things. I saw what I had to do to lead me to this moment. Weaken every foundation just enough that the whole thing would topple."

He looked back at Jack, a smile curving his lips. "What's that little rhyme? Ashes, ashes?"

"We all fall down," Jack croaked.

Legion nodded. "That's it. I have to say, I'm glad you're taking this so well, Jack. Humans have a survival instinct that borders on the idiotic. They fight against the inevitable even when everything has already reached terminal velocity."

"I'm not fighting," Jack said.

"Rejoicing, then?" Legion said. "Brave new world, Jack. You're going to be a part of history, one of the few humans there when all of the worlds became one."

Jack shook his head. His vision swam in concert with the movements. "Distracting you," he managed. Legion's smarmy grin smoothed out into the flat nonexpression Jack had come to recognize as the default of the deeply psychopathic.

"What?"

Jack flipped Legion the bird with his good hand. "*Sciotha.*" Usually a leg-locker was enough to knock someone down, get their attention, and take the wind out of their sails. The Black was so vast and so tumultuous here, though, that the hex slammed into Legion with the force of a lorry, knocking him off the edge of the roof. Jack heard the crunch of his body hitting the gravel.

"Fuck," he muttered, and tried unsuccessfully to stand. The gravel was too slippery, and he was too beaten to do much more than flip himself into a sitting position. The wound on his leg had started to bleed again, and he was so lightheaded from the pain that every sound and sensation felt like being bounced around the inside of a giant tin can.

He tried to put his scrambled thoughts in some kind of coherent order. Legion's ramblings aside, he needed to find Pete, make sure she was all right, and get them the fuck away from here. He'd failed in what he'd intended to do, but Legion had been right about one thing—he planned to survive.

The plan seemed like a good one until a form crashed onto the roof, and Legion strode toward him, brushing brick dust and debris off his clothes. "I did *not* fucking appreciate that," he snarled, grabbing a fistful of Jack's shirt and pulling their faces so close he could see almost nothing but Legion's eyes.

"You know," Legion breathed, "I can go anywhere with Azrael's machine. Time, space, future, past . . . all of it is open to me. I think when I'm done ripping down these walls I'll go back to your sad little childhood home and kill your mother. And then I'll kill you, you little shit, but not before you watch your guts fall out into your hands."

Jack stared at him. He'd never seen so much rage contained in a living body, never felt such malevolent black magic rolling off a creature. Human, demon, or whatever Legion claimed he was, he was the worst thing Jack had ever laid eyes on.

"You're full of shit," he rasped. Legion blinked, and then bared his teeth.

"Are you stupid, or do you just have a death wish?"

"I'm going to die either way," Jack said. He fumbled inside his coat with his good arm, hoping that Legion was too enraged to notice anything but his squirming. "I might as well say what I think—all that nonsense about tearing down walls and balance is crap. You're just kicking over your toys because you're mad at Daddy. Isn't that right?"

Legion snarled, a bone-deep sound that was definitely animal rather than human. "I am going to enjoy holding your heart in my hand, Jack," he said.

Jack whipped the Morrigan's blade up and into Legion's chest, aiming under the breastbone and for his vital organs. "Promises, promises," he said.

Legion grabbed his wrist in a crushing grip, looking down at the blade in Jack's fist. "You sneaky little bastard," he said. "I hope you're proud of yourself." He ripped the blade from Jack's grasp and shoved Jack down, onto his back so that he could see the sky. Dark thunderheads rolled across the skyline of London, and Legion whipped his head around as the sound of a million wings beat the air louder than thunder.

"Cavalry's here," Jack said. Talking was getting difficult again. Legion looked back at him, his grin wider than ever.

"All that you've accomplished, Jack, is that now I get to kill you twice." Legion raised the blade and with an economical movement drove it straight down into Jack's chest, planting it to the hilt.

He stood, looking up at the sky, and shook out his coat. "Gotta run. Armageddon time."

Legion hopped over the lip of the roof and disappeared. Jack couldn't move, couldn't even blink, could only stare at the sky as the darkness rolled in.

CHAPTER 38

The thing that surprised Jack most about dying again was the cold. All his pain vanished and he felt nothing. His body was just an object, abused and discarded, and he was behind the eyes but not a resident.

Ravens and crows soared overhead, so numerous that they blacked out the sun, and behind them Jack felt a pulse that vibrated through the Black all the way up to the sky. Not a ripple or a tear, like he'd felt when Nergal and Abbadon had tried to break through or open doorways between places that were too large to sustain.

This was a fundamental fracture, something that made him feel as if half of the power that he relied on as part of his talent, part of *him,* had disappeared. A skip in the record, a break in the transmission, a void filled with nothing but static.

The ravens had obscured everything, and Jack's vision was filled with roaring blackness. He couldn't breathe much at all any longer.

He'd thought the end of the line had come before, so it wasn't as if he hadn't expected it. Really, from the moment Belial pulled him in, he'd half expected to end up dead.

Then, as his vision started to swim toward that final blackness, Pete was there. Her expression was frantic, and she grabbed at him, checking his pulse and breath and touching the knife but not pulling it from his chest.

"No, Jack," she said, her face shattering from horror into an agonized sob. "No . . . not this . . ."

"I'm sorry," Jack managed. "I wanted . . ."

Pete shook her head. "Don't talk." She was pulling out her mobile, calling for 999, cursing and throwing the mobile to the ground as the operator squawked that all circuits were busy.

Jack fumbled for her hand, managed to grab at her wrist. "Pete, listen," he said. "I don't have long."

The rush of wings crescendoed and he saw her, standing behind Pete, her raven feathers gleaming blue-black and slick in the sunlight.

Poor Jack. Poor dead Jack, the Morrigan sighed. Pete paid her no attention, and Jack kept his hand on her wrist.

She can't see me, the Morrigan said. *Not this time. I told you that it would be this, Jack. That at last, there would be a day when you could no longer refuse me.*

Pete was crying, holding his hand, tears sliding down her face as she pressed her cheek to his.

"I'm fine with dying," Jack said to the Morrigan. His voice sounded fine again, which told him he'd slipped into that place where he was closer to the Land of the Dead than life. His soul was only tangentially attached to his body. One way or another, he'd belong to the Morrigan soon.

Ah, but dying would accomplish nothing, the Morrigan purred. *If you accept your place at my side, you will have what brought you to death today.*

Jack blinked at her. His vision was no longer clouded, and though his body had shut down, his talent was alive and burning with power as another shudder passed through the Black. Beyond the Morrigan, he saw a plume of smoke rise from the center of London. He was too late. Legion had kicked over the first domino, and there was nothing to reverse it. "Spit it out," he said. "I'm not coming over to you on some vague promise."

Come to me, Jack. The Morrigan held out her clawed hand. *Come to me. Lead my army of the dead, and you will have the prize you most desire. I will feast on Legion's beating heart, and he will no longer exist as anything but a memory.*

She, too, looked back toward the city, and at the vortex of ravens circling overhead. *But you must choose. Now. This world you love so much, where your wife and your child can live on, or you. One of the unshackled dead, drifting for eternity through a ruined universe that is nothing but a memory of life.*

Jack lifted his head. "Swear to me," he said. "Swear to me that Legion will die and I'll go with you willingly. You'll have what you've wanted all these years."

I have wanted you far longer than years, Jack, the Morrigan said. *You were always my child. The living man touched by Death. But yes—join me and Legion's death will be yours, to bring to him in any fashion you desire.*

"And Pete," Jack said, looking back at Pete as she held his body and shook with sobs. "She and Lily and Margaret will be safe?"

The Morrigan nodded, her yellow eyes aglow with anticipation. *She will be watched until her time of death, and taken into my bosom as my most favored citizen.*

Jack thought about Seth walking away from him. The mage had known something he hadn't. Jack could run, but he was always meant to end up right here.

There was no point in fighting it. He belonged to the Morrigan. He had always been a walking dead man, ever since he first saw the Morrigan on the altar twenty years ago. He could pretend things could be different, but Seth couldn't change it. Not even dying and going to Hell could change this.

This was the end, the period on his sentence. And this time, there was no way to pretend he was going to live out the life he'd pretended he could have.

Jack looked up at Pete, reached up with the last of his air to touch her cheek. "It will be all right," he said. "I promise I'll see you again."

Pete choked, but she put her hand over his. "You don't get to go leaving me," she managed, squeezing his fingers as tight as she could. "That's not on, I hope you know."

"Wouldn't dream of it," Jack whispered. He gave her hand a squeeze in return. "You're stronger than I ever was, Pete. Don't change that."

Pete lowered his hand gently to his chest, and put her hand against his cheek. "I love you, Jack Winter."

Jack gave her a smile as the ravens landed all around them, and the Morrigan advanced, and he could see that Pete saw her now, but she raised her chin and refused to show any fear. "I love you," she repeated, looking only at Jack.

He stood and joined the Morrigan, the ravens surrounding them. He looked back at Pete and gave her a nod. "I know, luv."

The ravens surrounded him, the Morrigan's feathers blending with the flock, the darkness sweeping in, and Jack found himself surprised that death didn't feel like coldness, like hotness, like pain, like a release. Death didn't feel like anything. He just felt his connection to Pete sever as the Black spasmed for a third time, and then everything was gone.

CHAPTER 39

The cloud of ravens lifted to reveal that they stood over the Thames, the scrollwork of Blackfriars Bridge dividing the river from the sky.

Jack looked down at himself. His tattoos were gone, his skin unblemished for the first time since he'd gotten ink from a shady friend of one of his bandmates who wanted someone to practice on. His scars were gone, the wound in his leg, and instead of being planted in his chest, the Morrigan's blade rested in his hand.

She looked at him. "I'm a woman of my word."

Her voice didn't rasp and echo. It sounded more like a stone being dropped into a deep well, hollow and inhuman, just as her face and eyes were. The blood still dribbled from her mouth, but Jack only half noticed it.

What he did see, with shocking clarity, were the dead. They stood shoulder to shoulder on the bridge, along the banks of the Thames, the riverfront prom-enades, everywhere that Jack looked, as far as he could see.

And they all looked at him, all stared at him, un-blinking, their silver-black forms fizzing and winking as their spirit energies interfered with the sputtering, fritzing wild magic of the Black.

Jack turned to the Morrigan. "What are they waiting for?"

The Morrigan gestured to Jack. "Their orders."

Jack was going to breathe, try to keep calm, until he realized that his heart didn't beat and his lungs didn't inflate. *Why should they?* he thought. He was dead.

He belonged to the Morrigan now, as her right hand. Her dead army was waiting. Waiting for him to tell them to march forth upon the world, unleash themselves on the living.

Jack scanned the bridge, the river banks. Parts of the city were in flames, sirens screamed, and the living were leaving in droves, abandoning their cars and flooding away from the City center.

"We have to do something," he said to the Morrigan. "The Black is starting to spill over. Things might already be too unstable to stop it."

"Then tell your soldiers," the Morrigan said. "Tell them of the man you wish to deliver unto death."

Jack gripped the broken blade tight in his fist. "Legion," he said. "I want Legion."

For a moment, nothing happened. The dead stared at him, unblinking, and then they began to move. They turned as one and marched north into the heart of the city that Jack had thought of as home for most of his life.

The Morrigan gave Jack a smile, her teeth stained with blood. "You're learning quickly," she said. "I knew I was right to choose you, Jack."

"I'm only doing this to end Legion," Jack said. "I don't care what you think."

"You should," the Morrigan said. "Because after this, you and I are going to be together for a very long time."

She passed her talons down his cheek, and it should have hurt, but Jack felt nothing. "Go," the Morrigan said. "Have your moment of revenge. Plant the blade into the treacherous heart that stole it from me. I wish you well."

Jack followed the dead, who passed straight through walls and buildings, not needing the benefit of streets and pavement as he did. He still had a body as the Morrigan did, but now he was inhuman as her.

London was in chaos. Emergency vehicles clogged the streets, and looting had already started along Oxford Street. Fires raged, people screamed, and the wounded tried to pull themselves to safety.

He saw creatures of the Black—zombies, lycanthropes, lesser things, dark-dwelling things. They ran through the daylight world with impunity, and the people of London panicked. The city had turned itself inside out, and Legion had barely started.

Jack walked faster.

The dead had stopped, arrayed in columns across the plaza in front of Buckingham Palace. The crown of the palace was on fire, and the Territorial Army had set up tanks in front of the gates, soldiers firing on rioters and zombies with equal prejudice if they came too close.

Legion watched the chaos around him with a bemused expression. Even though the entire city was eating itself alive, burning and screaming, spinning out toward the ashes-and-dust future that Jack's talent had shown him, nobody came within a hundred feet of Legion. He stood alone, holding Azrael's device, watching everything with the delight of a small child.

"You really couldn't be more obvious, could you?" Jack said. "Buckingham Palace, really? Is your ego that massive?"

Legion turned on him, face going from serene to poisonous in a split heartbeat. "I killed you."

"Oh, right and proper," Jack assured him. "You put that knife right in the sticking spot, and I died in agony. No need to feel bad on that score."

Legion turned in a slow circle, looking at the dead, then at Jack, and finally down at the device. His shoulders began to shake and Jack sighed. The Joker routine was getting old.

He didn't feel the rage, though, that he'd felt when he was alive. There wasn't any feeling, really, just as there was no air in his lungs. He was devoid of life, and only life brought the sort of rage that had gotten him killed.

"Jack, you still don't get it," Legion sighed. "You never did. I *made* you. Mage kind. My blood is the blood that gave the human race the spark. Azrael saw the wild magic of this world when it was new, and when he saw what sprang forth when he fused that magic into flesh, when he made me, he panicked. He saw his end in my eyes, and in the eyes of my line, of every human mage to come. When I escaped Azrael's vault, I came here. I saw the things that were thrashing in the mud and shit to become human, and I gave them a gift. It nearly ended me, but I knew I had to plant the seed that would grow into the race that toppled the Princes, toppled Hell itself. I waited and I hid among the elementals, and when I finally took Azrael's prize, I went to each of his pressure points and I squeezed. Nergal and Abbadon, and fostering mage-kind, pushing them along. Even making sure that a little council rat from Manchester found a shady Irish book dealer to teach him how his talent could aid my cause."

Jack tilted his head. What he remembered from life said Legion was trying to bait him, to torment him one last time before he ripped the universe apart.

Legion turned the orb in his hands. "I am not the end, Jack. I am life. A new world will come, and it will be better. Just as it was after I came here the first time. You see . . ."

He sputtered as Jack closed the distance between them, knocking the device out of the way and slashing the blade down. The device dropped, but Legion flowed backward.

He was fast, but Jack could see now. He could use his sight the way he had always been meant to—he was dead, and it couldn't harm him or drive him insane. It could always be on, searching for the dead and for the true face of the living. The soul that dwelled within the flesh, the thing that the Morrigan came for when the flesh gave out.

He had never seen a soul before. Demons didn't have them, and by the time a soul became a ghost, it was so corrupted and in so much pain it was unrecognizable.

Legion's soul looked like him, naked and painted with ancient woad, hair slicked with mud, eyes pure black and impossibly large in his face. He was alien, but he was alive.

He laughed, but Jack barely saw Legion's body any more. This was how the Morrigan saw the world, he realized. Saw the ordinary people as pinpoints, and the bright souls of things like Legion as beacons.

Jack wondered, just for a moment, what his own soul had looked like.

Legion snarled, and then screamed, as Jack grabbed him. He felt much stronger than he had in life. All of the aches and twinges he'd acquired had vanished, and he felt better than he had that night when he was eighteen, when he'd first climbed onto the altar with no idea of what lay before him.

"You can't stop me!" Legion howled. "I am this world's reckoning! I do not destroy, but I will create, and there's not a damn thing you can do, crow-mage! You hear me?"

Jack jammed the blade deep into Legion's soul, pinning it to his flesh, and it glowed for a moment before it exploded into ambient magic that ran all around the plaza, hitting off metal, causing people's mobiles to melt and the army's tanks to give off showers of sparks as their electronics blew.

"Second verse, same as the first," Jack said as he pulled the knife out. Legion's soul was gone, destroyed. His body was just an object. "Change the record, mate. Honestly."

Jack threw the blade aside and scrambled for the device as soon as he was sure Legion was dead.

The Black was convulsing, shuddering, and with each pulse more and more magic poured into the daylight world. People were starting to notice him, which in and of itself said just how much magic had already leaked out and taken over a realm that had no defense against it.

It was a radiation leak that was going to contaminate a fuck of a lot of people if he didn't do something. "Help me!" he yelled at the staring bystanders, pointing at the device. "I need that thing if I'm going to stop this!"

A foot came down on the object and crushed it just as Jack had it in his hands. The Morrigan tilted her head, looking down at the shards.

"Azrael thought he could remake the stars," she said. "Hang them in the sky any way he pleased. Legion may have set it to destroy rather than create, but it is the same. It is not something I will allow."

Jack felt as if a thousand-pound weight had dropped on him. All at once, he smelled the smoke again, heard the screams, saw exactly what was happening. What he was too late to stop. Had always been too late to stop.

"You bitch," he ground at the Morrigan. "You knew this would happen."

"Once the Black has fractured, it will proceed, whether we will it or not," the Morrigan said.

"And let me guess." Jack tasted bitter chemical smoke and blood against his teeth from where he'd slammed into Legion. "Now I'll lead your army of the dead, and overtake this broken place that used to be a world."

The Morrigan looked up at the sky. Crows circled above Buckingham Palace, but they were not the sweeping cloud of darkness he'd seen before Legion had killed him.

"No," she said. "This is not Legion's world. This is something new, something that you and I did not foresee."

Jack dropped to his knees. He'd failed. He was dead. London was burning. Pete was alone, and she and Lily were in danger.

"This is not a day of death," the Morrigan said. "It's life, Jack. Legion was correct—this is creation. Ashes are a beginning, you know. What grows out of them is the strongest of all."

Jack didn't lift his head. He was dead. He felt nothing, and he was glad. He had no air, no life, no blood.

Blood.

He tasted blood.

Jack snapped his gaze back to the Morrigan. "You tricked me!" he shouted. She spread her arms, her feather cloak flowing, her blood-coated smile wider than ever.

"I am Death, Jack. I choose my instruments wisely. You were dead, and as my avatar you used your blade as only my avatar could to end Legion's plans to terrorize this new life, this beginning." She came to him, and she lifted him as gently as anyone had ever touched him, her talons on either side of his face. "Life has its day, Jack. I learned that the hard way. You and I have another meeting, a long time from now, when we will spend eternity together."

She pressed her lips to his forehead, leaving a cool imprint of blood and magic. "Go back, Jack. You are alive, and with the living is where you stay."

His own banishment hex, used on more ghosts than he could count, said back to him was like a jolt to the heart. He gasped, fire filling his chest as his lungs sprang back to life.

Spasms threw him onto his back, and his heart sputtered like a defective motor while his nerve endings danced.

When he opened his eyes, the Morrigan had gone and Pete was kneeling over him.

"Fuck," he gasped. "What the fuck are you doing here? How'd you find me?"

"I followed you," Pete said, as if he were a very specific sort of idiot. "You got up and started walking like a zombie, and I followed you here. I saw you kill Legion."

Jack grabbed Pete and pulled her down, kissing her hard enough to bruise their lips. He tasted a tinge of her blood on his tongue. He wrapped his arms around her and didn't let her pull away until his heartbeat had decreased to a level where he didn't feel like it was about to explode.

When he did, he saw the Morrigan standing at the edge of the crowd, now being pushed back by a contingent of riot police clearing a path for ambulances.

Life has its day, she whispered, *but so does Death, and when that day comes, the two of us shall conclude our twined destinies. Until then, Jack . . . rise from the ashes, and live out your time.*

Pete flagged down an ambulance for them, and when Jack looked again, the Morrigan had vanished.

The paramedics cut away his shirt and attached a heart monitor, but Jack felt fine. Even the ever-present throb of his sight was quiet for the moment. Pete drew back, her fingers passing across his chest with the lightest touch.

"Your tattoos are gone. Your scars . . ."

Jack sat up, looking down at his arms. He'd gotten a clean slate once before, but it hadn't lasted long. His arms were bare, pale, and dusted with dark hair. He touched his face and didn't feel the scar on his cheek. Even his knee felt fit.

"I'm a new man, luv," he said. "From the ashes, and all that."

"Yeah, well," Pete said, helping him onto the gurney. "You're still going to the hospital."

Jack nodded. "I think that's a good idea."

He watched the chaos retreat as the ambulance drove away. The Black was everywhere now, no longer a hum and a tide but like the air around them, touching his skin, his mind, his talent. It was one with the daylight now, and the world was still here.

That's what's important, Jack told himself as the ambulance bumped through the streets in the old part of London.

Until that last day came, the world would be there. And so would he.

CHAPTER 40

Jack was glad that for once he didn't actually *need* a hospital, because he hated them more than any place on earth. The A&E doctor looked him over, saw that he wasn't gravely injured or bleeding out, and sent him on his way through a packed waiting room full of the aftermath of the riots and the incursion of the Black.

Jack stepped outside to the smoker's patio to call Pete and tell her that he'd be home soon. She'd left to be with Lily, and he hadn't minded a bit—he could handle a few pokes and prods just fine on his own.

After the day he'd had, a hospital actually seemed like a vacation, albeit a loud, crowded vacation that smelled of antiseptic and latex.

He watched a zombie shamble down the sidewalk and some lesser form of Fae flit among the gargoyles on top of the hospital. His sight showed him everything as if he were tuned to some kind of radar, pings of magic feeding back to him, but without any of the usual pain.

Jack sat on the steps and lit a cigarette. He could get used to this—magic in the daylight, creatures out in the open, people like him living in the human world like they should instead of living with one foot in the daylight world and one foot in the stuff of nightmares.

"Spare one of those?" Belial flopped down beside him, looking pressed and polished and utterly, utterly slagged off.

"Well look at you," Jack said, passing over the last of his crushed pack. "Aren't we a sight for sore eyes."

Belial lit his cigarette with Jack's proffered lighter and pulled a face. "These human brands are like sucking on a candy stick. Horrible."

"You enjoying yourself?" Jack asked. "Seeing everything all topsy turvy?"

Belial shook his finger. "Don't avoid the subject, Jack. You didn't give me that blade."

Jack rolled his eyes. "You threatened me. You couldn't even use it, anyway. And I did your job for you, so by the by, you're welcome."

Belial turned to Jack, and his expression was as stony as any of the gargoyles, dead as any of the zombies all around them. "I don't take this sort of thing lightly, Jack. We may all be neighbors now, but there is still a food chain, and I'm still the big bad wolf."

Jack exhaled his last drag and scraped out his cigarette on the granite next to him. His virgin lungs protested a lot more than the ones he'd spent decades torturing, and smoking no longer held its masochistic joy. "See, that's the thing," he said to Belial, when he'd dragged out the action long enough that the demon looked like he might be about to have a cardiac event. "I don't think so."

Belial's teeth flashed. Jack glanced back at the hospital. If this went wrong, at least they were near an A&E that was rapidly gaining experience dealing with demon attacks.

"Explain to me exactly why I shouldn't rip your balls off and make a tasty carpaccio to feed back to you," Belial said, voice as silky as the cut of a good razor blade through a willing wrist.

"Let's see." Jack ticked on his fingers, hoping as hard as he could that Belial wouldn't simply cut his losses and kill him. His brief brush with immortality had worn off, and now he was just sore and painfully alive. "Hell's only barrier is the Gates. The walls are down. Anyone can breach the Gates, from either direction, and I bet that you lot are going to be busy with revolt for the next, oh, say, five hundred years." He gave Belial a smile. "Elementals don't like being your slaves, Belial. Handy tip. Not to mention whatever science projects Azrael has tucked away, *plus* that prison holding Abbadon and his buddies has got to be pretty shaky by now, and I'd say that even if you *wanted* to take this Legion mess out of my hide your hands are already full."

"Don't test me, Winter . . . ," Belial started, but Jack held up a finger.

"Shhh, darling. I wasn't finished." He reached into the pocket of his coat, which Pete had grabbed when they'd started cutting off his clothes on the plaza. "Also—and this is the important part—you fucked up, Belial. You went against the Princes, misguided as they might be. You stole from them, violated their vaults, and made them look like fools. I'd say the chances of them treating you like a friend at this point are, oh, zero."

He pulled the key to the Gates from his pocket and held it up. "You have two choices, Belial, the way that I look at it. You can get all hot and bothered and try to get your pound of flesh, or you can walk away into this brave new world, keep that human suit on full time, and sample what the new deal has to offer."

Belial threw down his cigarette and stood up, glowering as he loomed over Jack. "Are *you* actually bargaining with *me*? That is *pathetically* hilarious."

"Not bargaining," Jack said. "Telling. Those are your choices, and these are your consequences: You walk away and you don't take to eating babies, and I'll let bygones be just that. I'll forget what you did to me. I'll do my best to forget what you are."

Jack stood, toeing up to Belial. He had a good inch on the demon's human form, and he gave Belial a stony look as he held up the key. "You ever come at me again or try to worm your way back into the Triumvirate by screwing me over, and I will use this on you. I'll deliver you to the Princes' doorstep in gift wrap, and I'm telling you, Belial, I won't be the one they'll have words with."

He tucked the key back into his pocket and folded his arms. "What do you say, Belial? Do you think we can be friends?"

Belial sucked in a breath. His nostrils flared, and Jack could count every one of his shark teeth, could feel his slender body as it vibrated with rage. "Go to

Hell, Winter," he finally spat, spinning and storming down the steps.

"Already been there!" Jack shouted. "And I'm going to want my lighter back, one of these days!"

Belial shot him the bird and kept walking. Jack sat back down, his knees feeling a bit more liquid than they had before. But it had worked. He'd backed off a demon. First step into a brave new world.

Jack tossed his pack into the bin and went back inside to wait for Pete. If this was the world, he could get used to it.

EPILOGUE

Two weeks to the day later, Jack stood glaring at Morwenna Morgenstern over the bonnet of her Bentley. "Keep staring," she said, curling her lip at Jack. "Maybe I'll do a trick."

"That would be far too much to hope for," Jack said. He watched Margaret give Pete a hard hug and kiss Lily on the forehead before she picked up her backpack and suitcase and slumped toward the car.

"Do I *really* have to go back with them?" she asked Jack. Jack sighed.

"You need real traning, luv, and after what happened it's too much of a mess here. You need to be safe, and much as I hate to admit it, these tossers will do a decent job of that." He returned to glaring at Morwenna. "Or they better, if they don't want me foot up their arses from here to eternity."

Morwenna gave a delicate shudder. "That literally sounds worse than actually going to Hell and being tormented by demons, Jack."

Jack grinned. "Going to Hell isn't so difficult these days. One could arrange it. . . ."

Morwenna jerked the back door of the Bentley

open. "Get in, dear," she said. Margaret rolled her eyes, but she hugged Jack and climbed aboard while Victor loaded her bags.

"I won't let them turn me into a posh twat like her," she whispered before the car pulled away. Jack patted her on the shoulder.

"You're going to lead all of us some day, kid. Stay in school, drugs are rubbish, they'll tell you dabbling in black magic isn't allowed, but it can be a lot of—"

Morwenna cut him off. "That's *quite* enough goodbye from you, Jack."

Margaret gave Jack one more wave before the Bentley pulled away, and Jack felt a pang deep in his gut. "Please tell me we're doing the right thing," he said to Pete, where she sat with Lily on the stoop.

"Sending the future Merlin to a place where she can't be kidnapped, eaten by zombies, or possessed by a demon? Yeah, just a bit," Pete said. "It's the best thing, Jack. Grandmother on my mum's side was sent to the country during the Blitz. This is the same principle."

Jack watched the Bentley disappear around the corner, zigzagging to avoid potholes and police cordons, and tried to tamp down his misgivings. Margaret needed a real teacher, not someone like him.

"Come on," Pete said. "Let's go inside. I'll put the kettle on, assuming we have power today."

Jack followed her upstairs and settled on the sofa with Lily while Pete bustled around the kitchen. His daughter cooed, smiling up at him. "Look at that face," Jack said to Pete. "Going to be a heartbreaker, just like her mum."

"And a hellion, no doubt, like her da," Pete said.

"No possible way," Jack said. "Our Lily is going to be an angel." He grinned at his daughter as she grabbed for his hands and whispered. "Be a bit of a hellion if you can. Life's more fun that way."

"Oi, I hear you filling her head with ideas," Pete said. "Don't you go thinking just because I was law and order I'm going to be the bad cop." She brought them tea and put on a Miles Davis record that had belonged to Connor. Jack let the music play uninterrupted as the sun went down and spits of rain coated the window glass.

The flat had mostly survived the riots and the subsequent cleanup unscathed. He'd boarded over a few of the windowpanes, and there had been some smoke damage from a fire next door, but they'd been able to go home within a week when half of London was still largely homeless.

"You know," Pete said, taking Lily from him as she began to fuss. "You'd think it would be more different."

"More how?" Jack said, raising his eyebrow.

"I mean, worlds *literally* merged," Pete said. "The Black fell on top of the daylight, and Hell floated up to the surface like some bloated corpse in the Thames. Magic exists now, in the world as everyone knows it. But everything out there is just a bit mussed. I don't understand it."

Jack shrugged. "Humans are survivors, luv. I mean,

plagues, fires, wars, disco music—they can stand up to a fuck of a lot of punishment and carry on."

Pete looked out the window, rocking Lily gently. "What do you think is going to happen?"

Jack had given that a lot of thought since he'd gotten out of the hospital. The Black was still there, ever present against his skin, but it felt less menacing somehow, like a monster that's terrifying as a shadow on the wall but only mildly bothersome when you drag it into the harsh light of day.

He could still do magic, but then again so could about ten thousand other blokes in London who'd suddenly discovered a scrap of latent talent that hadn't been able to cross the old barrier. Which might be a good thing, since 666 demons and their assorted rent boys were waiting just out of sight beyond the Gates to surge up and turn the world into their buffet. That is, Jack thought, if they ever stopped fighting each other in the chaos wrought by Legion.

"You know," he said, "for the first time in a long time, Pete, I think we'll be all right. Life rolls on, is what happens. It'll be interesting, and sometimes I think it'll be fucking awful in a way it's never been before, but it'll be life."

Pete considered this and then nodded. "I can live with that," she said, giving Lily a kiss and standing up to take her to her crib.

Jack heard a thump on the sill and hurried to the glass, opening the pane and looking out into the rain. He locked eyes with the Fae balanced on the top of the burned-out flat block across the alley for just a moment before the thing flitted away.

The noise had come from a smooth, flat piece of stone etched with the tri-horned sign of the Faerie King, and below it a sprig of rowan bound in black thread.

"What is that?" Pete said, and Jack jumped. Sometimes he really wished the Morrigan had left him that handy unflappability that came with being dead to human feeling.

He shut the glass and showed her the tablet. "It's a death note," he said, running his thumb along the rough edge of the stone. "The Faerie King has put a price on my head. This is their way of being polite and giving me a day to get out of town."

Pete raised an eyebrow. "Fae? Threatening us?"

Jack nodded. "I'm guessing he's not too happy about me spoiling his little alliance by killing his best pal Legion and, you know, dropping the barriers so any old human can find himself trespassing in Faerie."

"After all this," Pete sighed. "You'd think we'd get a break. Just for a moment."

Jack dropped the death threat on the side table and put his arms around Pete. She smiled at him, sliding her arms around his waist in turn, slotting them together like they'd been made for that purpose. "Like you said: interesting life we're going to have."

Jack dropped a kiss on Pete's forehead. "I wouldn't have it any other way."